THE DARKNESS KNOWS

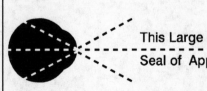

A VIV AND CHARLIE MYSTERY

THE DARKNESS KNOWS

CHERYL HONIGFORD

THORNDIKE PRESS
A part of Gale, Cengage Learning

GALE
CENGAGE Learning·

Farmington Hills, Mich • San Francisco • New York • Waterville, Maine
Meriden, Conn • Mason, Ohio • Chicago

GALE
CENGAGE Learning

LIBRARY OF CONGRESS CATALOGING-IN-PUBLICATION DATA

Names: Honigford, Cheryl, author.
Title: The darkness knows / by Cheryl Honigford.
Description: Large Print edition. | Waterville, Maine : Thorndike Press, 2016. |
    Series: A Viv and Charlie mystery | Series: Thorndike Press large print historical
    fiction
Identifiers: LCCN 2016034983 | ISBN 9781410494986 (hardcover) | ISBN 1410494985
    (hardcover)
Subjects: LCSH: Radio actors and actresses—Fiction. | Radio serials—Fiction. |
    Murder—Investigation—Fiction. | Large type books. | GSAFD: Mystery fiction. |
    Historical fiction.
Classification: LCC PS3608.O4945 D37 2016b | DDC 813/.6—dc23
LC record available at https://lccn.loc.gov/2016034983

Published in 2016 by arrangement with Sourcebooks, Inc.

Printed in Mexico
1 2 3 4 5 6 7 20 19 18 17 16

For Barak and Kate

CHAPTER ONE

October 27, 1938

Vivian's scream was a thing of beauty — startling and pitch-perfect, as usual. She caught her breath, waited a beat, and leaned into the microphone. "A gun!" she cried.

She scanned the page, searching for the next line in the script. It belonged to the villain in tonight's episode, and Vivian felt Dave Chapman tense next to her in preparation.

"That's right, sweetheart," Dave said. "And you're a goner."

The organ music swelled, rose higher, reached a crescendo. Vivian held her position for a few seconds and then relaxed when she heard the first few bars of the Sultan's Gold cigarette jingle.

You'll be sold on Sultan's Gold.
The cigarette that's truly mellow . . .

Her eyes caught Graham's over the microphone. He winked at her, and she felt that wink slide slowly down her body to settle in the tips of her toes.

Graham Yarborough had the kind of looks that were thoroughly wasted on the radio, she thought: dark, debonair, and eminently distracting. Working with him had been somewhat of a challenge, because gazing at Graham tended to make her lose focus.

Not that Vivian was anything to sneeze at either: petite with strawberry-blond hair and doe-brown eyes. She caught appreciative glances from the men at the radio station, on the streetcar, everywhere really. She'd had several marriage proposals in her short life, but Vivian had turned every one of them down. None of them had been remotely suitable choices, but even if they had, she'd decided she wanted some excitement before she settled down and had to start worrying about developing dishpan hands.

She was still ruminating on her escape from drudgery when she noticed that silence hung heavy in the studio. Not merely a silence, but an utter vacuum of sound. Vivian's stomach lurched, and she turned to Dave. He jabbed a finger at his script, eyes wide with urgency. They were back from sponsor break, and it was her line.

"I think Mr. Diamond will have something to say about that," she said, the line bursting from her lips in a nearly incoherent rush of air. She didn't dare look into the control booth. Dead air was anathema in the radio business.

Instead, against her better judgment, she sneaked another peek at Graham, Harvey Diamond himself. At the moment, he appeared every bit the tough, troubled hero of *The Darkness Knows,* his face a mask of scowling intensity as he waited for his next line.

"Mr. Diamond?" Dave said. "Your Mr. Diamond will never make it in time. You'll be dead, and the emeralds will be mine."

"That's what you thought, Glanville," Graham interjected, leaning toward the microphone. He paused for a short burst of organ music. "You thought tying me up in a deserted mine shaft was going to keep me away? Now you're going to pay."

The well-choreographed struggle began on cue. The organ hummed. The soundman punched a fist into his open palm once, twice while he scuffled his feet through the small tray of gravel in the corner. Graham growled, "Take that!" There was the sound of a single gunshot — a blank fired into the air from a real pistol — then a beat of silence.

Vivian glanced into the control room. Joe McGreevey, the director, held a stopwatch. Looking panicked, he started bringing his open palms together in front of his chest. "Hurry up," he mouthed. The timing was off, and they were behind.

"Harvey!" Vivian shrieked. "Oh, Harvey, are you all right?"

"It's over," Graham said. "I've disarmed him, and he's out cold. There's a jail cell with this mug's name all over it."

"Oh, thank goodness. But how did you ever escape from that mine shaft?"

"Well, that's a long story," Graham ad-libbed. The original script contained three lines of extra dialogue detailing Harvey's harrowing escape. He looked up at Vivian and smiled as he delivered his final line: "How about we talk about it over dinner, doll?"

The theme music crept in from the organ in the far corner of the room, signaling that another episode had reached its dramatic conclusion.

Bill Purdy, the show's announcer, stepped up to the microphone to end the show. Vivian held her breath until she heard ". . . and Vivian Witchell was heard as Lorna Lafferty." She didn't think she'd ever grow tired of hearing those words.

Bill deftly sped up to complete the voice-over before the second hand of the large studio clock swept up to the hour indicating the very dot of 8:30 p.m. Then the chimes rang to signal a change of programming. As soon as the on-air light switched off, they all heaved a collective sigh of relief.

"Good work, everyone," Joe said over the speaker from behind the thick glass of the control room. "But there's no time to rest on our laurels. We do it all again at ten o'clock for the folks on the West Coast." He switched off the microphone, paused, and then switched it back on. "And let's all try to remember our cues next time around."

Vivian quickly dipped her head to avoid meeting anyone's eyes and pretended to study her script.

She'd been doing small parts on shows at WCHI for over a year now, and there was certainly no excuse for missing a cue. Lorna Lafferty and *The Darkness Knows* were by far the biggest and best things to ever happen to her, and she couldn't afford to muck them up — not when she was just starting to get noticed.

In fact, Vivian had just gotten her first mention in the Chicago "Tattler" section of this week's *Radio Guide* magazine. She'd read and reread the blurb so many times she'd committed it to memory: "Former WCHI secretary Vivian Witchell gets raves for her new role as sidekick to popular gumshoe Harvey Diamond. She replaced Edie Waters, who left the show for marriage and the stork. I hear Vivian's a class act and that everyone who knows her thinks the world of her, including her costar Graham Yarborough. The two have been seen out on the town together more than once and may, in fact, be Radioland's newest couple."

Vivian smiled ruefully at the idea. Sure, she and Graham had been out on the town together — strictly for publicity photos.

"Nice work."

Vivian looked up at Graham and smiled. He looked especially rakish this evening; no jacket or tie, shirtsleeves rolled up to expose muscled forearms.

"Thanks, but I think you saved the show," she replied, cocking a thumb at the control room. "And you may have also saved Joe from a massive coronary . . . The timing's all wrong in the second half." She flipped absently through the pages of her battered script.

"Well," Graham said, bending slightly forward. "We'll have to fix that."

Vivian could feel his warm breath on her cheek. It smelled lightly of menthol cigarettes and coffee.

"Yes," she said, eyes flicking up to meet his gaze. "We will."

They regarded each other for a few seconds in silence.

"Viv . . ." Graham began.

"Yes?"

Someone lurking just outside Vivian's field of vision cleared their throat.

"Speaking of bad timing," Vivian muttered under her breath.

She turned and saw Peggy Hart's eyes just visible above the tower of cigarette cartons in her arms. The ornate script of the Sultan's Gold logo partially obscured the image of the lounging Turk who regarded Vivian through narrowed eyes, a delicate tendril of smoke curling from the cigarette perched on the end of an impossibly long, thin holder.

"Your weekly cigarette allotment," Peggy announced, pushing the leaning tower toward Vivian.

"No thank you. I don't —" she replied. The carton on top tumbled off, and Vivian had just enough presence of mind to catch it before it landed on the floor at her feet.

"Oh, and here are some notes on your

13

performance," Peggy said, thrusting a sheet of paper at Vivian. "Most are Joe's suggestions, but some are mine." Peggy Hart regularly sat in the control room of various shows, observing and taking notes on the actors' performances and helping with the productions. She also handed out cigarettes, as she was tonight. Since Peggy was the station owner's indulged only child, Vivian assumed it would be a short leap from the all-girls' academy Peggy currently attended to a position as head writer or even featured actress on a high-profile show.

"Thank you, Peggy," Vivian said. She tucked the notes into the pocket of her skirt.

Graham reached over, plucked a carton from the top of the pile, and flashed a thousand-watt smile in Peggy's direction. Peggy's eyes held Graham's for an instant before she glanced away. "I should go." She swiveled on her heel and set off in the opposite direction.

Vivian eyed the girl as she walked away. She was only seventeen and deeply entrenched in her awkward phase, all knobby knees and pimples. She seemed not to have inherited any of her glamorous parents' looks or manner. A pity. Vivian liked Peggy, and she was certainly no threat to Vivian. Still, she wasn't keen on the idea of watching yet another woman go sweaty and red-faced in Graham's presence.

"So, Viv, before we were so rudely interrupted . . ." Graham continued.

"Yes?"

"I was going to ask if you'd like to join me for some coffee before the ten o'clock show. We can talk about the timing in the second half."

"Sure," she said.

"I mean some decent coffee," he said with a smirk. "Not the stuff they peddle in the lounge here."

"Oh . . . Oh, sure. Let me get my bag."

She rushed off before he could change his mind. Graham had never before asked her to do anything outside the studio, not personally. Their dates, of which there had been precisely two, had been arranged by the publicity department. Vivian would receive a note that read *Meet Mr. Yarborough at the College Inn at Hotel Sherman at 9:30 p.m. There will be cameras.* At the College Inn there would be a few drinks, some light banter, and a couple of dances — all within sight of at least one photographer. Vivian was no wide-eyed ingenue; she knew that the hint of a romance between costars would get *The Darkness Knows* — and the station — into the gossip pages. The listening public loved love, even the blatantly manufactured kind, and the publicity department knew that. Gossip spelled ratings, and ratings spelled revenue.

Still, it would be nice if, at the end of the evening, Graham wouldn't just politely see her to a waiting cab without a second glance. But this time was different, she thought. This time he'd asked her himself.

Vivian ran up the flight of stairs to the twelfth-floor lounge, nodding hello to at least a dozen people on the way, and plucked her purse from the back of the chair. Her eyes snagged on the poster tacked to the announcements board. *WCHI Halloween Masquerade! Costume Contest! Prizes! Dancing! Palmer House Empire Room — October 28.* That was tomorrow night. With the whirlwind of starting a starring role on *The Darkness Knows,* the masquerade had slipped from Vivian's mind. She hadn't had time to get a costume. Besides, choosing a costume was a precarious thing. It needed to be a delicate balance of interesting and alluring, and she hadn't yet hit on the perfect combination.

She realized that she was still clutching her unwanted box of cigarettes. After a moment of consideration and a glance at the man eating a sandwich at the table on the far side of the room, she left the carton of Sultan's Gold next to the mountain of unwashed mugs in the lounge sink. She could always claim she'd set it down and forgotten it if someone asked. And if all went well, some lucky smoker would swoop in and take it, no questions asked. She had to remember to ask Graham why her initial refusal had been such a glaring faux pas. There was still so much about this business that she didn't understand.

Her eyes fell on that morning's edition of the *Chicago Daily Tribune,* left under an overflowing ashtray near the sink. The headline squawked "Germans Oust Polish Jews." The threat of war had loomed heavy since September, and the papers had been filled with nothing but Hitler's threats. Things had seemed to calm down when the British allowed Germany to take part of Czechoslovakia, but that's all Vivian knew. She rarely read the papers except to scan for mentions of herself or *The Darkness Knows* in the entertainment section, and this morning's paper had neither; she'd already checked at breakfast.

Vivian rushed from the room, riffling through her purse for her lipstick and compact, and felt her shoulder brush against someone walking in the opposite direction.

Vivian looked up in time to glimpse Marjorie Fox staring intently at a piece of paper, her brow furrowed in concentration.

"Oh, sorry," Vivian said. She stopped, but Marjorie continued down the hall as if she hadn't heard or, more likely, didn't care. Vivian stared after her, wrinkling her nose at the distinctive waft of cheap whiskey left in the woman's wake.

Marjorie Fox was the star of the station. She'd played Evelyn Garrett on WCHI's popular family drama *The Golden Years* for three years now. The show followed the trials and tribulations of the Garrett family in a small, indeterminate Midwestern town and was the station's crown jewel. Evelyn was the perfect wife to Roger and model mother to Rosemary, Bill, and Susie. Her catchphrase was an exasperated "Good heavens . . ." because members of the family were always doing things like tracking mud across the freshly waxed kitchen linoleum.

It was a blow to Vivian's ego to know that she had made no impression on someone as important as Marjorie Fox. In her former position as secretary to the head of the station, Mr. Hart, Vivian had greeted Marjorie at least twice a week, and now the woman had the nerve to act like she'd never seen

Vivian before. Even when Marjorie *had* deigned to speak to Vivian, she'd never had a kind word to say. Once, she caught Vivian powdering her nose at her desk and had the audacity to announce, "Don't worry, honey. It's not your *nose* he's interested in." Even now Vivian felt a phantom blush begin to creep up her collar at the years-old affront.

But as Vivian watched Marjorie shuffle away, she comforted herself with the thought that the older actress was on her way out. Her star was on the wane, and Vivian's was on the rise. She had nowhere to go but up. Vivian smiled to herself and pushed the ladies' room door open.

She studied her reflection in the bathroom mirror and rubbed a smudge of Ravishing Ruby lipstick off her front tooth. She patted the wave of hair over her forehead lightly and straightened the comb holding her hair back on one side. The high neckline of her green wool dress complemented her rosy complexion and strawberry-blond hair, she thought, at least in that dim light. Satisfied, Vivian gathered her things and headed out. But as she opened the bathroom door, an angry female voice pushed its way in.

". . . won't keep my voice down . . ."

Even though the line was delivered in a low hiss, Vivian recognized the voice immediately: it could only belong to an extremely unhappy Marjorie Fox. Instinctively, Vivian let the door fall closed. Marjorie's voice and a much lower one belonging to a man rumbled through the thick wood, both from right outside the restroom.

"Now, Marjorie, I'm sure it's a misunderstanding . . ." The rest of the sentence was muffled.

". . . possibly be a misunderstanding? Look at this. You told me you took care of everything."

The man sighed. "I *always* take care of it, don't I?" he said. "There won't be any more trouble."

Vivian leaned closer and held her breath but heard nothing more. Without warning, the door flew inward, and Vivian jumped out of the way. She lost her grip on her handbag and watched with horror as everything within — including wads of lipstick-smeared tissue — spilled on the floor at Marjorie's feet.

"Sorry," Vivian said for the second time in as many minutes.

Marjorie sniffed dismissively, stepped over the mess, and headed straight into the last stall, slamming the door shut behind her. Vivian crouched and scooped the items into her open bag, muttering under her breath about her own carelessness. She paused to tame her swirling thoughts before pulling the door open to find Graham sauntering toward her down the hallway, hands in pockets.

"There you are," he said.

"Here I am," she agreed. She glanced down the hallway in both directions. It was empty. In the time it had taken her to collect her things, the other participant in Marjorie's hushed conversation had disappeared.

"Shall we?" Graham asked, holding out his arm.

CHAPTER TWO

Vivian was halfway through her cup of coffee before she realized that Graham did just want to talk about the timing in the second half of the show. She'd let herself imagine they might discuss more personal matters, but Graham showed no sign of getting any more personal than his fictional alter ego's motivation.

In fact, he'd already segued into a list of possible plotlines for Harvey Diamond. It seemed he'd thought long and hard about the direction his character should take, not merely in the next episode, but in the next several dozen. He called it the character's "arc," which, Vivian was sure, was something he'd just overheard one of the writers say.

She'd also been hoping to go somewhere more exotic than the Tip Top Café, the tiny coffee shop on the lower level of the Morrison Hotel across the street from the station. The station staff frequented this place due entirely to its proximity rather than the quality of its food or service — both of which left much to be desired. A dozen or so people were clustered in twos and threes throughout the smoky room, most of them couples either coming from or about to go to one of the half a dozen movie palaces in the neighborhood. The McVickers Theater, just one block east, was showing the last night of *Carefree,* an Astaire and Rogers picture, and many people were likely taking their last chance to see the film before it closed.

The reed-thin waitress who had halfheartedly taken their order returned with the coffeepot. Vivian placed her hand over her cup as Graham said in a booming voice, "Sure, doll. Top it up."

He flashed the waitress a smile, which she self-consciously returned. Then he turned his attention back to Vivian.

"I don't want Harvey to remain so one-dimensional, you know?" Graham took a deep drag from his cigarette, and Vivian noted that even though he'd taken it from a Sultan's Gold box, complete with the knowing Turk on the cover, the cigarette did not have the distinctive Sultan's Gold band around it. She opened her mouth to comment but instead caught Graham's smoky exhalation.

She coughed as politely as she could into her hand and turned her head to the side to escape the unswerving plume of smoke. As she did, she noticed the two women in the booth opposite. They were pretty young things, glancing at Graham and whispering to each other behind white-gloved hands. Graham seemed to take no notice of his admirers, but Vivian didn't doubt for one second that he knew he'd attracted their attention. She just hoped they wouldn't come over and ask for his autograph.

"I want Harvey to be a full-fledged human being with a dark side as a counterpoint to his inherent goodness," Graham continued.

"I think that's admirable," Vivian said, raising her voice slightly for benefit of the eavesdroppers. "Few radio actors truly care about character development."

Graham looked at her thoughtfully, then flicked the end of his cigarette in the general direction of the ashtray. "Do you think Mr. Hart has any influence on the writers?"

"Well, of course he does," Vivian said. "He's the head of the station."

"Yes, I know that," Graham said impatiently. "But can he pressure the writers to write about certain things?"

Vivian smiled at Graham's naïveté. Mr. Hart was The Boss. If he wanted a serial drama about pigeon racing in Pocatello, Idaho, he'd get it. She'd seen plenty of evidence of his influence when she'd been his secretary: sponsors being worked into lines of dialogue, his wife's name used as a minor character in a women's serial on their anniversary, even allowing an unprofitable opera review to remain on the air just because he liked watching the star soprano's bosom heave as she hit the high notes.

"Well . . . I don't think 'pressure' is the right word," she said, attempting to tread lightly on the topic.

"So what is the right word?"

Vivian stuck her lower lip out and exhaled, ruffling the wave of hair lying over her forehead.. " 'Influence,' perhaps . . . ?"

It was a cop-out, but Graham seemed to consider it thoughtfully, staring off into middle distance.

Mr. Hart had certainly influenced the producer of *The Darkness Knows* to give Vivian a try as the new Lorna Lafferty after Edie quit. Vivian knew her previous minor acting credits at the station wouldn't have won her the job alone. Vivian had heard whispers around the station speculating

25

about the true nature of her relationship with Mr. Hart, and she knew Graham had too. Was that the reason for Graham's sudden interest in her? Did he think she had any influence with Mr. Hart because of her previous position as his secretary? Vivian braced herself for Graham's next question. He'd certainly ask whether she could put a bug in Mr. Hart's ear for him about Harvey's character arc.

"Harvey Diamond is merely a stepping-stone for me, of course," Graham said instead, speaking as smoothly as if he were giving an interview to a reporter for a glossy magazine. He leaned back into the padded red vinyl of the booth. "I have greater ambitions."

"You do?" Vivian tried to sound surprised. After all, who *didn't* have greater ambitions? She looked at Graham expectantly: no doubt Hollywood, the pictures. He'd probably already signed a contract with Paramount.

"I've written a play," he said solemnly.

"A play?" Of all the career ambitions she'd imagined for Graham Yarborough, playwright was not among them. Perhaps he had hidden depths after all. "That's marvelous, Graham. What's it about?"

"It's about communism."

"Communism," she repeated doubtfully.

"It is, but it's not," he said, lowering his chin and glancing about him. His face grew flushed, and he lowered his voice. "You can't write about communism outright these days, of course."

"Of course."

"It's sort of a veiled allegory about communism."

A veiled allegory about communism. Vivian repeated the phrase in her head several times, and the repetition only served to make the idea less interesting to her.

"I see," she managed to say. "Are you a . . ." Vivian also looked around to make sure no one was listening. The two girls at the booth opposite were chatting animatedly with each other; eavesdropping had apparently become tiresome. "Communist?" she finished in a whisper.

"Oh, good lord, no," Graham answered quickly, relaxing back into his seat again.

Vivian sighed. Well, that was a relief. It wouldn't do at all for Harvey Diamond to be associated with the Red Menace. That kind of thing ruined careers.

"But I do think the ideas of the movement are interesting," he continued in a matter-of-fact tone. He looked off into the distance again for a moment, and then his attention

27

snapped back to her. "Anyway, I'd love for you to read it and give me your impression."

Vivian's eyes widened with surprise. "Me? Read your play?"

"When it's finished, of course," he said, looking deeply into her eyes. "I trust your professional opinion implicitly."

Vivian's breath caught in her throat. Her professional opinion? No one had ever suggested she might have a professional opinion before, especially not someone like Graham Yarborough. He was a bona fide star.

"Say," he said, placing his hand over hers on the table. "Would you like to have dinner with me this Saturday night?"

Vivian felt her pulse quicken at his touch, but she forced herself to wait a beat before answering. She still wasn't entirely sure that he wasn't charming his way into a favor. Then he beamed that movie-star smile at her, and her resolve softened. *So what if he is?* she thought. With a smile like that, he could charm her into almost anything.

"I'd love to," she said.

Graham tipped his wrist to glance at his watch.

"It's after nine already," he said, releasing her hand. "We should head back for the ten o'clock. I want to give my thoughts on the timing to Joe."

■ ■ ■ ■

The WCHI studios occupied the top two floors of the outwardly unimpressive dark stone Grayson-Cole Building. It was wedged among hotels, movie theaters, and drugstores on Madison between Clark and Dearborn in Chicago's Loop, just a stone's throw from "that great street," State Street. The cavernous lobby was deserted at this time of night, but the elevator was waiting as Vivian and Graham approached, the sign above proclaiming "Express to 11 — WCHI." The doors were open, and Angelo, the operator, sat on his stool in the corner, flipping a nickel with his thumb into the open palm of the other hand. He jumped up immediately when he spotted them, a smile lighting his face.

"Mr. Yarborough, Miss Witchell," he said, bobbing his head respectfully toward Vivian.

"Quiet night, Angelo?" Graham asked, jingling the keys in his coat pocket.

"Yes, sir." Angelo brushed imaginary lint off the front of his immaculate maroon uniform and closed the elevator doors behind them.

Vivian smiled at him as he set the elevator

into motion with a jerk of the floor lever. She felt a certain solidarity with people like Angelo. Not so long ago she had been just a lowly receptionist, overlooked and put upon.

"I heard there's a chance of rain tonight," Graham said, idly adjusting the cuffs of his shirtsleeves.

"Rain? Oh, shoot!" Vivian exclaimed in irritation. "I left my umbrella in the upstairs lounge."

"I'll go up and fetch it for you," Graham offered.

"No, no. That's okay. I think I'll go up and get a glass of water for the ten o'clock while I'm there," she said. "My voice was a bit hoarse at the end of the last show."

The elevator jerked to a stop, and Angelo opened the doors to the eleventh floor.

"Watch your step, sir."

Graham hopped up the inch from the elevator to the hallway floor. He turned with a flourish. "I'll see you in the studio," he said to Vivian, giving Angelo a little salute before the doors closed again.

Another few practiced jerks of the controls and they arrived at the twelfth floor. It seemed to have cleared out almost completely since Vivian retrieved her purse only thirty minutes earlier. She stuck her head tentatively out the elevator door and surveyed the hallway in both directions. No more than half of the hallway lights were illuminated.

Angelo also poked his head out of the car to survey the atmosphere. He sniffed, as if testing the air. "Would you like me to walk with you, miss?"

Vivian stepped out into the hall. Something felt wrong. Were the lights always turned off this early in the evening?

"Oh, no, Angelo," she said, squinting into the semidarkness. "Thank you for the offer. I'm not going far." She waved her hand toward the end of the hallway with a confidence she didn't feel and headed toward the lounge, wincing as every step echoed on the marble floors. Vivian glanced at the closed doors of the studios she passed. Most of them were small and used for news broadcasts or lectures.

The other half of the floor was occupied by rehearsal space and administrative offices, which were usually deserted by seven o'clock. Even Mr. Hart rarely worked later than that. She started to hum "Jeepers Creepers" in an effort to lighten the mood but stopped after a few bars. It was a poor choice of song. She increased her pace, heels clicking madly.

Vivian walked quickly, breezing right past

the closed lounge door, then stopped so abruptly that she lost her balance and stumbled, the flat side of her right heel scraping the slick floor. She righted herself, and as she bent over to rub out the offending scuff mark her shoe had made, she saw a sign pinned to the door.

She leaned in to get a closer look, and the remaining hallway lights silently blinked to life. Vivian gasped and jumped backward. Her hand flew to her chest, and she felt her heart thumping beneath her open palm. She took a few deep breaths to calm herself, and when she finally turned back toward the elevator, she saw that Angelo had found the light switch. He stood just outside the elevator doors, watching her with an anxious expression on his face. She waved her thanks to him and sighed at her skittishness.

She returned her attention to the note. On what appeared to be the blank side of a piece of a script was written "Closed for Cleaning" in large block letters. She pushed the door with the tips of her fingers. It wasn't latched and swung open with more force than she had intended, hitting the wall with a bang.

The interior room's lack of windows made the darkness almost complete. She could see nothing but the soft yellow glow of the radio in the corner of the room, which was tuned to *The Kraft Music Hall.*

Bing Crosby quietly crooned a love song as Vivian felt around the corner to flip the switch. She sighed with relief when light flooded the room. It looked just as it had a few hours earlier: dirty coffee cups scattered about, ashtrays overflowing. Her discarded carton of cigarettes still rested near the sink. Clearly, no one had been cleaning anything in here.

She was sure her umbrella had fallen under a chair at one of the tables on the far side of the room where she'd had her lunch earlier in the day. As she approached, she thought she spied the tip of the black handle peeking out from underneath the table closest to the sink. Vivian sighed with relief and crouched down to retrieve it.

Her eyes were drawn to the admonishing note pinned above the sink in front of her: "Please rinse out all cups PROMPTLY." She rolled her eyes as her fingertips brushed the floor. Her hand closed around something soft, but when Vivian pulled, it didn't budge. She wrinkled her brow and pressed the object with her fingertips. It gave a little under her touch. She prodded it for a moment in confusion before she finally glanced under the chair with an exasperated sigh.

When her eyes fell upon what she'd been touching, she sucked in her breath sharply and staggered backward into the table behind her. A wooden chair fell to the floor with a clatter. Vivian realized with shock that she'd been poking the stockinged calf of a woman lying on the floor under the table.

"H-hello?" she said, her voice a barely audible squeak. There was no movement, no sound except for the quiet mumbling of the radio. The announcer's voice registered somewhere in her mind, saying with gusto, "Miracle Whip is America's favorite salad dressing, the favorite of millions of men and women . . ."

Vivian gathered her courage, tiptoed slowly around the side of the table, and froze.

The woman was lying on her stomach with her face turned toward Vivian, her gray eyes fixed and staring. There was a trickle of blood drying at the corner of her mouth, and a sticky mess of it covered the side of her head.

It was Marjorie Fox, and she was dead.

CHAPTER THREE

Vivian opened her eyes, and Graham's face came into focus above her, his brow furrowed with concern.

"There's my girl," he said, straightening up with an unconvincing smile. "Feeling better?"

Vivian glanced around and was surprised to find herself lying on the leather sofa in Mr. Hart's office, shoes off, stockinged feet perched atop two pillows. The only source of light was the green-shaded lamp on the desk, and there was the faint smell of smoke in the air. Vivian squinted into the dimness and spotted the remains of something smoldering in the ornate crystal ashtray. She wrinkled her nose at the acrid tang in the air.

"I'm . . . well, I'm not sure how I am. What happened?" she asked, rubbing her forehead with the tips of her fingers.

"You fainted."

"Fainted?" She sat up in alarm.

"You've been out quite a while," Graham assured her. "You gave us a good scare. It's a good thing Angelo was there to catch you when you fainted; otherwise, you might have a nasty bump on your head as well."

Angelo, she thought. *I fainted, and Angelo caught me.*

"I did?" She started to replay the evening's events in her mind. She remembered having coffee with Graham, riding in the elevator, going to fetch her umbrella . . . Then everything caught up to her in a rush: the blank stare, the blood.

She gasped, covering her mouth with her hands. "Marjorie!"

Graham sat down next to her and coiled his arm around her shoulders.

"Now just relax, Vivian." Mr. Hart walked into the room with a small glass of amber-colored liquid. He leaned down and tried to put the glass to her lips, but Vivian snatched it from his hands. She was in shock, but she wasn't an invalid.

Mr. Hart shrugged and pulled one of the matching leather armchairs that had been facing his desk closer to the couch and took a seat. He watched her sip at the brandy for a few seconds. Then, in complete silence, he took off his wire-rimmed spectacles and cleaned each lens slowly and carefully with a handkerchief pulled from the inside breast pocket of his jacket. His hands were shaking.

Mr. Hart was just shy of sixty, but he looked significantly younger — quite a handsome man for his age, Vivian had always thought. He'd aged gracefully, kept a trim figure. His hair was completely gray, but it suited him. It lent him an air of distinction. In the two years she'd worked as his secretary, he'd made at least two dozen passes at her. She'd politely deflected all of them. In secretarial school they'd warned her about the propensity for an employer's attentions to become amorous, after all.

Despite the fact that she'd turned him down repeatedly, gossip about them had still made the rounds at the station. She hadn't done anything untoward, yet everyone believed she had. So it was strange, uncomfortably intimate somehow, to be here with him now — in his office at night — even though Graham sat right beside her.

At the same time, she was glad Mr. Hart was here. If anyone could handle an awful situation like this, it would be him.

"The police are here," Mr. Hart said. "They're . . . taking care of things." The slight quaver in his voice was anything but reassuring.

"The police are here?" Graham stood up. "They'll want to question us."

"Vivian, at least."

Graham rubbed his hands on the front of his trousers and glanced at the closed door. "I think I'll go see if I can be of help," he said. He sprang for the door, reaching it in two long strides. As he grasped the doorknob, he turned back to Vivian. "You'll be all right here with Mr. Hart," he said. Before she could protest, he was gone.

Vivian shook her head and watched the door close behind him. She could see where she ranked in the grand scheme of things as far as Graham was concerned — somewhere below Harvey Diamond and the entire Chicago Police Department.

Mr. Hart had also gotten up from his seat and was pacing back and forth between his desk and the floor-to-ceiling windows on the opposite wall. All they afforded him was a view of the mammoth brick structure of the Morrison directly across the street. Silhouettes flitted across the Roman shades in some of the hotel windows.

"This is horrible," he said in a low voice, shifting his gaze to the street below. "Just horrible. It's all gone wrong."

Vivian made a vague noise of agreement in her throat. A dead woman in the lounge — something had gone horribly wrong indeed. She straightened her skirt, smoothing it over her knees. She slipped her feet back into her shoes, wondering which man had taken them off.

"I'm feeling much better, Mr. Hart," she said, anxious to remove herself from this awkward situation. Mr. Hart was clearly not himself. "I think I'll just —"

He turned sharply and fixed her with such a bewildered expression that she paused midsentence.

"— walk around a bit," she finished in a faltering voice. "Clear my head."

"No, no," he said, looking down at the polished leather of his shoes. "This won't do at all . . . The police will want to question you first thing." He glanced out the window and then back to Vivian.

"Of course," she said, confused.

She sat for a minute in silence as Mr. Hart continued wearing a path in the carpet: from the desk to the windows, the windows to the desk.

"Were you here when it . . . it happened? Did you see anything — the person that could have done this?" Vivian glanced at the ashtray on his desk where the remnants of something still smoldered. That wasn't cigar smoke in the air.

"I was working late, but I didn't notice anything unusual." He turned from the window briefly to glance at her, then turned back before adding, "Until I heard you scream, that is."

Vivian felt the color drain from her face as the image of Marjorie's dead body popped into her mind. She didn't remember screaming.

"Do you need anything?" she asked. She had been the one who fainted, but Mr. Hart seemed to be the one who needed support. "A drink?" When he didn't answer, she continued in a small voice, "I'll just go out and see if I can be of help to the police then, shall I?"

Mr. Hart grunted. "Yes, yes, go see what you can do." He turned to look at her and attempted a smile.

Vivian took another sip of the brandy and then set it on the side table. She left Mr. Hart staring silently out of the window at the lights of the city.

The whole floor was abuzz with activity. Vivian walked a wide berth around the scene of the crime. The lounge was taped off, but she could see that the "Closed for Cleaning" sign remained on the door and was now hanging slantwise from one corner. She wondered if Marjorie was still in there, if her eyes were still open.

Vivian poked her head tentatively into Studio K, which seemed to be the hub of police activity, and heard Graham before she saw him.

"So you're saying this most definitely wasn't any sort of accident?" he said, voice booming in the perfect acoustics of the studio.

Vivian locked eyes with Graham over the top of the head of the policeman he'd been addressing. She couldn't hear the policeman's response, but Graham replied with a grave "I see" as he motioned Vivian over with a quick flick of his fingers.

As she approached, another man came into view. He was standing to Graham's right, saying something to the group that she couldn't make out. He stood an inch or so taller than Graham, and his golden-brown hair was smoothed back from his forehead in two sharp waves. There was something slightly unfinished about his features — the nose too sharp, the brow too prominent. They didn't work separately, but in combination they made him look rugged, Vivian thought, and maybe a little dangerous. His tie was loosened, his shirt wrinkled, and stubble shadowed his jaw. He also looked, Vivian decided, like she felt — like this was not quite the end of a very long day.

The man's eyes flicked over to meet hers, and she felt herself flush instantly under his gaze. His face was hard, his mouth drawn into a scowl. He looked her up and down, then, without a change of expression, returned his attention to what the detective was saying.

"Viv," Graham said as she stepped forward. "This is Sergeant Trask." He motioned to the shorter man, and she nodded politely.

"Miss Witchell." The policeman acknowledged her with a slight nod of his head, and she shook the officer's hand.

There was an awkward pause before Vivian thrust her hand out to the taller man and said, more forcefully than she'd intended, "Vivian Witchell."

The strange man hesitated a moment before enveloping her hand in his. He stared into her eyes, and Vivian felt her knees weaken a little. This was real intensity, she thought, not the fake Harvey Diamond kind.

"Charlie Haverman," he replied.

He wasn't wearing a uniform, and Vivian had never seen him around the studio before. "Viv plays my sidekick on *The Darkness Knows,*" Graham said. "Lorna Lafferty."

"Is that right?" Mr. Haverman's mouth curved up on one side.

"She's the *new* Lorna," Graham clarified. "Just started last week to replace Edie, who went and got herself married." Graham clucked in bewildered amusement at the idea.

Vivian glared at Graham.

"And Chick here," he continued, pointing at Mr. Haverman with his index finger and thumb at a right angle like a gun, "is the special consultant to the show."

"Special consultant to the show . . . *Our* show?" She hadn't been aware they even had a special consultant.

Graham opened his mouth to explain, but Sergeant Trask jumped in.

"Miss Witchell," he began. "You discovered the deceased?"

Vivian reluctantly turned her attention to the policeman, his pencil poised at the ready. "Yes," she answered quietly.

"Can you tell me exactly what happened, please?"

"Detective," Graham said. "Does Viv

43

really have to go through all of this right now? She's been through a hell of a shock. You've already heard what happened." He placed his hand protectively on her shoulder.

"I'd like to hear Miss Witchell's version."

Vivian nodded to Graham and took a deep breath.

"Well," she began, "Graham and I had grabbed a cup of coffee across the street between shows. Graham walked me back to the station, as he's probably already said."

"Did you see anyone in the building when you arrived?"

"Just the security guard," she said slowly. "And Angelo. He operates the elevator."

The policeman nodded, and his eyes darted to the far corner of the room as he wrote. Angelo sat next to the security guard. Morty Nickerson, the show's engineer, was slumped in a chair beside them, nervously biting his fingernails and staring at the floor. She glanced around the room and noted others from *The Darkness Knows* production staff. There seemed to be someone missing, but her muddled mind couldn't place who.

"I . . . I left Graham on the eleventh floor and took the elevator up to the twelfth to retrieve my umbrella. He had mentioned

44

that it might rain." Vivian took a deep breath and steadied herself. "The twelfth floor was deserted . . . or at least it seemed deserted. I didn't see or hear anyone. The lounge door was closed when I reached it, and there was a sign on it that said 'Closed for Cleaning' . . . which was odd."

"Odd how?" the policeman asked.

"Well, I couldn't tell you the last time the lounge was cleaned. It's a pigsty," she said with a nervous laugh. "Anyway, I opened the door, and all the lights were off, but the radio was on in the corner."

She paused. She'd meant to glance at Graham for some encouragement, but she caught the special consultant's eye instead. He nodded soberly at her. Vivian took another deep breath and focused back on the sergeant.

"I turned the lights on," she continued, unable to keep her voice from shaking. "And I didn't see anything out of the ordinary at first. I walked into the room and reached for what I thought was my umbrella under the table near the sink, and instead, I . . ." Vivian shivered. "Well, then I saw her. Marjorie was lying in a pool of blood. Then I don't know what happened." Vivian shrugged. Graham squeezed her shoulder, and Vivian leaned into him.

45

Sergeant Trask smoothly noted the end of her story with the last strokes of his pencil.

"Apparently, you screamed and ran into the hallway, where the elevator operator caught you as you fell," the policeman said, succinctly completing her story.

Vivian felt her face grow warm with embarrassment as she glanced over at Angelo. He was fidgeting in his chair, probably uncomfortable with all the attention and anxious to get back to work.

"So what killed her?" Graham asked.

Vivian winced at his lack of tact.

Sergeant Trask looked up at Graham with narrowed eyes. "A blow to the back of the head with a heavy glass bottle," he answered matter-of-factly. Then he turned to Vivian. "Canadian Club. There are shards of glass all over the floor. I'm not sure how you didn't notice that when you walked into the lounge, Miss Witchell."

Vivian exchanged glances with Graham. Everyone at the station had known about Marjorie's closet drinking. She was no doubt in the process of making her coffee "Irish" when she'd been struck over the head with her own whiskey bottle. Her manner of death was so fitting that it was almost laughable.

Almost.

"You're positive you didn't see anyone suspicious around the station at all tonight, Miss Witchell?" the sergeant asked.

Vivian shook her head, afraid that if she opened her mouth she might start laughing out of hysteria.

"Well, it seems that Miss Fox had something of an enthusiastic fan." The policeman grimaced slightly.

"Enthusiastic?" Graham said.

The policeman nodded before adding in a near-whisper, "There was a threatening letter from this fan found with her body."

Vivian sucked air in sharply through her teeth, and Graham's fingers tightened around her shoulder.

"I saw her with a letter after the eight o'clock show!" Vivian said. "You think the person that wrote the letter . . . hurt Marjorie?" Goose bumps had sprung up on her arms, and she rubbed them furiously.

"It's a distinct possibility," the policeman answered. "You never heard Mrs. Fox mention anything about fan letters?"

"No . . . Well, I don't — didn't — really speak with Marjorie . . . Mrs. Fox." Vivian felt her face flush again, both at her stumbling over the clumsy explanation and the fact that Marjorie Fox had found her unworthy of conversation.

Sergeant Trask raised his eyebrows. "Any particular reason for that?"

"I barely knew her," Vivian said with a shrug, hoping that the policeman wasn't suggesting she'd had some sort of falling-out with the dead woman. "I don't think I was worthy of being spoken to, in her opinion. Not many people at the station were."

"Can you think of anyone else around here that might want to hurt Mrs. Fox?"

"Well, I don't personally know of anyone . . ." Vivian said, hoping she wouldn't have to finish the thought.

"But?"

"But she wasn't the most popular person at the station." She didn't like to speak ill of the dead, even Marjorie, but it was true.

"Funny how many times we've already heard that tonight," said Mr. Haverman. There was nothing in his tone to suggest that he found it funny at all.

"Oh, Sergeant Trask, there's something else," Vivian said. "I don't know how much it helps, but I heard Marjorie arguing with someone — a man — earlier, just before Graham and I went for coffee."

"Heard them?"

"Yes, through the ladies' room door. It was definitely Marjorie, but I don't know who the man was. She was angry, and she said she wanted him to take care of something, but I couldn't follow what they were talking about."

"About what time was this?"

"Well, it was after the first show . . . eight forty or so?"

"I see." The policeman snapped his notebook closed, sticking the pencil stub behind his right ear. "Thank you, Miss Witchell. We'll let you know if we need your further assistance."

She nodded, then turned to ask Graham about that argument in the hallway — surely he'd seen something — but he'd already started off after Sergeant Trask, who was heading briskly in the direction of Morty Nickerson. If Graham had seen Marjorie arguing with anyone, he would've told the police. Wouldn't he?

"So you're Lorna Lafferty."

Vivian looked up to find herself standing alone with the special consultant, Mr. Haverman.

"That's me, I guess," she answered, her eyes returning to Graham and the policeman on the other side of the room.

"You guess?"

Vivian forced her attention back to Mr. Haverman and searched for an appropriate

49

response. "I've only been Lorna Lafferty for a week," she replied, realizing too late just how stupid that sounded.

Mr. Haverman smiled though, and the whole geography of his face changed. The dangerous scowl was gone, and in its place was the smile of a man who could charm his way through most anything, and probably did.

"You know, you're not what I expected," he said.

"I'm not?"

Mr. Haverman shrugged, broad shoulders lifting and falling in one smooth movement. "I guess I expected someone with more of a face for radio." He fixed her with an unnerving stare.

"I . . . Well, um . . . thank you," she said, glancing away, flustered by the compliment. "So, Mr. Haverman," she said quickly, meeting the tall man's eyes again. "Graham said you were a consultant to the show. What does that mean, exactly?"

"Well, it means I tell the writers and Mr. Yarborough" — he motioned toward the corner of the room where Graham hovered over the shoulder of the beleaguered Sergeant Trask — "what the life of a private eye is like."

Vivian's eyes widened. "A private eye?"

He nodded.

"That makes you the real Harvey Diamond then."

One corner of his mouth curled in a crooked half smile. "I suppose I am."

"Vivian!" Joe McGreevey ran toward her, holding up one hand, fingers splayed. "We're on in five!"

It took a moment for the import of that information to sink in.

"We're on?" she asked, heart thudding. "We're doing the ten o'clock?"

"Of course we're doing the ten o'clock." The director shook his head. "Murder or no murder. The West Coast is waiting." Then he scurried off to gather the rest of the cast and crew.

Vivian closed her eyes for the briefest of moments, and when she opened them, the room was swimming in front of her. She swayed on her feet and held one arm out to steady herself. She grabbed the closest thing to her, which happened to be Mr. Haverman's sleeve, and held on for dear life. He took hold of her shoulders and pulled her firmly upright.

"Whoa there," he said softly. He crouched down to look directly into her eyes. "Are you all right?"

Vivian held his gaze, and soon the room

slowly began to right itself. His eyes were a beautifully calm shade of blue green — like Lake Michigan in the summer, she thought.

"No, not really."

"Let's sit you down," he said. He took her elbow and began steering her toward an unoccupied folding chair.

She stopped abruptly and shook his hand off her arm. "I can't," she said as forcefully as she could muster. "I have to do the ten o'clock show."

"Miss Witchell, I don't think you're in any condition —"

"I have to get to the studio."

CHAPTER FOUR

Vivian had no illusions about her talent. She was a capable actress, but just that. She had no doubt that if she had demurred tonight, as acceptable as it may have seemed under the circumstances, another girl — almost certainly that horrible Frances Barrow — would step in and do Lorna as well as Vivian had ever done her, and that would be the beginning of the end of her short career. Vivian knew she had to hold on to Lorna Lafferty with everything she had, and if that meant navigating a live show while her stomach roiled and her vision clouded with images of a dead Marjorie Fox, then so be it.

She clutched her script with one hand and brushed away the beads of sweat that had formed along her hairline with the other.

"That's right, sweetheart. And you're a goner." Dave Chapman spoke his line smoothly, without conveying the tension apparent in his face. He glanced at Vivian, then nervously into the control room.

Bill Purdy stepped to the mike, looking just as dapper as he had during the eight o'clock show — not a hair out of place. She'd seen him give his statement to the police right before they went live. Then he'd just sauntered up to the microphone and done his job as if nothing had happened. He raised his right hand to his ear and gazed off into the middle distance as he began the sponsor's announcement.

"That's right, folks. You'll be sold on Sultan's Gold. The mellow choice of cigarette smokers everywhere . . ."

Graham stood slightly apart from the others as he usually did. He ran a hand through his oil-black hair, never taking his eyes from the script.

The organ music came in to wrap up the sponsor's jingle.

"I think Mr. Diamond will have something to say about that," Vivian said after a perfectly timed beat, hitting the cue she had missed earlier.

She glanced into the control room. Joe gave her a sharp nod, the highest praise he was willing to give under any circumstances. Vivian smiled nervously and nodded back. The control room was especially crowded

54

for this performance. Joe was surrounded by Mr. Hart, Mr. Haverman, Sergeant Trask, and two other uniformed policemen. Morty was sitting at his control panel. Vivian's eyes wandered to each man in turn. Mr. Hart looked beside himself with either worry or excitement — she couldn't tell which. The police detectives and Mr. Haverman simply observed the performance, their faces impassive. She wrinkled her brow as she reviewed those assembled in the control room again. Someone was missing. Someone else had been there for the eight o'clock show who was not here now, but neither the name nor the face would come to her.

She glanced around at those assembled on the studio floor. Dave, Graham, Bill Purdy, the soundman, the organ player. Could one of them have hated Marjorie Fox enough to kill her?

The scuffle between Harvey Diamond and Glanville, his nemesis, began again. Then the shot rang out, followed by a beat of silence.

"Harvey!" Vivian shrieked. "Oh, Harvey, are you all right?"

"It's over," Graham said. "I've disarmed him, and he's out cold. There's a jail cell with this mug's name all over it."

Graham liked having a live audience — paying customers or policemen, it seemed to make little difference to him. He'd worked up a sweat, and his gestures were even more exaggerated in this performance than they had been two hours before. He'd nearly knocked Dave's script right out of his hands during the fight scene.

In fact, they all seemed to thrive under pressure because the timing in the second half was perfect this go-around. When the on-air light went out, Vivian almost collapsed with relief.

"Well done, everyone," Joe announced over the speaker.

"Nice work, Viv," Graham said, rerolling the cuff on his right sleeve. "You really came through tonight."

Vivian shot him a feeble smile. "I'm a professional."

"That you are, Miss Witchell. That you are." Graham smiled warmly at her. "Say, Viv —"

Vivian glanced up through her lashes at him, but he didn't get a chance to finish his thought.

"Miss Witchell?"

Her shoulders slumped, and she turned reluctantly toward the source of the interruption. Mr. Haverman stood just behind her, hands in his jacket pockets.

"More questions?" she asked him wearily.

"I was just going to offer you a lift home," he said.

"Oh." She sighed. "No, thank you."

"But I insist," he said firmly. His face softened, and he glanced to Graham. "Mr. Yarborough can vouch for my character."

Vivian glanced at Graham, who was looking at the detective through narrowed eyes.

"I have no doubts about your character, Mr. Haverman." She offered him a tired smile. "You are the real Harvey Diamond, after all."

Vivian regretted the words as soon as they came out of her mouth. Graham's ego was a remarkably fragile thing. There was a long pause, and then Mr. Haverman held out his arm to her.

"Then shall we?"

She looked at Graham, but his face was unreadable. She hoped she hadn't offended him too terribly. She knew how much he identified with his character. Wordlessly, she took the detective's arm. After all, any ride home was better than taking the streetcar — especially after the night she'd had.

"I'm parked across from the LaSalle." The detective tilted his head to the west and the general direction of the large redbrick hotel on the far corner of the next block. Madison Street was crowded even at this time of night with well-dressed couples ducking into the hotel nightclubs for a late dinner and a show. There were several choices in this small strip of the city alone — the Terrace Garden at the Morrison, the Brevoort's Crystal Bar, and, of course, the LaSalle, near where Mr. Haverman had parked.

A red-and-cream streetcar clanged past them heading west, and Vivian flinched at the sudden loud noise. She exhaled slowly and, to distract herself, glanced up at the La Salle Theatre's marquee to see what was playing. *Crime and Horror Show Tonight!* the sign screamed. She hesitated a second, blinked, and looked again. It was a B movie double feature of *Boys in the Racket* and *Phantom G-Men.* The detective had stopped walking when she had, and she felt Mr. Haverman's forearm tense under her hand.

"Something wrong?" he asked.

Nothing except that Vivian felt like she was starring in her own crime and horror show tonight, and she had to stop herself from laughing at the nearly perfect coincidence. Somehow she didn't think Mr. Haverman would get the joke.

"I just realized that I never got my blasted

umbrella," she said instead. It was the first thing that had come to mind, and it sounded ridiculous. She avoided looking at him, instead glancing up toward the night sky, which had been rendered a useless, rusty-brown haze by the lights of the city.

"I'll go back and get it for you."

"No, no," she said. A train thundered over the elevated tracks a block west at Wells Street. A car horn honked, another streetcar clattered past, and suddenly everything was too loud, too much. She wanted to be home very badly and tugged Mr. Haverman forward again by his jacket sleeve.

They walked on without speaking, stopping at LaSalle and Madison in front of a nondescript black sedan, its wheels hugging the curb. He opened the passenger-side door.

Vivian stepped forward, and her eyes swept the length of LaSalle Street — an artificial canyon made by the lofty buildings on either side and capped at the end by the imposing Chicago Board of Trade Building. She glanced up at the illuminated Ceres statue, goddess of agriculture, standing sentinel at the very top. Then the sky behind the statue flickered, and she heard what could only be a rumble of thunder somewhere in the distance. She shivered.

"Miss Witchell?"

She shot the detective an apologetic smile, meeting his eyes only briefly as he helped her into the passenger seat.

The sodium lights lit the streets of the Loop bright yellow, and neon lights blinked, advertising beer, cigarettes, chop suey, and dancing to Dick Jurgens and his orchestra at the Aragon Ballroom in Uptown. She eyed the happy couples strolling arm in arm as the car turned right onto Washington Street, and she envied them having nothing on their minds other than where to find a good time.

"So where exactly am I taking you?" he asked.

"Sorry." Vivian sighed. "Left on Michigan up here. Then another left on Scott shortly after Michigan meets Lake Shore. I'm at Scott and Astor."

They stopped at a red light, the engine rumbling unevenly in its idle. She shot a glance at the detective's sharp profile, and then her eyes fell on the glowing red sign of the Stop and Shop on the street beyond him.

Vivian's mouth flooded with the taste of the delicate, sugary, violet-flavored Italian Majani candies that her father brought home from that store at Christmastime.

Sometimes he'd stop on his way home from the office and pick up an exotic item like a kumquat or a pomegranate, presenting it to her triumphantly upon his return as if he were giving her a bag of gold. She wished he were here now. He would know what to do. It would comfort her just to hear his voice. She closed her eyes against the tears that threatened and immediately saw Marjorie dead, hair matted with blood, on the black screen of her eyelids. Vivian opened her eyes and folded her arms tightly across her chest as the car lurched into gear again.

"Are you all right?" Mr. Haverman asked, briefly taking his eyes from the road.

Vivian sighed. "I'm a little rattled, to be honest."

He grunted sympathetically. They passed under the El at Wabash and then made a left onto Michigan Avenue to head north. *Speed West with Streamliners to California!* the brightly lit billboard announced off to her right. What she wouldn't give to get on a screaming-fast train headed anywhere right now, she thought.

"So what's it like to be a private eye?" she asked. "Is it terribly exciting?"

"It depends."

"On what?"

"On what I've been hired to do."

"I think Graham has the impression that it's terribly exciting all the time," she said.

"I let him believe what he wants to believe. It makes for a better show."

The lights of the city sparkled off the black mirror of the Chicago River as they rumbled over the Michigan Avenue Bridge.

"Do people really call you Chick?"

"Only Mr. Yarborough."

She smiled. "And I bet you've never been tied up and left for dead in an emerald mine."

"Can't say I have," he replied drily. Then he returned her smile, his teeth a flash of muted white in the semidarkness of the sedan.

Vivian broke from his gaze and turned back to the window. The activity outside had quieted. Traffic was light, and they'd just passed the elegant white wedding cake of the Wrigley Building and the towering gothic spire of the Tribune Tower across from it. North Michigan Avenue was subdued, the immediate hubbub of the Loop behind them on the other side of the river. The soaring Palmolive Building was ahead, the recesses in its limestone facade lit impressively with floodlights and the blazing white Lindbergh Beacon at the top swiveling 360 degrees to guide airplanes into Chicago Municipal Airport southwest of the city from more than two hundred miles away.

"So what is it that you do exactly — assuming you aren't always disarming kidnappers and saving damsels in distress?"

"Oh," he said. "Usually a lot of waiting around, trying to catch people doing things they shouldn't be doing."

Vivian glanced sidelong at the detective. "Like cheating husbands?"

"And wives . . ."

Vivian tried to imagine what *The Darkness Knows* would be like every week if all Harvey Diamond did was lurk outside hotel rooms waiting to catch unsuspecting couples in flagrante delicto. Less dramatic, she thought, and decidedly not suitable for radio.

"I can only assume you have a lot of leggy, mysterious brunettes showing up in your office asking you to look into wayward husbands, missing heirs, things like that?"

"Not nearly as many as I'd like."

"Is that why you became a private detective, Mr. Haverman?"

"The promise of leggy women in need had a lot to do with it, yes." He took his eyes off the road for a moment to fix her with a curious stare. "Why the third degree? Interested in giving up your career in radio for the life of a private dick?"

"Oh no," she said, ducking her head. "It's just helping take my mind off . . . off the situation."

"I don't mind."

Vivian's attention was again drawn out the passenger-side window, gazing at the vast, inky void of Lake Michigan. Mr. Haverman turned the car left onto the quiet side street. "The short answer is that it's the family business. My father, that's Charles Haverman Sr., taught me everything I know." He paused a few seconds and then added, "No one calls him Chick either."

Vivian smiled.

"And what's the long answer?" she asked. "Oh, here it is. You can let me off on the corner."

"The long answer is a story for another time," he said as the car slowed to a stop. "This is your . . . house?"

Vivian heard the strange lilt in his voice and glanced out the window, realizing she'd forgotten to warn him. Her circumstances, such as they were, usually surprised people.

They'd arrived in front of a large, elaborately carved stone house at one of the toniest addresses on the Near North Side. The house, though much larger than her family had ever needed, was actually one of the smallest in the neighborhood. It was dwarfed on either side by much larger expressions of wealth in brick and stone, and the famed castle of Chicago scion Potter Palmer was only a few blocks away. The porch light burned brightly, but all of the interior windows were dark, the lace curtains still. It was well past eleven o'clock now, and Mrs. Graves, the elderly housekeeper, would have long since been in bed. Vivian's mother was likely out at some society soiree.

It was still difficult for Vivian to think of this monstrosity as her home. They'd moved here from an only slightly less stylish neighborhood in Lincoln Park not long before her father's death seven years ago. He'd purchased the house from a former client who had hit hard times. A lot of people had hit hard times during the Depression, but her father, a prominent attorney, had flourished. Now that Vivian's younger brother, Everett, was at Northwestern, just she and her mother were rattling around this ridiculous old place.

"Pretty grand," Mr. Haverman said simply.

"Yes, well, it's my mother's house," she answered. "I'm only staying here until . . .

until I can get a place of my own." The stone lions stared reproachfully at her from their perches on both sides of the massive stone staircase leading to the double-hung front door.

"I see."

"Well, thank you for the ride, Mr. Haverman." She extended her hand, and he shook it. "I very much appreciate it."

"I'll walk you to the door."

"No need —" she began, but he'd sprung out of the car before she could finish.

They walked in silence, dry leaves crunching under their feet. The thunder seemed to be moving off into the distance, the promised rain skirting the city. The night had grown frosty, and Vivian pulled her flimsy jacket tighter around her shoulders, wishing she'd opted for something a little more substantial when she'd dressed that morning.

Mr. Haverman unhooked the wrought iron gate and swung it open. He paused briefly in front of one of the stone lions, hands in his pockets, raising an eyebrow but saying nothing as Vivian hurried up the stairs. She pulled the key from her handbag as she went to unlock the thick mahogany door with a quick flick of her wrist. She turned on the threshold, already fantasizing

66

about soaking in a nice, hot bath. Mr. Haverman took the wide limestone steps two at a time.

"Again, thank you for the lift home. Maybe I'll see you around the station sometime?" Vivian tried to smile, but it was all she could do to keep her eyes from closing as she said her good-byes.

"Actually, I'd like to come in," he said.

Vivian's mouth opened in reply, but words momentarily failed her. She searched her memory for anything she'd said during the drive that might have led Mr. Haverman to believe that she was anything but the most respectable of ladies.

"Perhaps we can have a nightcap some other night, Detective." Her voice was tipped with ice. He was charming, but this was a bit too forward. She held his gaze for a long second and then began to close the door, but the detective stopped it with his hand.

"No, Miss Witchell," he said. "I don't think you understand. You're in danger."

CHAPTER FIVE

"Mr. Hart wanted to keep this under wraps for as long as possible." Mr. Haverman took off his dark gray fedora and placed it atop the coat-tree in the entry hall. "He doesn't want a lot of loose talk around the station."

"Yes, yes, I understand," Vivian said, even though she didn't. She strode straight through the entryway and into the den. "Would you like a drink?" she asked over her shoulder. She didn't wait for a response before opening the paneled oak doors of the extensive liquor cabinet and surveying the contents. "Scotch all right?" She named the first bottle she recognized that contained enough liquor for two.

"Sure."

She poured the drinks with a shaking hand, the bottle bouncing against the lip of the glass. She handed Mr. Haverman his drink and took a mighty gulp of her own. She coughed and then sank into the armchair nearest the fireplace, wishing it had been lit. She was suddenly chilled to the bone.

"Okay," she said, feeling the scotch slide down her throat, her strength artificially buoyed by the trail of warmth the alcohol left. She took a deep breath. "Let's have it."

Mr. Haverman set his glass on the fireplace mantel and reached into the breast pocket of his jacket. He spoke as he slowly unfolded a plain piece of paper. "This isn't the original, of course, but I was able to jot down the contents of the letter that was found with Mrs. Fox's body before the police took it as evidence."

Vivian took the paper from him and held it gingerly between the tips of her thumb and index finger. She looked up at Mr. Haverman, who nodded his encouragement, and began to read aloud.

Dearest Evelyn,
My heart leaped into my throat when I heard you say the secret words today. Our secret words. I like how you dropped them so smoothly into your speech about Bill missing football try-outs, clever girl. I'll come for you right away.

Vivian shot the detective a questioning glance, took another deep breath, and continued.

I'm not upset that you haven't answered any of my letters. I know you're busy, and I know you think of me as much as I think of you. I know Mr. Garrett will be angry when I take you away from him, but it has to be done. You belong here with me. Don't you see that? He'll have to see that too. See you very, very soon, darling.

Your Walter

P.S. Tell Lorna that I'm waiting for her secret words too.

"I don't understand," she said slowly, staring at the words written in the detective's large, looping script. "What does this mean? It's addressed to Evelyn and mentions Bill and Mr. Garrett from *The Golden Years* . . . This man, this Walter, thought Evelyn was real?"

"It appears so."

"And he mentions Lorna . . . He thinks *Lorna* is real too?" She looked up at the detective, eyes wide.

"Which is why Mr. Hart has hired me to keep an eye on you."

Vivian's eyebrows knit together with worry but then relaxed as a thought struck her. The whole thing was a mistake, of course. "But this Walter can't mean *me*," she said. Her voice was strong, buoyed by her sudden certainty. "I just started as Lorna. He'd be after Edith Waters, the original Lorna."

Charlie shook his head slowly. "I wouldn't be so sure. I think this Walter is after Lorna. Period. He thinks she's real, and as of last week, *you* are Lorna Lafferty."

Vivian slowly slumped back into the chair. *Talk about bad timing,* she thought. "Jesus, Mary, and Joseph," she said under her breath. "Why would someone want to kill me?"

"Not you, Miss Witchell," the detective corrected. "Lorna Lafferty."

"Yeah, yeah," she muttered. "Well, if Lorna dies, then so do I." Her attempt at a carefree laugh came out as a cough, and she stifled it with her hand.

Mr. Haverman paced silently in front of the mantel for a few moments before speaking again. He turned to Vivian, frowning. "I suspect that Mrs. Fox's death was an accident, or at least unplanned."

"Why do you say that?" Her voice sounded flat and small in her ears.

"I think that this Walter is delusional. He

71

may have come to see Evelyn — that is to say, Mrs. Fox — fully expecting her to go with him willingly, and when she resisted, he panicked and hit her with the first thing available."

"The bottle of whiskey." Vivian considered that information for a moment. She brought the glass to her lips, but there was no scotch left. She couldn't remember finishing it. "I know that's meant to be comforting in some way, but it's not."

"You're sure you haven't received any letters?"

"Like this? I would have remembered." She held the note in front of her and then placed it on the side table.

"You don't recognize the name Walter?"

She shook her head.

"Can you think of anything that you and Mrs. Fox might have had in common?"

Vivian shrugged. "We work with a lot of the same people — engineers, soundmen, writers, directors, actors, announcers, musicians. All the staff work on everything at the station. But as I told you earlier, Marjorie and I weren't the best of friends. We were barely even acquaintances."

"Right," he said, nodding. He stood deep in thought for a moment. "And I suppose you don't have any idea what the secret words might be?"

"I haven't a clue," she said, defeated. She suddenly sat stiffly upright as a new and terrible thought struck her. "If I don't know what they are, how will I know if I've said them?" Her eyes darted over Mr. Haverman's face, searching for some tiny bit of reassurance, perhaps even an outright declaration that the secret words mentioned were just a bit of delusional nonsense.

The detective looked Vivian squarely in the eye. "You got me."

At that moment, the front doorknob rattled. They could hear the muffled curses of someone trying to force a key into the lock. Charlie tensed and reached inside his jacket. "Expecting someone?"

Vivian glanced at the time on the grandfather clock, then relaxed back into the chair. She pinched the bridge of her nose with her thumb and forefinger.

"Just Mother," she said with a sigh.

Vivian heard the front door open and shut again quickly, followed by the thump of the bolt being set into place. Her mother burst into the room soon after, pulling one long, white glove off as she walked. She was dressed to the nines, and Vivian recalled that her mother had planned to attend a benefit at the opera this evening. She had kept her active social and charity schedule after Vivian's father's death and was out at least four nights of every seven. Her mother had the same strawberry-blond hair as Vivian, except that hers was liberally streaked with gray and swept back into a classic chignon at the base of her neck. She was a bit plump — pleasantly, Vivian would say — but her eyes were bright, her skin was clear, and even Vivian had to admit that she looked like her older sister rather than her mother. Unfortunately for Vivian, her mother didn't act much like an older sister.

"Well, that was a disaster. Whoever planned that benefit had no idea —" Her mother stopped suddenly as her eyes fell upon Mr. Haverman. She pulled the second glove off with a flourish. "You have a gentleman caller at this time of night?" she asked smoothly, addressing Vivian as she appraised Mr. Haverman with a cool eye.

Vivian fought the urge to laugh at her mother's use of the antiquated phrase *gentleman caller.* "Mother, this is Charles Haverman."

"Pleased to meet you, Mr. Haverman. I'm Vivian's mother, Julia Witchell," her mother said, holding out her ungloved hand. She took the detective's hand with only her fingers, made the briefest of downward motions with her wrist, and then immediately released it. She turned her attention back to Vivian, one eyebrow arched in expectation.

"Mr. Haverman is a private detective and a special consultant to *The Darkness Knows,*" Vivian explained. "He graciously offered me a ride home after the ten o'clock show tonight."

"I see." Her mother's eyes fell upon the bottle of scotch sitting on top of the open liquor cabinet. "Are you feeling all right, Vivian?"

Vivian paused as she considered how to answer the question. Where to begin? With her fingernail, she tapped the glass she was holding.

"There's been an incident at the station, Mrs. Witchell," Mr. Haverman said.

"An incident? What kind of incident?"

"A murder," Vivian clarified. "Marjorie Fox. She played Evelyn Garrett —"

"On *The Golden Years,*" her mother finished. "I listen to that every day!"

"You do?" Vivian asked, surprised.

Her mother waved the question away impatiently. "What on earth happened?" Her eyes darted from Vivian to the detective and back to Vivian, where they narrowed with suspicion. "You're not involved, are you, Vivian?"

"I may be," Vivian said quietly. She stood, retrieved the letter from the side table, and handed it to her mother. "This was found with Marjorie's body. I'm mentioned. Well, Lorna is. I may be in danger if this Walter person was responsible for Marjorie's murder."

Mr. Haverman and Vivian watched in silence as her mother read the letter.

"This is horrible," her mother said in a low voice. "No, this is really horrible." She looked up sharply, as if they were about to argue with her. "You have to go away."

"Go away?"

"Your life is in danger, Vivian. You can't stay here."

"Yes, I can. Mr. Haverman's going to look after me." Vivian glanced at him. "Mr. Hart hired him to do just that."

The detective slid his hand into his inside jacket pocket and produced a calling card for each of them. Vivian glanced at it.

Charles Haverman Jr.
Private Inquiries
HAR–7998

"I'm sure Mr. Haverman is competent at whatever it is that he does," Vivian's mother said, holding the card at arm's length and gazing doubtfully at it. "But I don't trust him with my daughter's life."

The detective showed no sign of offense. Vivian had to admire his calm in the presence of the formidable Mrs. Witchell.

"You're going to have to, Mother, because I'm not leaving." Vivian crossed her arms across her chest. "I have shows to do."

"Oh, the shows . . ." Mrs. Witchell threw her hands out as if to push the idea away, the letter flapping in the space between mother and daughter. "You can do those shows when you come back safe and sound."

"Mother, that's not how it works," Vivian said.

"Posh on how it works. Mr. Hart will understand."

"Of course he'll understand," Vivian agreed. "And they'll find another girl to do all my parts while I'm away."

"I don't really think that would be such a bad thing."

"Oh, Mother, don't start."

"You can go up to our cabin in Wisconsin for a few weeks," her mother continued in a softer tone of voice. "Everett was just up there with some friends. I'm sure it's in fine condition."

Vivian rolled her eyes at the idea. If

Everett had been up there with his fraternity brothers, the cabin was sure to be in less than fine condition. "I'm not sitting alone in a freezing cabin for a few weeks while my radio career goes right down the toilet," she said.

Her mother scowled at the inelegant phrasing. "I'm only thinking of your safety."

"So it's fine if I freeze to death?"

"Don't be smart."

Vivian turned to Mr. Haverman. "Mother would love me to drop all this radio nonsense, get married, and have babies. Right, Mother?"

"Now, Vivian. That's not fair." Her mother added a glare that said, *And certainly not an appropriate conversation to have in front of a guest.*

Vivian grunted, amused at the barely noticeable blush on the previously unflappable detective's stubble-darkened cheeks.

Mrs. Witchell looked at the letter again and then turned to him. "So what do you suggest we do, Mr. Haverman?"

"I suggest that your daughter go about her daily routine as usual," he said, pausing to assess Mrs. Witchell's reaction. She said nothing, so he continued. "I'll be with her at all times. She'll be as safe as a kitten." He brushed his jacket back ever so slightly so that the butt end of a revolver was visible, tucked into a holster on his hip.

Vivian's mother's eyes widened, but she said nothing. The sight of the gun shocked Vivian — and thrilled her a little too.

"And I'm to be used as a sort of lure for this Walter?" Vivian asked suddenly.

The detective had no time to answer before Mrs. Witchell admonished her. "Vivian!"

"Well, how else do you think they're going to catch him, Mother? It's exciting, don't you think? I've read about things like this in *True Crime* magazine."

Mrs. Witchell sighed. "Your father never should have let you read those silly rags. Giving you ridiculous ideas . . ." She rubbed her temples.

"I'm afraid it's far too late for that now, Mother."

Mrs. Witchell glared as she finally removed her expensive-looking, black Persian lamb coat, laying it carefully over her arm. She moved back toward the entryway, Charlie and Vivian following behind. She paused at the base of the stairs and turned back to face them.

"Oh, I have a splitting headache," she said. She sighed again, this time more dramatically. "You're staying, Mr. Haverman? I'll phone Mr. Hart right now to verify your story, of course. Assuming that you are who you say you are, I'd feel much safer with a detective in the house." She didn't wait for his response before continuing. "The guest room is at the end of the hall upstairs. It should be ready for use."

She started climbing, then stopped and turned back.

"Oh, and don't go near the room next to the stairs," she said to Mr. Haverman. "That's the housekeeper's room. She keeps a baseball bat next to the bed, and she's likely to knock you out cold."

"Thanks for the warning." The detective caught Vivian's eye and smirked.

"Good night, Mother," Vivian called sweetly. She watched her mother disappear up the front stairs, then returned to the open bottle of scotch and refilled her glass. "I'd forgotten all about Mrs. Graves and her bat. She's always saying that three women living alone together need to be able to take care of themselves."

"I agree completely."

"And we don't often have strange, gun-toting men in the house . . . Once or twice a week at most."

"This isn't a laughing matter, Miss Witch-ell," the detective said in a low voice.

"Oh, I know. Believe me, I know," she said with a sigh. She turned to face him but continued staring down at her drink as she spoke. "All that silliness with Mother was an act so she wouldn't worry." She swished the amber liquid around in her glass. Then she looked up at the detective, the false bravado wiped from her face.

"I assure you, Mr. Haverman, I'm terrified."

CHAPTER SIX

Marjorie's murder had pushed Hitler below the fold of the morning papers. Vivian's mother held up that morning's copy of the *Tribune* wordlessly as Vivian entered the dining room. A photo of a much younger Marjorie graced a full one-third of the front page. It appeared to be a publicity photo taken when *The Golden Years* was first catching on. She'd been quite a striking woman before the booze really took hold, Vivian thought. Amazing what it could do in only half a dozen years. Vivian took the paper and quickly scanned the story.

The article held scant detail about the murder itself, and Vivian was not mentioned at all. The contents of the mysterious fan letter still seemed to be under wraps. Mr. Hart had no doubt worked his magic, or more likely his muscle, with the staffs of the city's major newspapers.

The *Chicago Patriot* had identical information, but also ran a side story trumpeting access to Marjorie's secret diaries, which would be published in tomorrow's edition. Giving them enough time to be fabricated, Vivian mused. Secret diaries were a staple of the *Patriot.* There was little cause to think that anything they published would be the remotest neighbor to the truth. Marjorie didn't seem like the type to keep a secret diary.

"You're not mentioned in either paper, Vivian," her mother said. "Thank goodness."

"The *Patriot,* Mother?" Vivian raised an eyebrow. She buttered a slice of toast and applied a hefty dollop of strawberry jam. Unfortunately, being in mortal danger had done nothing to quell her appetite.

Her mother sniffed as she glanced at the tabloid.

"Yes, well, I had to see what the papers were saying . . . All the papers."

"Mmm," Vivian mumbled, her mouth full of toast. She didn't want a rehash of last night. She wasn't going to spend a few weeks in that dreary cabin in the Wisconsin wilderness, and that was final.

Mrs. Witchell appraised her only daughter. "Vivian, darling, you look awful."

"Why, thank you, Mother."

"Such dark circles under your eyes . . ."
She tut-tutted.

"I didn't sleep very well last night, as you
can imagine."

"I *can* imagine," her mother said. "With
this mess you've gotten yourself into."

Vivian glared at her. "Gotten myself into?
I did absolutely nothing wrong, I'll have you
know, besides walk into the station lounge
at the wrong time."

Her mother sighed heavily. She didn't
have to say another word. Vivian knew the
lines of this particular argument by heart:
Julia Witchell didn't think Vivian should be
walking around the halls of WCHI at all, let
alone at night. She shouldn't be messing
around with radio. She shouldn't pursue
this silly acting business. She shouldn't have
a job at all. She shouldn't. She shouldn't.
She shouldn't.

Vivian fumed silently. She was determined
not to let her mother get her goat this morning, even though preventing that would take
something akin to a Herculean effort. She
knew better than to think she could have a
rational conversation about something like
this with her mother. What she needed was
to talk this through with someone who was
on her side, someone who was always on
her side — someone like her best friend,

84

Imogene Crook.

She wasn't supposed to tell anyone about the letter, but Vivian had picked up the telephone several times during the course of her sleepless night. She'd never completed the call. Not because she didn't trust her best friend to keep a secret, but because it had been too late to give her a ring. She didn't want to wake Genie and get her stewing about something she couldn't do anything about. Besides, she'd see her at the station today. Genie was the station program manager's secretary.

"Nothing new with the investigation," Mr. Haverman said, entering the room oblivious to the tense atmosphere. "Good morning, Miss Witchell."

"Good morning," Vivian said. She didn't look up from the grapefruit she was studiously dissecting on the plate before her, suddenly feeling self-conscious about her newly acquired dark circles.

"So what's the schedule for the day?" he asked, clapping his hands together with enthusiasm.

Vivian jumped a little at the noise. She paused to recover her nerve before speaking. No doubt she was on edge.

"Well, I should be at the station by at least 10:30," Vivian began. "There's a rehearsal for *Love & Glory* at 11:00, and then we go live from 11:30 to 11:45. I have another rehearsal after lunch. Another live show from 2:00 to 2:15. And there's some publicity to do in there somewhere . . ."

"That's quite a schedule."

"Welcome to the world of an up-and-coming radio star," she said with a tight smile.

"You aren't going anywhere today, Vivian," her mother said, setting her spoon down with sharp finality next to the grapefruit half on the plate.

"I have to. I have two shows and a photo shoot for —"

"I don't care what you have," her mother interrupted. "When I spoke with Mr. Hart last evening, he advised very strongly that you stay at home where we can all keep an eye on you."

"Mr. Hart advised, did he?" Vivian looked to the detective for confirmation.

Mr. Haverman nodded. "He did. But —"

"But nothing." Mrs. Witchell's gaze at the detective was cold.

"But the threat against Vivian is not verified," he continued, returning her cold gaze completely unfazed, "and I see nothing wrong with Miss Witchell going about her normal routine."

There was a tense silence while Vivian's mother considered his statement. She seemed to be taking stock of the detective. She held his gaze for a few seconds, and Vivian noted with satisfaction that her mother was the first to look away.

"You'll be with my daughter the entire time, Mr. Haverman?" Mrs. Witchell asked finally.

"I won't let her out of my sight."

"Don't you have other cases?" Vivian asked. She found herself inordinately pleased to be the focus of so much special attention.

"I do," he said. "But Mr. Hart has made it worth my while to put those on hold for the time being."

"All for me?"

"All for the *station*," he corrected.

CHAPTER SEVEN

Mr. Haverman's car was even less impressive in the full light of day. It was an unremarkable Packard sedan, black, with some rust spots beginning to form near the wheel wells. It was clean inside and out, but the cloth upholstery was shabby and had certainly seen better days. Vivian began to wonder how well his business was doing and, consequently, just how good a detective he truly was. But Mr. Hart seemed to trust him, and Mr. Hart didn't trust just anyone.

They drove south down Michigan Avenue toward WCHI. It was a rare treat for Vivian to be driven anywhere. She usually walked or took the streetcar. She didn't have a driver's license, and her mother had been nearly shocked to apoplexy a few years back when Vivian suggested she wanted to study for one. A woman of means didn't drive themselves anywhere, her mother had told her. But she had adamantly refused to use her mother's chauffeur at any time. It was a small act of defiance, but it pleased Vivian to shock her mother by bucking social convention. When Vivian had argued that she was an independent working woman who needed a car, the mere idea had sent her mother into a fit and ended the conversation.

Vivian rested her head against the seat back in Mr. Haverman's car and smiled at the memory. "I want to thank you for helping me out with my mother," she said. "I was afraid I was going to have to shimmy down the drainpipe or something." Vivian glanced sidelong at the detective. She noted his rueful smile and added, "I've done it before."

Mr. Haverman raised his eyebrows at the thought and said, "I have no doubt, Miss Witchell." Then he added, "But I don't blame her. She's worried about you."

"Worried about me," Vivian repeated with a scowl. "Worried about my reputation, you mean. And hers." Vivian affected the boarding-school-polished, mid-Atlantic tones of her mother and added, "Murder is so working class."

"Hey, you sounded just like her." He slapped the steering wheel in surprise.

"Ah, she's easy," Vivian said, waving her hand in dismissal. "You should hear my Mae West."

"You're a pretty good actress, you know," he said, his smile fading slightly.

"Thank you," she replied. Her brow wrinkled. "But you've only seen me perform one *Darkness Knows* episode."

"I mean that, sure. You're certainly better than the previous Lorna. She couldn't act her way out of a paper bag . . . But I also mean the act with your mother and with me. The stiff-upper-lip charade."

Vivian laughed nervously. "Oh yes, well, if I act devil-may-care, I may start to believe I actually am."

"Is it working?" The detective glanced over at her, then back to the road.

"Not so far," Vivian admitted. She absently fingered a worn spot in the upholstery of her seat, scraping her nail against the individual threads.

"You know, I don't think anyone would question you taking some time off right now," he said.

Vivian took a deep breath and let it out slowly. "If this is some sort of reverse psychology, Mr. Haverman, it won't work. I was serious about what I told my mother last night," she said. "If I bow out of anything now, I'll be a has-been before you can say 'Jack Robinson.' "

"And then you'll have no choice but to get married and have babies."

Vivian's brow furrowed, then she smirked when she realized he was teasing. "Exactly," she agreed.

They stopped at a red light next to the stone column of the historic Water Tower, and Vivian watched the commotion of early morning commuters rushing past her window. People scurried to and fro on the sidewalks of Michigan Avenue. The men were a blur of gray flannel, the women clad in smart fall dresses with matching hats and gloves. It was a gorgeous, crisp October morning. They were in the middle of a true Indian summer, the days warm and sunny. Vivian had always thought Indian summers were a cruel trick. They gave everyone false hope that winter might not come. But winter always came to Chicago.

"I'm going to be a star, Mr. Haverman," she said firmly. "I'll do whatever it takes."

The detective narrowed his eyes. "Whatever it takes?"

Vivian didn't like his tone: teasing, sarcastic, implying something devious in her ambition. She opened her mouth to unleash a scathing retort when her eyes fell on the newsstand on the corner. Marjorie's face stared back at her from the front page of every paper, dozens of them lined up for sale. "Radioland Murder!" the handwritten advertisements screamed.

Vivian shuddered and closed her eyes, opening them only when the car started moving again and they were past the newspaper stand. "So what *are* we going to do about finding this Walter?"

"I don't know what you mean."

"I mean, how do we find this awful person before he comes after me too?"

"I have no plans to find any Walter," Mr. Haverman said.

"But you're a private detective —"

"Who is being paid simply to keep one client from harm. Mr. Hart didn't hire me to find a killer. The police are handling that."

"Posh," Vivian said. "It's part of your job, the way I see it. Find the killer and you don't have to protect me anymore. It's two birds with one stone, really."

"Very sensible."

"I'm nothing if not sensible," she replied, inspecting her manicure before primly placing her hands on her lap.

The detective smirked and said nothing.

Luckily, the Michigan Avenue Bridge was

down, the flags lining both sides flapping in the breeze blowing in off the lake. If the drawbridge had been up, as it often was, they would have to wait at least ten minutes before they could cross. Vivian gazed out at the river and the buildings rising on either side to create an artificial canyon of steel and stone. The morning sunlight sparkled off the water. Vivian spotted another newsstand on the south side of the bridge, and she closed her eyes until they'd passed it.

"If it's about money," she began, tentatively opening her eyes again, "I'll be more than happy to pay for your services."

Mr. Haverman glanced sidelong at her, a lazy grin sliding onto his face. "Well, why didn't you say so?"

"So that's it? You'll do it?" Vivian asked, incredulous. She hadn't expected his motives to be that transparent.

"For the right price."

"A little money can persuade you that easily?"

"I hope we're talking more than a little . . ."

Vivian dismissed the comment with a wave of her hand. Money could be discussed later, she thought. At the moment, she was just thrilled at the prospect of being able to do something productive about her situation.

"So where should we start with the investigation?" she asked.

"Now wait a second," the detective said, holding up one large hand. "There's no *we* about it."

Vivian frowned and pursed her lips. "I just want to ask some questions around the station. That wouldn't hurt anyone, would it?" She turned to the detective, lowered her chin, and peered up at him through carefully mascaraed lashes.

The detective's eyes remained on the road. "I'll handle all the questioning, Miss Witchell."

Vivian let her breath out through her nose and narrowed her eyes in irritation. "Well, I'm not just going to sit around and wait for someone to smack me on the side of the head with a liquor bottle," she said.

Mr. Haverman took his eyes from the road only briefly to glance at her, one eyebrow arched. "I wouldn't recommend that, no," he said.

Vivian glared at the man's sharp profile for a few seconds, then sat back in her seat. "Well, I'm going to ask some questions," she said quietly. "And you can't stop me." She sucked her lower lip between her teeth, conscious that the man's eyes were on her again.

He didn't answer right away, but when he did, his voice was serious. "And just where would you start with your *questioning*?"

Vivian ignored his condescending tone and answered with confidence. "Marjorie's costars on *The Golden Years*. I think they'd know her better than anyone."

"Good a place as any, I suppose."

Vivian scowled. "You're just humoring me."

He continued to steer the car down Michigan Avenue, the fading green of Grant Park flashing briefly to their left. He made a right onto Madison, and when they passed under the El, a train overhead rendered any conversation fruitless for a few seconds. Vivian eyed the fall hat display in the front window of Mandel Brothers Department Store as they paused at the corner of State and Madison.

"I don't care if you are," she said with a wave of her hand. "As long as you help, I think you'll find that I'm not quite the flibbertigibbet you think I am."

"Oh, I think you're an immense flibbertigibbet," Mr. Haverman said, pulling smoothly into an empty parking space in front of the Grayson-Cole Building. He put the Packard in park and turned to face her with a smile. "But it suits you," he said. He held her gaze for a few seconds longer than strictly necessary.

Vivian turned back to the window and exhaled through her nose. Suits her indeed, she thought, as if that were some kind of compliment.

"This is a real stroke of luck," the detective said, opening his door. "There are never any spaces right out front."

He jogged around the back of the car and opened the passenger door with a flourish. He held out his hand to help her. "Miss Witchell . . ."

She glared at him for a moment before taking his hand.

"Oh, enough with this Miss Witchell business," she said, stepping from the car. "It's driving me batty hearing that every other sentence. You can call me Vivian like everyone else."

"Okay, Vivian."

"Actually, I prefer Viv," she said, straightening her hat — a black, schoolgirl-style beret with a green velvet ribbon band.

"Okay, Viv," he said seriously. "And I'm just Charlie, please."

"Not Chick? Graham will be crushed."

"He'll get over it."

Vivian smoothed the skirt of her suit and turned to face the building. She groaned at the sight. At least a dozen reporters milled around the entrance, firing questions at anyone who approached. She watched them follow one unsuspecting man to the entrance, swarming around him like flies and dispersing when he escaped inside. Then they backed away to stand together in small groups, chatting among themselves until the next poor person moved toward the entrance where the whole scene would replay itself.

"I can't do this," she said.

"Having second thoughts about going back to the station?"

"No, it's not that," Vivian said impatiently. She glared at the reporters. "I just don't want to walk through all of those vultures." Usually, the idea of photographers hanging around to take her picture would be a dream come true, but those reporters were here because of Marjorie, not her.

"I'll protect you." Charlie moved to put his arm around her shoulders, but she sidestepped it.

"Actually, I have a much better idea," she said. "Follow me."

Vivian led him in a long loop around the block to the alley directly behind the building. She smiled as the grungy, deserted back entrance came into view. Stepping over puddles of God knows what, she held her nose against the stench. At the entrance, Vivian pulled the handle, and the heavy metal door swung open with a screech.

"I guess luck really is on our side today. I wasn't sure the door would even be open. This staircase goes all the way up to the top floor," she said, craning her neck to look up into the darkness. "But there's also an entrance to the lobby through the door at the other end of this hall."

"Smart girl," Charlie said.

"I wasn't born yesterday. The elevators went on the fritz once, and I had to climb down all twelve flights."

"You weren't wearing ridiculous heels like these, were you?" Charlie nodded toward Vivian's formidable footwear.

"I always wear ridiculous heels like this," she said and smiled. "Come on."

She hadn't walked but a few steps toward the stairs when she slipped, her feet flying out in front of her. Charlie caught her just before she landed on her bottom and set her back upright, holding on to her until he was sure she was steady.

"Maybe you should rethink the heels."

"Pfft," she said, dismissing the idea. "I

just slipped on something." Vivian scanned the floor until she spotted the small black-and-gold object that had rolled to the far corner of the stairwell. She picked it up and examined it, holding it out on her outstretched palm.

"A cuff link," he said.

Vivian wrinkled her brow. "It looks like ones I've seen Graham wear."

"Maybe he had the same idea about avoiding the press this morning."

"Maybe . . ." Vivian put the cuff link in the pocket of her jacket, but something about the idea of Graham avoiding the press didn't sit quite right. Graham never avoided reporters.

CHAPTER EIGHT

Angelo's mouth fell open in surprise when the elevator doors parted and he spotted Vivian waiting impatiently for the express elevator to the eleventh floor.

"Miss Witchell!" he cried. Eyeing Mr. Haverman warily, he held out a protective hand to help her into the waiting car. "What are you doing here? You should be at home resting!"

Vivian made a concerted effort not to roll her eyes. "I have a show to do, Angelo," she said, stepping into the elevator and politely shaking the older gentleman's fingers off her forearm. She set her jaw determinedly. Angelo was the first of many run-ins she was likely to have today, all with acquaintances concerned for her welfare, and all of those encounters a nuisance.

"But is it" — he leaned in and lowered his voice to a whisper — "*safe* for you to be here?" He glanced from Vivian to Charlie, his eyes round.

"Don't be silly," she replied, making an effort to keep her voice light. "I'm safe as a kitten." She glanced at Charlie, who was studying the elevator inspection papers. Then she looked meaningfully at Angelo, willing him to stop talking about it already.

"Ah," he said with a nod toward the detective. "This is the man Mr. Hart hired for you, eh?"

Before she could respond, someone called, "Hold the elevator!" A harried-looking man hurried toward them, waving his arms. Without a word, Angelo closed the heavy metal doors. He pulled another lever, and the elevator jerked to life. Vivian's stomach lurched at the sudden movement, and she grabbed Charlie's arm to steady herself.

Vivian blinked. "Yes, but how do you know about that?" she asked, surprised.

"Graham told me on his way out yesterday."

Of course Graham would have talked about the letter found with Marjorie, Vivian thought. It was his chance to be part of a real-life detective case, not just one written for radio. By now, gossip about the letter's contents could have spread through the whole station.

"What's it all about?" Angelo asked, as if

she would be able to supply the answer right there in the elevator.

Vivian shrugged. "I wish I knew," she said.

"There's some crazy man after you?" With a self-conscious shrug, Angelo added, "That's what I hear anyway."

"Honestly, I don't know." Vivian heard her voice crack, and she felt her eyes begin to sting. She blinked several times, warding off the tears that suddenly threatened.

"The police are looking into it," Charlie said, his voice strong and reassuring. He placed his hand over hers.

The elevator jerked to an unceremonious stop at the eleventh floor. Angelo placed his hand on the door lever, but before pulling it, he turned to Vivian and said, "You be careful, miss."

Vivian leaned over the ladies' room sink and let cold water from the tap drip from her fingers onto the back of her neck. She was no longer close to tears, but she still felt that nagging fear in the pit of her stomach. Lifting her head, she met her gaze in the mirror. She looked like a terrified rabbit ready to run at the slightest hint of danger. That wouldn't do. It *couldn't* do. If she wanted to feel confident, she had to look the part. She made herself smile and pinched her cheeks to increase the blood flow.

The door of the stall farthest down the row opened. Vivian's eyes met Imogene's in the mirror over the sink.

"Viv!" Imogene squealed, rushing toward Vivian, her face alight with concern. "Are you all right? I heard what happened from one of the engineers first thing this morning!"

Vivian had met Imogene on her first day at secretarial school. They'd shared a stick of gum and a wisecrack about the generous proportions of Mrs. Hepplebottom, the shorthand instructor. "She should be called Mrs. Amplebottom," Imogene had whispered, and Vivian had had to fake a sneeze to cover her snort of laughter.

From there they'd both gone on to garner swell positions at WCHI — quite a coup for brand-new graduates. It didn't hurt that both girls were cute young things with a penchant for flirtation. Actually, if Vivian was honest, Imogene had talked her way in the door at WCHI and then dragged Vivian along with her. It was only happenstance that Vivian, instead of Imogene, became Mr. Hart's secretary. Imogene was better at shorthand, typing, and taking dictation —

but Mr. Hart preferred redheads to brunettes.

Vivian's forced smile became genuine, and she felt some of the tension leave her body. Imogene was exactly the person she needed to see right now. They hugged, and then Imogene pulled back and assessed Vivian with a critical eye. She didn't seem fooled by Vivian's newly pinkened cheeks.

"You're not all right," she said.

Vivian sighed and shook her head.

"I'm so sorry, Viv. That must have been a terrible shock." Imogene lowered her voice to a barely audible whisper. "Was it ghastly, seeing Marjorie dead like that?"

Vivian recalled the spongy flesh of Marjorie's lifeless calf under her fingertips, and she swallowed the bile that rose in her throat. "Yes," she said, pressing one hand against her stomach. "It was."

"You didn't have to come in today. They could have found a replacement for your parts, you know."

"I know," Vivian said grimly. "That's what I was afraid of."

"Right, right." Imogene sighed. The name *Frances Barrow* went unspoken between them. "Do you really think it was murder though? I mean, couldn't it have been an accident? You know, with all her . . ." She mimed tipping a bottle into her mouth.

"It was most definitely murder."

Imogene sighed again. "So who do you think did it? Do you think it was really this crazed fan?"

Vivian glanced sharply at her friend, but she wasn't surprised that Imogene had already heard about the letter. Word traveled fast at the station, and Imogene always had her ear to the ground.

"We both know how popular Marjorie was here," Vivian said. "I could think of at least five people off the top of my head who might have wanted to do her in."

"So can I," her friend agreed. "Including me from time to time."

Vivian frowned at her.

"Sorry. But do you think it could really be a fan?" Imogene continued. "It makes my skin crawl to think some crazy man might have been lurking around here, waiting for his chance to strike."

That man could be lurking and waiting again — this time, to strike her, Vivian thought. Her knees weakened, and she steadied herself against the sink, feeling the color drain from her face. Her hands grew cold. She glanced up at the mirror and saw Imogene's eyes widened in alarm.

"Oh God, Viv. What is it?"

Vivian hesitated. She knew she wasn't supposed to tell anyone, but if she kept this to herself any longer, she would burst. And if she couldn't trust her best friend with something like this, who could she trust?

"You know the letter they found with Marjorie?" Vivian said. Imogene nodded. "Well, it would seem that this crazy Walter person is also interested in Lorna Lafferty. *Very interested.*"

"No!" Imogene raised the back of her hand to her forehead. "But why you of all people?"

"I don't know. I really don't."

"What are you going to do?"

"What can I do? I have no idea who this Walter person is, and I haven't received any letters myself. The police aren't even sure this is a solid lead."

"But what are you going to *do,* Viv? You have to protect yourself. I have a revolver you can borrow. Well, it's my father's, and I'm not sure it still works, but you could use it just to scare someone, I suppose."

Vivian could see Imogene's gears turning and moved to stop her before this conversation took a real turn toward the ridiculous.

"Genie," Vivian said sharply.

Imogene stopped talking midsentence.

"I have someone to protect me," Vivian

said, turning back to face her friend. "Mr. Hart's hired a private detective."

"A private detective?"

Vivian nodded. "He's already a special consultant to *The Darkness Knows.*"

"Oh," Imogene said, her eyes lighting up. "I think I've seen him around here. Tall drink of water?" She leaned in, smugness in her voice. "Dangerously handsome?"

"Charlie Haverman," Vivian supplied, glancing away from Imogene's knowing gaze. She also wasn't surprised that Imogene already knew about Charlie.

"Right. I might find myself in some danger too, if you know what I mean." Imogene winked.

"Genie, this is serious."

"I know, I know," she said. "Just trying to lighten the mood a little." She gave Vivian another quick, bone-crushing hug. Then she glanced at her wristwatch and started. "Oh shoot! Sorry, Viv. I have to go! I promised Mr. Langley I'd get him those scripts *tout de suite.*" Imogene was secretary to Mr. Langley, the head of programming at WCHI. If Mr. Hart was the boss, Mr. Langley was a very close number two. "I'll tell you first thing if I hear anything. You'll be okay?" Imogene asked, already backing toward the door.

Vivian nodded, hoping the doubt didn't show on her face. As Imogene opened the door to the hall, she turned.

"Take care of yourself, Viv," she said. "A murderer might be lurking the halls of this station as we speak." She shuddered dramatically and was gone.

CHAPTER NINE

In fact, the halls of WCHI were always so crowded and chaotic that lurking was quite unnecessary. The murderer could be sauntering down the hallways right now in broad daylight. Pages scurried in every direction. Actors, musicians, and writers chatted and mingled as they made their way between studios. Vivian knew perhaps half of them by sight. She found herself scanning each unfamiliar face and wondering if he or she had taken that whiskey bottle to the back of Marjorie's head. And Vivian wondered, not without trepidation, where Charlie had gone.

Studio F was one of the smaller studios on the main floor. *Love & Glory* was a quiet serial with a small cast, almost all of which was already assembled for rehearsal when Vivian entered the room. Ralph Murphy, the director, pointed to his watch, and Vivian said defensively, "It's ten fifty-nine,

Ralph. By my watch that's right on time."

The group chuckled.

Vivian reached for the last script on the table, but it disappeared under one of the other actor's hands. She turned around in frustration. "Any other scripts around?"

Peggy stepped forward and handed her the copy she'd been holding. Vivian smiled her thanks and glanced at it as she poured herself a glass of water from the carafe on the refreshment table.

"Horrible what happened to Marjorie . . ."

Vivian swallowed the water with a gulp and peered over the edge of her glass at Dave Chapman. He was looking decidedly the worse for wear this morning. The purple bruises under his eyes were only highlighted by his sallow complexion, and he yanked on the knot of his tie with one finger as he spoke as if the tie were strangling him.

"Yes," she agreed. "Horrible."

"I just had to say it," Dave said with the slightest trace of a smile. "Elephant in the room and all . . ." He poured himself a glass of water. "Did you speak to the police last night?"

"Of course," she replied.

"Yes, that's right," he said grimly. "You found her."

Vivian winced. "Did *you* speak to the

police?" she asked.

"Yes, yes, of course. But I really had nothing to tell them. I barely knew the woman . . ." Dave looked off over Vivian's shoulder instead of meeting her eyes.

Vivian recalled that Dave had also worked with Marjorie off and on throughout his time at WCHI. They'd even starred on a short-lived show called *Night at the Theater* in which they'd played a bickering newly divorced couple. It had aired for fifteen minutes nightly for two months last year before it failed to find national sponsorship and was canceled. Working with the woman day in and day out for months qualified as "barely knowing" Marjorie? Vivian wondered what would have to occur between him and someone else for Dave to remove the qualifier "barely." After all, he currently played Vivian's on-air husband in *Love & Glory,* and she'd feel terrible telling someone that she "barely knew" Dave, especially if he'd just been murdered.

"Nice of you to join us, Frances!" shouted Ralph Murphy.

Vivian turned to the studio door. Frances was never a welcome surprise.

"I'm sorry," Frances said, out of breath. "I got stuck on the other side of the bridge . . ." She paused to make sure every-

111

one knew she meant that the Michigan Avenue Bridge had gone up and she'd had to wait for it — shorthand for the fact that she had been on another show on another network, from which they were all to infer that she was *in demand.*

"I got here as quickly as I could," she continued, dropping her bag on the floor near the door. "I ran all the way from the elevator."

"Where are you working?" someone asked enthusiastically. "Wrigley?"

"Merchandise Mart," Frances said. "It's a new historical reenactment program. Very dramatic. I'm playing Mata Hari." She looked directly at Vivian and smiled.

A collective "ooh" arose from the few other women in the room at the mention of the exotic, doomed spy.

Frances Barrow was beautiful. There was no denying that. With blue-black hair that curled under in a soft wave just above her shoulders and a creamy complexion, she looked like the cartoon Snow White sprung to life.

Frances had started as an actress at WCHI around the same time that Vivian had decided to make the switch from typewriter to microphone. Frances had broken into the business as one of the cowgirls on *Chet*

Whibley's Country Cavalcade, a hokey, hoedown-type show WCHI had added to contend with the farm stylings of competing station WLS. But she'd quickly moved on from square dance calls, and in the past year Vivian had found herself in direct competition with Frances for most of her roles. Vivian's recent triumph with Lorna Lafferty had dealt Frances's ego a substantial blow, and she'd been unbearable in the weeks since.

"All right, everyone. Let's get going. No time to waste." Ralph nodded toward the glass-enclosed control room where a fleshy woman had just entered and taken a seat.

Vivian's stomach lurched. Edith Gill-Davison, the grand dame of all dramatic daytime serials and producer extraordinaire, had come for a rare visit.

"Better scurry," Dave said under his breath. He hurried to the far side of the room to await his cue.

Vivian thought Mrs. Gill-Davison more closely resembled a washerwoman than a dramatic genius. In fact, she was more than a genius. She'd single-handedly created the genre of the family daytime drama and had no fewer than three sponsored serials on the air at any given time, dictating the story lines for all of them on a weekly basis.

Vivian knew Edith Gill-Davison could make or break your career. If she didn't like you, she made damn sure that no one else did either. She hadn't visited a live performance of *Love & Glory* for months. And today she looked to be in a foul mood, fouler than usual, probably because the star of her linchpin serial, *The Golden Years,* had just been bludgeoned to death. That would ruin anyone's day.

Vivian caught Frances's eye and was satisfied to see that her rival seemed equally terrified by the older woman's presence.

Vivian glanced at the first page of today's script. She was playing Donna Riley, wife of respected heart surgeon Delbert Riley. Donna was the supportive-woman-behind-a-successfulman type, and she'd had little to do until recently because the focus of the show had been on Dr. Riley's turbulent office life. But Donna had suspected for a week's worth of episodes that Delbert had been getting a little too close to his surgical assistant, Nancy. And today apparently was the day she was to confront the suspected other woman. Vivian smiled. This was just the type of juicy script she'd been waiting for. Maybe coming into the studio today wasn't really such a bad idea after all.

"Okay, let's begin."

Vivian glanced around but didn't see the actress who played Nancy. Surely, they couldn't start without her. She carried half the script.

Ralph pointed to the organist in the corner, and the theme music began quietly. He then pointed to the announcer, who stepped up to the microphone, one hand to his ear.

"Wickman's Laundry Soap presents *Love & Glory* . . . We return to Morgan Creek where the travails of a young successful heart surgeon are nothing compared to the troubles at home."

The theme music grew louder as the organist pounded on the keys with fervor and then died away again as the announcer continued.

"We find ourselves again in the home of eminent heart surgeon Delbert Riley. His wife, Donna, has finally acted upon her suspicions and invited Delbert's beautiful young assistant, Nancy, for a serious talk. Donna paces nervously before the front door . . ."

Ralph pointed to the soundman. He knocked on the prop door, waited a few seconds, and then opened it. Ralph pointed to Vivian.

"Hello, Nancy. Please come in," Vivian said.

Frances stepped up to the microphone.

"Hello, Mrs. Riley," she said, her voice smooth as butter. "Thank you for inviting me. I've wanted to meet you for such a long time."

Vivian looked up sharply at Ralph, one eyebrow raised. Ralph just shrugged his shoulders and jerked his thumb toward Mrs. Gill-Davison. So that was it? Frances had somehow weaseled her way into the woman's good graces and into a plum role on the show? Vivian narrowed her eyes and forced herself to focus on the task at hand. She had fifteen minutes of scripted melodrama to rehearse, and there was only time for one rehearsal before the live broadcast.

She turned the first page and something white slipped to the floor — an envelope. Vivian glanced at it as she picked it up and shoved it into her jacket pocket.

After a moment of panic, Vivian found her place in the script. "Would you like some coffee?" she asked.

"Yes, cream and sugar." Frances paused and then added with hesitation, "Mrs. Riley, is something wrong?"

"Why?"

"You're wringing that poor handkerchief

to pieces."

"Oh." Vivian laughed nervously. "I suppose I am."

She glanced at Mrs. Gill-Davison. The older woman watched the scene play out before her, her expression unreadable. Where had that envelope come from? The silly thing had broken Vivian's concentration. She took a deep breath and fought the threatening nerves. She couldn't have her voice quaver, not now.

"Ahem." Frances cleared her throat in irritation. "Your line, Viv."

Vivian jerked her head back down to the script.

"I . . . uh . . ." The lines were reeling before her eyes. She blinked them back into focus. She'd made a mistake during *The Darkness Knows* last night. She couldn't make another now. "I have something important I need to discuss with you, Mary."

"Nancy," Frances corrected in a flat voice.

"I'm sorry. Nancy." Vivian shook her head in an attempt to clear it. She needed to get back on track. She couldn't afford to flub in front of someone as important as Edith Gill-Davison. "I have something important I need to discuss with you, Nancy," Vivian repeated with her eyes closed, focusing as

117

hard as she could on the task at hand. She needed to make it through this show. She opened her eyes again and saw the older lady frowning at her, her lips pursed into a thin, white line.

Vivian made it through the rest of the rehearsal by the skin of her teeth. The appearance of the envelope had rattled her, and Frances's spiteful presence only made matters worse. She knew Frances was hanging on her every word, waiting to pounce on any mistake. To Vivian's immense relief, the live show went without a hitch. Even Dave held his own, showing no signs of the nervousness he'd exhibited before the rehearsal.

She risked another glance at the grande dame after the on-air light was turned off. Mrs. Gill-Davison wasn't smiling, but she wasn't frowning either.

Vivian watched Frances surreptitiously out of the corner of her eye. She had to admit that Frances was perfectly cast as the cunning, man-stealing Nancy. She'd finally found a role that truly suited her. Vivian opened her mouth to tell her just that when Frances fired the first shot.

"It seems we'll be working together a lot now," Frances said sweetly.

"Seems so," Vivian agreed. "Congratulations on the new role."

"Oh, it was nothing," Frances said, her tone implying that it actually was everything. "Talent opens a lot of doors."

Vivian grunted skeptically at the implication that Frances's talent alone had landed her the role.

Frances narrowed her lovely sapphire eyes at Vivian. "You're not the only one who can play the game," she said, the pleasant tone of her voice in sharp contrast to the biting words. She glanced over at Mrs. Gill-Davison.

"I don't play any games," Vivian answered, rolling her eyes toward the ceiling.

"That's not what I've heard," Frances said with a smirk. "I've heard you like to play all sorts of games with a certain head of this station . . ."

Vivian's focus snapped back to Frances. "You know that's not true," she hissed.

"Do I?" Frances asked. "You, a former *secretary,* stole Lorna Lafferty from me, and I can only figure one way that could have happened." She raised her eyebrows. When Vivian didn't take the bait, Frances continued, her face a picture of innocence. "On your back," she mouthed, each syllable distinct so the message could not be misinterpreted.

Vivian took a deep breath, everything in her aching to reach out and grab Frances by her scrawny neck. The insinuation was rich, coming from the likes of her, Vivian thought. Everyone had heard how Frances got that up-front role on the *Country Cavalcade,* and it certainly wasn't because of her acting talent — not the on-air kind anyway. She was about to let Frances have it when she noticed that Peggy Hart was standing behind Frances, listening to their exchange. Vivian snapped her mouth shut. Had she been there this whole time?

Sensing an audience, Frances smiled warmly at Vivian. She leaned in closer and said loud enough to be overheard, "You don't look at all well, Viv. Are you sure you're doing all right? You seemed off your game today. Honestly, I wasn't sure you were going to make it through."

"I'm fine," Vivian replied tersely. She caught Peggy's eye, and the girl glanced away.

"I'm glad to hear it," Frances said without emotion. "But if you need anything, let me know. A few days off, a break . . . anything . . ." She raised her perfectly formed eyebrows suggestively.

"Gee, thanks," Vivian answered, not bothering to hide the sarcasm that crept into her voice. "Well, as pleasant as it is to chat with you, Frances," Vivian said, "I simply must dash." She made a show of checking the time on her wristwatch. "A photo shoot for *Radio Stars* to get to, you know." She flashed her most saccharine-laced smile at Frances and watched her rival's face fall. It was childish, but she knew Frances was foaming at the mouth to get a mere mention in *Radio Stars,* much less a photo.

Vivian rushed to the door before Frances could slip in the last word.

"Viv, wait!"

Vivian turned just outside the doorway to find Peggy bearing down on her.

"I needed to tell you that Daddy — Mr. Hart — wants to see you as soon as possible. I would have told you sooner, but I didn't want to interrupt you and Frances." The girl glanced down shyly.

Vivian snorted through her nose. "I wish you would have," she said with a roll of her eyes. "And on top of everything, Mrs. Gill-Davison . . . today of all days," Vivian said under her breath and began walking.

"Oh yes," Peggy said, falling into step beside her. "Your flub wasn't that terrible. In case that's what you're worried about."

"Just one of the many things I'm worried about, Peggy," Vivian said with a sigh.

Peggy shot Vivian a knowing look and then lowered her voice. "Mrs. Gill-Davison is really in a tizzy over losing Marjorie. I wonder what she'll do with *The Golden Years*?"

"End it, I suppose," Vivian said. "How can they go on without the lead?"

"I haven't heard one way or the other yet," Peggy said breathlessly. "Boy, I'm almost disappointed that I missed all the excitement last night."

"Lucky you," Vivian said ruefully. "I wish I could have missed all the *excitement* last night."

Peggy's face flushed pink. "Sorry, it was a poor choice of words. I meant that I wish I could be around the studio more, but with school and Mother . . ."

"How's your mother doing?" Vivian asked in a quiet voice. Peggy's mother, Mr. Hart's wife, had been ill for some time, bedridden with a serious ailment that no one called by name but everyone knew was cancer.

Peggy's face clouded over. "She's doing okay," she said. She looked up, tears glistening in her eyes. Vivian felt sorry for the girl, just a teenager and about to lose her mother.

"Give her my best, would you?" Vivian said.

Peggy nodded and hugged the papers she

was holding tighter to her chest. "Hey, where's your shadow?"

It took Vivian a moment to realize Peggy was talking about Charlie. He'd hardly been her shadow at the station so far today. In fact, she wasn't sure where he was. "He's probably already upstairs with your father. Do you know Mr. Haverman?"

"We've met," she said.

Vivian glanced down and realized she was still holding the script for today's *Love & Glory*, the edges tattered where she'd ripped the pages in nervous agitation. She thrust the crumpled stack of pages at Peggy. "Can you toss this for me?" she asked. Her mind was already upstairs in the executive suite. What could Mr. Hart have to tell her? Was there a development in the investigation?

CHAPTER TEN

Mr. Hart seemed to be taking Marjorie's death considerably harder than Vivian would have expected. Usually a dapper man who never left the house without looking every inch the gentleman, today a day's growth of salt-and-pepper stubble covered his cheeks, and he was wearing the same gray suit and shirt Vivian had seen him in the evening before. The dark circles under his eyes were on par with Vivian's own (prior to the two layers of pancake makeup she'd applied, that is).

He'd likely spent the night here in his office. She glanced at the sofa, but if the station head had slept there, it had been tidied since. His office smelled stale, of cigar smoke and sweat. The decanter of brandy that she'd sampled from the night before sat empty on the desktop, but the ashtray was now empty.

Mr. Hart hadn't spoken since Vivian had

entered the room. He'd simply tapped the mother-of-pearl-handled letter opener against the side of his desk and stared at the rug, deep in thought. Sergeant Trask sat in a leather chair identical to the one Vivian had perched on and was equally silent. He was scratching notes on his ever-present notepad with the swift, even strokes of a sharpened pencil. Charlie stood at the window, his back to the room. He'd turned briefly when she entered, nodded his acknowledgment of her arrival, and then returned to his post without a word. Vivian was dying to break the silence, to say something, anything, but she didn't dare.

Instead, she watched the dust mites dancing in the shaft of late-morning sunlight that streamed from the window and tried not to let her mind wander back to this morning's rehearsal.

Vivian sighed. The real problem was that she'd let Frances get to her. Vivian couldn't bear to think about that disapproving look on Mrs. Gill-Davison's face. She just hoped she'd recovered well enough during the live show and that the swirling drama of Marjorie's murder would push the disastrous rehearsal out of the woman's mind.

Mr. Hart's new secretary, a buxom young thing with a mass of fiery red hair, swept in with a tray of refreshments. She refilled his coffee cup without asking, stirring in a generous dollop of cream. He nodded his thanks and lifted the cup to his mouth with a trembling hand.

"Coffee? Tea?" she asked Vivian, dipping the tray toward her.

Vivian waved her off. Coffee or tea would only make her more agitated.

The secretary offered refreshments to Sergeant Trask and Charlie, both of whom refused, before turning and sashaying out the door. Mr. Hart waited until the door clicked shut behind her before speaking.

"I trust you know by now about the letter?" he asked Vivian solemnly. His voice was raspy. There was a sadness etched into the deep lines around his mouth, and Vivian began to wonder just how well Mr. Hart had known Marjorie. Perhaps better than she'd suspected.

"Yes," she answered. "Mr. Haverman has explained everything to me."

Charlie shifted when he heard his name mentioned, but made no move to join the conversation.

"Good, good . . ." Mr. Hart looked like he was about to say something else, but he lost his grip on his letter opener, and it clattered to the desktop.

126

Vivian jumped, and a self-conscious giggle escaped her lips.

"Miss Witchell," Sergeant Trask began, leaning forward in his chair and narrowing his pale eyes at her. "Anything to report since we spoke last night?"

Vivian felt her palms start to sweat. "About what exactly?" she asked.

"Any more letters? Anything suspicious happen?"

"Oh, nothing like that, no," Vivian said. "Charlie stayed over, of course." She heard the way that sounded and felt her face burn with embarrassment. "I mean . . . Well, I mean . . . for my protection . . . as Mr. Hart hired him to do."

The sergeant only nodded and made a note on his pad. "That's good. Of course, I — we — want you to be on your guard, but there's no real cause for concern at this point."

Vivian blinked and leaned toward the policeman.

"No real cause for concern?" she asked, incredulous. "Someone wants to kill me."

"Now, Vivian," Mr. Hart interjected, waving his hands impatiently. "We don't know that."

Vivian opened her mouth to protest, but the policeman spoke first.

"Mr. Hart is right," he said. "We have no evidence at this point that the letter found with Mrs. Fox was related to her death."

Vivian's head jerked from Mr. Hart to Sargent Trask and back again.

"Not related?" She wasn't sure she'd heard that correctly. "Not related? Someone threatened Marjorie's life in that letter, and then she ended up dead. Explain to me how that's not related."

"I don't recall there being any threats on Marjorie's life in that letter," Mr. Hart said. His tone was patronizing, but, Vivian acknowledged reluctantly, he was technically correct. The letter had made her skin crawl, but this Walter person hadn't specifically mentioned anything about wanting Marjorie dead. Vivian sighed heavily.

"Would you like me to read the letter again?" the policeman asked. "I have it right here." His hand started toward the breast pocket of his uniform, but Vivian held up one hand to stop him.

"No," she said, her stomach doing a sickening flip-flop at the thought. "That won't be necessary."

"We're following a number of leads right now, Miss Witchell," Sergeant Trask said.

She looked pointedly at the policeman. "But particularly related to this letter?"

128

"Of course," he said, briefly meeting her gaze. "There's no need to worry."

No other phrase could have possibly made her worry more.

"I have every confidence that Mr. Haverman will keep you out of any danger until everything gets straightened out," Mr. Hart added.

Straightened out, she thought. Mr. Hart made Marjorie's murder sound like a bookkeeping error. Vivian looked to Charlie, who shrugged his shoulders in response.

"Everything's been satisfactory with the arrangement so far, hasn't it?" Mr. Hart continued, glancing from Vivian to Charlie and back again. "I assume that Mr. Haverman has been both professional and courteous?"

"Well, yes," Vivian responded. He had, of course, but that wasn't the point. She was opening her mouth to say that when Mr. Hart stood up abruptly.

"Good. Then if you'll excuse me, I have some very important meetings to attend. There is much to be discussed involving the station and recent incidents. I'm sure you understand."

Vivian understood all right. She was getting the brush-off.

She turned to the policeman who was also

standing in preparation to leave. "Sergeant Trask," she said. "You'll let me know if there are any developments in the investigation, won't you?" She smiled sweetly at him, but he remained stone-faced.

"Of course, Miss Witchell. You'll be the first to know."

"It's imperative that you not worry, Vivian," Mr. Hart said, looking like that was exactly what he'd spent all night doing. "It's also imperative that the existence of this letter not be leaked to anyone outside this room." He pointed a finger at each of them in turn, including Sergeant Trask.

Vivian studied her shoes to avoid meeting Mr. Hart's gaze. *Imogene doesn't count,* she thought. Because Imogene had already known.

"Vivian."

She looked up to Mr. Hart staring at her. He knew her too well. "Yes, Mr. Hart," she said obediently. She resisted the urge to cross her fingers. "No one outside this room."

"And especially no talking to the press," he said sternly. "We don't need anything else about this leaking to the papers."

Vivian nodded and watched Mr. Hart and Sergeant Trask walk briskly from the room. They had nothing. The police had nothing, and now they were trying to convince her that she wasn't in danger. But the persistent gnawing in the pit of her stomach told her otherwise. Someone had threatened Marjorie in the letter, then followed through on that threat. And that same someone had threatened Vivian. Someone was out to get her. But who?

CHAPTER ELEVEN

The atmosphere of the neighborhood changed abruptly just south and west of the Loop. It was run-down and slightly seedy, not the Chicago of postcards and travel brochures. Vivian wouldn't have come here alone, but it was broad daylight and Charlie seemed unfazed. So Vivian clutched his arm tighter and glanced surreptitiously up at the art deco–style marquee of the burlesque house they were passing. The Gem stated proudly that inside you could find "Live Girls Onstage and On-Screen." And it was all just a few blocks from where little old ladies sipped tea in their Sunday best, Vivian thought with a delicious little thrill.

Charlie had promised to take her to lunch somewhere they could talk in private. Apparently the somewhere he had in mind was a tiny cubbyhole nearly hidden down a short flight of stairs sandwiched between a liquor store and a tobacco shop in a long row of dilapidated buildings. There was no sign out front. Perhaps the place had no name. A simple, handwritten placard propped in the grime-covered front window advertised the specials: ham sandwich, fried chicken, twenty-five cents. It certainly wasn't Henrici's. It wasn't even the Tip Top Café, but it would have to do. At least Vivian could take comfort in the fact that no one she knew would see her in a place like this, and maybe that was the whole point.

The interior did nothing to improve her overall impression of the place. It was dark and cramped and clouded with cigarette smoke. The dark-stained wooden paneling lent a particular air of claustrophobia to the atmosphere — not an easy feat on an otherwise bright, sunny day. Vivian and Charlie found a table as far from the crowded counter as they could get and ordered two egg-salad sandwiches with coffee.

"I don't think the police are taking the threat against me seriously," Vivian said in a low voice as soon as the waitress left with their order. "Telling me not to worry," she huffed. "And that no evidence connects the letter to Marjorie's murder. I don't think they know the first thing about who killed her."

"Unfortunately, I think you may be right,"

Charlie answered.

The waitress returned with the coffeepot and filled both of their cups to the brim. Vivian frowned and dropped a sugar cube into her coffee, watching it dissolve into the blackness. "What did Mr. Hart have to say before I arrived?"

"Not a lot, actually. He wanted to make sure you were being looked after. He was very concerned about the effect Mrs. Fox's murder will have on the station — financially, of course. He was nervous, jittery, altogether a mess, I would say."

"He looked awful," Vivian whispered. "I don't think he went home last night, and I'm certain he didn't get any sleep." Vivian thought of the empty brandy decanter.

Charlie eyed her suspiciously.

"He was chummy with Mrs. Fox then?"

"Chummy?" Vivian snorted softly. "I can't imagine Marjorie being *chummy* with anyone. Say, I guess you've been around the station awhile," she said. "Hadn't you run into her once or twice and experienced her particular brand of charm for yourself?"

"Me?" Charlie looked surprised.

"Everyone runs . . . ran . . . into Marjorie at some point. She was hard to miss."

"I'd met her, but just in passing. I heard she was difficult."

134

"Difficult," Vivian repeated with a wry smile. "That's a nice way of phrasing it." She leaned in toward the detective. "None of her costars on *The Golden Years* could stand her. She liked to be the one and only star and caused a big ruckus if anyone else got a bigger story line in an episode."

"A real prima donna, eh?" he said.

"I'd heard Marjorie had the biggest problem with little Sammy Evans. He played her son on the show."

"A little boy?" Charlie asked, incredulous.

Vivian laughed. "Little Sammy Evans is forty years old. The 'little' in his name is literal."

Charlie looked at her in confusion.

"He's a midget," Vivian said.

One of Charlie's thick golden eyebrows arched. "A midget?"

"It's pretty common in the radio industry to have a midget play a child's role," she explained. "Midgets have high-pitched voices like children, but they're far more experienced and reliable. Hit their cues perfectly, things like that."

Charlie shook his head slightly in amused disbelief. "So what was Marjorie's problem with little Sammy Evans?" he asked.

"He was becoming a fan favorite and getting plum story lines. You know, playing the precocious little kid. The audience just eats up that kind of thing."

"Her worst nightmare."

"Exactly."

The waitress hurried to the table and dumped their sandwiches in front of them with a clatter.

"This is quite the popular place," Vivian said, looking around. All of the clientele, excluding herself, were male. And males of the extremely hardworking — or perhaps not working — variety. She met the gaze of a particularly large and unwashed man at the counter and immediately looked away, but she felt his eyes linger on her.

"I come here a lot when I'm working," Charlie said, looking around as if he'd never really studied the place before. "It's open all night."

"You do a lot of your work at night?"

He nodded. Vivian tried to picture this Charlie, the charming Charlie, lurking in dark alleys and mixing with shady characters, but she just couldn't. There must be another side of him that she hadn't seen yet. He sat chewing his egg-salad sandwich with a thoughtful expression for a few minutes before speaking again.

"I assume by the 'Mrs.' that there was a Mr. Fox in Marjorie's life at some time,"

Charlie said.

Vivian shrugged. "I assumed so too, but I'd never heard anything about her being or having been married."

"What about children?"

"Search me." Vivian stared down at the egg salad and tried to muster an appetite. All of this talk of Marjorie had squashed it. She looked back up at the detective and watched him chew his sandwich with gusto. His eyes caught hers, and his mouth curled in something like a smile. He was a terribly attractive man, Vivian thought, especially when he really played up being a hard-nosed detective. "So let's hear your story for another time," she said.

Charlie's brow furrowed. "My what?" He shoved the last bit of sandwich into his mouth.

"When I asked you last night how you became a detective, you told me it was a story for another time," Vivian said.

"And now is that time?" Charlie looked less than thrilled at the prospect.

"Well, we seem to have exhausted my firsthand knowledge of Marjorie Fox." Vivian took a sip of her coffee.

"Okay, well, where do I begin? My father, the senior Mr. Haverman, is a private detective, as I believe I mentioned. He started out as a track detective at Hawthorne Race Course. But then he branched into other areas as sort of a hobby. He also owns a furniture store."

"And how did you get into the business?"

"I was always helping him out, even when I was a little kid, but I never wanted to be a private eye myself. I wanted to be a cop. I started at the police academy, and I got a few months in, and then my mom got sick. Dad couldn't handle everything on his own, so I dropped out to help. Then after she died, I stayed on with Dad. That's about it." His eyes flicked off to concentrate on something over her shoulder when he mentioned his mother's death, but then they returned to Vivian's face.

"How did you get involved with *The Darkness Knows*?"

"Mr. Hart had hired me for a few jobs in the past year or so — just some small things, checking out business associates and the like. And when the show came up, he asked me if I could assist Mr. Yarborough with some of the finer points of being a PI, help him flesh out his character or something like that." Charlie smiled.

"Help him with his arc," Vivian said, nodding.

"His arc?"

"Oh, nothing," she mumbled. "So how is it? Working with Graham, I mean?"

Charlie leaned back in his chair, knitted his fingers across his abdomen, and smiled slightly. "Interesting," he said.

"That's it? Just interesting?"

"Mr. Yarborough," he said, "doesn't want to hear what my job is really like. He wants pulp novel plots about smugglers and white slavers."

"And that's what you give him?" Vivian asked.

"I aim to please," Charlie answered with a shrug. "But if he only knew he could subscribe to *Black Mask* magazine himself and cut out the middleman, I'd be out of a job."

Vivian smiled at the idea: if Graham only knew, he'd be livid. "You don't like Graham very much, do you?" she asked, leaning back in her chair.

Charlie shrugged again noncommittally.

"He's just very focused on his career," Vivian said quickly as if that explained any of Graham's character flaws — his intense self-interest, for one. She narrowed her eyes at Charlie, considering. "You know, Mr. Hart must have hired you for those jobs shortly after I left my position as his secretary last spring. I'd have remembered you otherwise," she said.

The detective's eyes opened comically wide. He leaned forward in his chair, elbows planted on the table on either side of his plate. "Wait a second. You were Mr. Hart's secretary?"

She nodded.

"You were," he repeated, pointing one long finger at her.

"Yes," she said, a little miffed that he hadn't already heard her story. Apparently, he didn't read "The Tattler" section of the *Radio Guide* magazine.

He seemed to consider this for a long moment. "So how on earth did you go from being Mr. Hart's secretary to the illustrious Lorna Lafferty?" he asked.

Vivian glanced down at her coffee cup, suddenly self-conscious. "I was in the right place at the right time," she said. "I filled in for a screamer, and the acting bug bit me." She looked back up at Charlie, whose brows had come together over the bridge of his nose.

"A screamer?" he asked.

Vivian smiled. "Someone who screams on the air for the lead actress so she doesn't ruin her voice," she explained. "You'd be surprised how often they have women screaming in these shows. Lorna Lafferty

140

screams at least once an episode, sometimes more."

"Oh," he said.

"There are women who specialize in crying like babies too," she added. Charlie smirked, and Vivian added defensively, "It's a real talent."

"I don't doubt it," he said, sitting back in his chair again. He eyed her speculatively for a long moment. "So you went from being a screamer to a star just like that?" He snapped his fingers.

Vivian couldn't tell whether he was teasing her, whether he'd already heard the gossip at the station. Charlie looked at her expectantly. There didn't seem to be any malice in his expression. Perhaps he hadn't heard anything — or perhaps he was exceptionally good at not betraying anything he already knew. "Hardly." Vivian picked at her egg salad. "It took a year of slogging through bit parts before I got my break. Edie eloping was a godsend for me. Right place at the right time."

Charlie returned the smile with one of his own. "You still appear on shows besides *The Darkness Knows* though . . . like that sappy melodrama. What's it called?"

"*Love & Glory,*" she supplied. Then she shrugged. "I take whatever I can get. Usually just bit parts, but the role in *Love & Glory* is pretty plum. It's a daytime serial though. Those aren't nearly as high profile as the nighttime shows. Unless you're a huge star — Jack Benny, Edgar Bergen — you have to do more than one show to get by."

"From the looks of the pile of bricks you live in, you don't need to just get by," he said. His smile had turned into a knowing smirk.

Vivian pushed her plate away and sat for a moment with the palms of her hands resting on the table.

"That's my mother's house, my mother's money, Mr. Haverman," she said slowly. "Not mine." She knew her tone was too severe, but he'd struck a nerve.

Charlie smiled lazily and leaned toward her.

"I was only teasing you, Viv. No need to start calling me Mr. Haverman again."

Vivian looked away. "I'm sorry," she said. "It's just a sore subject for me. My career, my independence, is very important to me."

Charlie held up both hands in mock surrender. "Understood," he said seriously.

Vivian sighed, sorry she'd been so harsh. Her eyes flicked to the counter, and she made eye contact with the same large, threatening-looking man. He didn't turn away, but smiled at her in a menacing way and rubbed the steak knife next to his plate with this thumb and forefinger. Vivian dropped her head and shielded her face with her hand, and Charlie's head swiveled in the direction she'd been looking.

"That man," Vivian said without moving her lips, "is staring at me."

The man hadn't turned away even though Charlie had taken notice of him, and he hadn't averted his gaze. Before she could say another word, Charlie leaped out of his seat and sauntered toward the man, hands in his pockets.

"What's the idea, pal?" he asked. Suddenly, the room was quiet, no one actually watching the altercation, but everyone with an ear tuned.

"Whaddya mean?" The man snorted dismissively, still fingering the steak knife.

"I mean . . ." Charlie's hands tightened into fists, but his voice stayed level. "What's the idea makin' eyes at my girl like that?"

"Makin' eyes? Who's makin' eyes?"

"You are. You're making her uncomfortable." Charlie pulled his right hand out of his jacket and rubbed the large ring situated there before he spoke again. "And you're making me angry."

The man blinked and looked down at his plate for a moment. His eyes met Charlie's again, and he shrugged. "Sorry, mack. Just noticing a pretty girl, that's all. Last time I checked, that's not a crime." He laughed nervously.

Charlie didn't bother to answer. He returned to their table, cracking his knuckles as he walked, and the noise level of the room returned to normal as if someone had adjusted the volume control knob. "Just a regulation lowlife. No one to worry about," he said in a low voice. "Let's go." He dumped a couple of bills on the table and helped Vivian into her jacket.

She took his arm and risked a glance at the man as they passed. He was studying the ham-salad sandwich on his plate, obviously intimidated. Vivian's eyes darted to Charlie's face in profile. He was scowling, eyes trained on the front door. Now *this* was the back-alley Charlie, she thought, the one that got things done. This Charlie was interesting.

CHAPTER TWELVE

Vivian had the dress rehearsal for the *Millicent Morris* live performance in less than half an hour, and she hadn't even seen the script yet. *Millicent Morris* was another sentimental melodrama about a poor little rich girl who was always running into some sort of exotic trouble: smugglers, jewel thieves, gold-digging love interests, scheming archrivals. Vivian only had a bit part in today's show as a conniving French maid, but every part was important. Every part kept her working.

She should probably practice her accent at least. That was one thing she had over Frances Barrow. Frances was horrible with accents. Vivian was staring at her feet as she walked toward the studio on the twelfth floor, repeating "Ah, *oui,* madame" over and over again, when she ran into something solid. She looked up, surprised, to find Morty Nickerson, the station engineer.

"Oh, Morty!" she cried. She felt her face flush with surprise.

"You walked smack into me, Viv," he said congenially. "Are you okay?" he asked, his boyish face full of concern. Everything about Morty was boyish — his wide blue eyes, the splash of freckles across his cheeks, the way he talked that made it seem like all of the world was one big surprise.

"I'm fine," she said. "I'm just a little flustered today."

"I can imagine," he replied. He glanced around the crowded hallway. "Do the police know any more about . . . you know?" He jerked his thumb toward the room where Marjorie had been found.

Vivian glanced toward the lounge and shook her head.

"Do they still think it was a crazed fan?" he asked.

"I don't know what they think," she said, studying Morty's open, guileless expression.

"Have there been any more letters?"

Vivian shook her head again.

"Strange," he said softly. "I mean, I would have expected another by now. One just for you perhaps . . ."

Vivian's throat grew dry. "How do you know what was in Marjorie's letter?" she croaked.

"I've been keeping my ears open. You know, listening to people when they don't know I'm listening." He smiled, and his gaze grew soft. "People say a lot of crazy things when they don't think anyone's listening."

Vivian shivered. She'd assured Charlie that she'd be perfectly fine while he popped into the men's room for a moment, but now she wasn't so sure. Even though the hall was crowded and people were rushing past in every direction, she suddenly felt very alone.

"I really have to get going, Morty," she said, stepping to the right to walk around him.

He matched her step, remaining in front of her.

Vivian looked up sharply. "Morty," she said firmly. "I have to go. I have a rehearsal soon."

"I know," he said, but he didn't budge. He was standing so close that she could see herself reflected in the pupils of his light blue eyes. "Don't you want to know what I have behind my back?" he asked.

"Morty, I really have to —"

His closed fist appeared in front of her face. He turned his hand over and slowly uncurled his long fingers to display a small gold locket without a chain. "I found this on the sidewalk outside," he said. "I thought it might be yours."

Vivian blinked at the piece of jewelry, the dulled gold surface etched with an elaborate set of initials she couldn't make out. She glanced up at Morty, trying to read his expression. Had he really found it? He was smiling eagerly down at her, pushing the locket toward her.

"Thank you," she squeaked, her throat closing. "But I can't accept it."

Morty's face fell. She'd be the first to admit that she'd flirted with the poor boy in the past. He was an engineer. He could make her sound good on the air, take care of her. Didn't all of the actresses at the station do the same? Looking up into his very young, very disappointed face, she suddenly wasn't so sure.

Morty shrugged and shoved the locket into his pocket without another word. He stepped aside after a few seconds, threw his arm out in the direction Vivian wanted to go, and bowed formally at the waist. It was meant to be an amusing, theatrical gesture, but Vivian couldn't force herself to smile. "Say hello to Millicent for me," Morty said in a bright voice.

Vivian managed a grunt in acknowledgment and gratefully went on her way.

"Viv, there you are!" Graham made a show of looking at his wristwatch. The gold cuff link in his sleeve glinted in the glare of the hallway lights.

"Here I am," she agreed, trying to sound casual.

"Are you okay? I wasn't sure you'd be in today." Graham was playing Millicent Morris's current boyfriend, a playboy from Monte Carlo who was not as he seemed. Millicent's boyfriends were never as they seemed.

"I'm okay," she answered, mustering a genuine smile for Graham. She nodded toward his sleeve. "Say, I think I might have something of yours."

She pulled the cuff link she'd found that morning from the pocket of her jacket, along with the envelope she'd hastily stashed there. She frowned at the memory of the envelope slipping from her *Love & Glory* script as she held the piece of jewelry out for Graham to see.

"My cuff link! I'd wondered where this had gotten to." He plucked it from her palm and held it up for a better view.

"When did you lose it?"

"Yesterday," he said. "I took my cuff links off so I could roll up my sleeves during *The Darkness Knows*. It was hot in that studio. Where'd you find it?"

"In the back stairwell."

Graham's brow wrinkled, and he dropped the errant cuff link into his jacket pocket. "What was it doing there?"

"You didn't take the back entrance this morning?" Vivian asked.

"The back entrance?" Graham seemed genuinely befuddled. His nose wrinkled in disgust. "Isn't that through the alley? I'm not sure I've ever used it."

Vivian tried to hide her smile. She had been right: the last thing Graham would ever do was avoid reporters — *any* reporters — or enter from the back when he could go through the front entrance where everyone could see him.

"Did you happen to say anything to the rabble out front when you came in?" she asked.

Graham feigned offense. "Of course not. I gave them no comment." He leaned in and added, "And a smile."

Vivian nodded her approval.

"What's that?" he asked, pointing to the envelope in her hand.

"Oh, nothing." Vivian regarded the envelope for a moment. But she had the distinct feeling that it *was* something. She grabbed Graham's lapel, tugging him a few feet farther away from the door of the studio. "Listen, Graham. I have to tell you something, and you have to promise not to tell another soul."

"Sounds serious."

"It is. Promise?"

"Of course."

Vivian swallowed and paused dramatically to impart the gravity of the situation on Graham. "I was mentioned in the letter found with Marjorie's body," she said.

"What do you mean?"

"I mean that letter mentioned Lorna Lafferty — and *me* as well."

Graham looked first over one shoulder, then the other. "Someone's after you?" he whispered.

"Well, not right this second . . . I don't think. The police don't seem to believe it's anything to worry about. But I don't want you to worry, and I also don't want you to wonder why Mr. Haverman is hovering around."

"Chick? What's he got to do with this?"

"Mr. Hart's hired him to watch over me until this thing has blown over."

Graham scowled at her. "To watch over

you?" he repeated.

Vivian nodded.

"I see," he said in a low voice.

Vivian watched his jaw work as he considered that piece of information. Was that a glimmer of jealousy she saw rising to the surface?

"We have rehearsal in a few minutes," she said, glancing at her wristwatch. She met Graham's eyes. "Not a word to anyone about the letter. Mr. Hart is adamant that it not get into the papers."

"He doesn't need to worry about me." Graham mimed zipping his lips and then locking them with an imaginary key. "But, Viv," he said, placing his hand on her arm. When he lowered his chin and looked directly into her eyes, she stopped breathing for a moment. "Please be careful."

"I will," Vivian said. She absently brushed the spot near her elbow where Graham had touched her and managed an upbeat smile until Graham turned to enter the studio.

As soon as he disappeared through the studio door, the smile faded, and she turned the envelope over in her hands. It was unmarked. She tore it open and pulled out a single sheet of white paper that had been neatly folded twice.

There were only a few short lines, typed

in the middle of the page. Vivian read it and gasped, swaying slightly and steadying herself against the wall. She blinked rapidly, once, twice. She heard someone talking to her, their voice muffled as if there were cotton in her ears. Strong arms pulled her upright and held her steady. Charlie's face appeared inches from her own. She could see him mouthing her name, but she couldn't quite hear him.

She read his lips. He was repeating "What's wrong?" over and over again.

"I . . . I . . . got a letter . . ." she whispered. Her voice sounded like it came from the end of a long tunnel.

The letter had slipped from her fingers, and Charlie managed to retrieve it while continuing to hold her upright. He read the letter rapidly and grimaced.

"Let's sit you down," he said.

He helped her into Studio G, where the cast members waiting to rehearse crowded around her.

"What happened? What's going on?" A jumble of voices assaulted her from every direction.

Vivian stared at the tips of her shoes and ignored all of them.

"Miss Witchell is just feeling a little under the weather," she heard Charlie say.

"Poor thing," someone clucked.

"Understandable," said another.

"Is that Viv?" she heard Graham ask as he pushed his way toward her.

"Is she going to make the rehearsal?" The director's voice boomed above the din.

Vivian looked up at Charlie and shook her head. No, she would not make the rehearsal or the live show this time.

CHAPTER THIRTEEN

Above the panic and fear rose the overriding feeling of guilt. Vivian was missing a show: a job, an opportunity to prove herself. It was only a small part, barely more than a few lines, but it was something. She didn't know who'd replaced her, and she didn't care — just as long as it wasn't Frances.

Mr. Hart was not in the building, but Sergeant Trask suggested they meet in his office anyway.

"It's a good thing I was already here," he said, making himself comfortable in the same leather chair he'd occupied a few hours before when he'd so blithely assured Vivian that there was no cause for concern. He pulled a fresh pencil out of his pocket and flipped to a clean page in his notebook.

Vivian perched on the edge of her seat, her body rigid, trying to calm her racing mind. This unknown person, this "Walter," had the upper hand. This person was likely inside the station right now and knew where she was and what she was doing every second. How could she fight that? Maybe she *should* just disappear for a while. She wasn't able to do her job properly now anyway. Earlier, she'd flubbed spectacularly in front of one of the most powerful people in radio, and she'd just bowed out of *Millicent Morris.* It was all too much to bear, and maybe it was time to admit that. Admit that maybe the killer had already won — he'd killed her career by barely lifting a finger. Ending her life couldn't be much harder, could it?

Mr. Hart's secretary came in and pressed a mug of hot tea into Vivian's hands. Vivian nodded her thanks and rubbed her thumbs along the ceramic sides until they ached from the heat while watching the thin tendrils of steam rise from the milky gray liquid.

Charlie smiled at the secretary as she handed him a cup of coffee. "You're sure it's all right if we talk here?" he asked.

"Oh yes, Mr. Hart is having a late lunch at Henrici's," she replied with a pert smile. "I don't expect him back for hours."

Vivian's stomach flipped. He must be meeting with Mrs. Gill-Davison to talk over *The Golden Years* and very likely Vivian's momentous flubbing during *Love & Glory* earlier in the day.

When the secretary had gone, Sergeant Trask licked the tip of his pencil and trained his eyes on Vivian.

"How did you get the letter?" he asked.

Vivian continued to stare at the steam rising from her mug as she spoke. "I think it was in my script for *Love & Glory,*" she said. Then she nodded sharply, remembering. "Yes, the envelope fell out of my script as I turned the pages. I just picked it up and shoved it into my pocket since we were beginning rehearsal and there wasn't time to read it. Then I forgot all about it." She looked up at Sergeant Trask and shrugged apologetically.

"Any idea how it got there?"

"No," she said quietly.

He scratched a note onto the notepad, then asked, "How did you get the script? Was it delivered to you somehow?"

Vivian looked up at the ceiling, trying to jog her memory. "I guess Peggy handed it to me," she said. "But I don't really recall. Things were so distracting today."

"How so?" the policeman prodded.

"Mrs. Gill-Davison was visiting," Vivian said, her stomach clenching. "Everyone was in a tizzy."

"Mrs. Gill-Davison?"

"The creator of *Love & Glory.* She's terribly important. I assume that's who Mr. Hart is lunching with right now." Vivian considered for a moment how lucky it was that she hadn't read the letter right away. If she'd read it before the rehearsal, she wouldn't have been able to continue at all — and that very likely would have been the end of her role in the show. She glanced over at Charlie, who offered the slightest smile of encouragement.

"Do you mind?" the policeman asked.

Vivian swiveled her head back toward him. Sergeant Trask held the letter up.

Vivian winced. Of course she minded.

He began reading without waiting for her answer.

```
Dearest Lorna,
I'll be seeing you very soon.
I've been watching you, and I
know you'll be more co-
operative than Evelyn. I don't
really want to hurt you, you
know.
                   Lovingly,
                   Walter
```

158

"Short and to the point," Charlie said grimly.

Vivian took a sip of her tea, trying to keep her hand from shaking as she brought the cup to her lips. Charlie took the note from the policeman's hands and studied it, laying it out flat on his thigh to give her a chance to look again too, if she wanted. She didn't want to, but her eyes strayed to that seemingly innocuous piece of paper anyway. The message had been typed, even the name at the bottom, and something about the whole thing was off somehow. She leaned forward, studying it more intently. There was something familiar about it, but her head was swimming, and her thoughts wouldn't focus long enough to make any sort of connection.

"Has anything suspicious happened to you today, Miss Witchell? I mean, anything besides this letter, of course." Sergeant Trask was staring intently at her. "Anything at all?"

Vivian wrinkled her brow in thought. "There was that man in the coffee shop . . ."

The policeman leaned forward and asked, "What man?"

"That was nothing," Charlie said, waving his hand dismissively.

"He certainly seemed menacing," Vivian

159

said, glancing sidelong at Charlie. "I didn't like the looks of him."

"Me neither, but he wasn't your letter writer," Charlie replied, lips pursed. Then he addressed the sergeant. "In fact, I'm sure the man could barely read. Just a garden-variety thug not used to seeing a pretty girl up close, that's all."

Sergeant Trask scribbled more notes, and Charlie leaned toward Vivian, speaking softly. "I shouldn't have taken you there. I just didn't want you to be around all of the usuals from the station. I wanted you to feel free to talk."

The "usuals" from the station. The idea made sense. It wouldn't do to feed the fire of gossip, and all of this likely had something to do with one of their own. Vivian shivered at the thought, and some of the tea spilled from the cup and splashed onto her hand. She started, rubbing it on her skirt.

Charlie placed one strong hand on her shoulder while he took the cup out of her hands with the other.

"Miss Witchell," Sergeant Trask said quietly. His voice was almost soothing now, and the change of tone scared her more than anything. "Can you think of anything else that happened today that might be helpful?"

Vivian shook her head slowly as she stared at the red welt beginning to form where the hot tea had burned her.

"There *is* something else . . ." she said slowly.

Both men waited silently for her to continue. A clock ticked somewhere in the room as she considered how to phrase what she was about to say.

"It's just that Morty was acting strangely this afternoon." She looked up, alarmed at what she'd just implied. "I don't want to get him in trouble or anything. Morty's a nice boy."

"What do you mean by 'strangely'?" Charlie asked, his fingers tightening their grip on her shoulder.

"Well, it's hard to explain, but he knew about the letter found with Marjorie's body. That's not so strange in itself," she added quickly. "People like to gossip around here. But he also seemed, I don't know, *surprised* that I hadn't received one myself. It was almost as if he knew that I was supposed to get another letter."

Charlie's voice was urgent. "When was this?"

"In the hallway before rehearsal. Just before I remembered the letter in my pocket."

"Why didn't you tell me?" he asked.

Vivian shrugged. "It all happened so fast. There wasn't any time."

"I'll need to talk to Morty. Morty Nickerson, is it?" The policeman flipped through his notepad. He tapped a page with his pencil. "The engineer on last night's program."

Vivian nodded. Her mind whirled with the possibility. Could Morty have put that letter in her script? Why on earth would he want to hurt her? To hurt Marjorie?

"He worked on *The Golden Years*," she said, more to herself than to anyone else.

"Did he?" Charlie said.

Vivian nodded. "Every evening. It's on from 6:00 to 6:15."

Sergeant Trask leaned toward her, no longer taking notes. "How well did he know Mrs. Fox?"

"I don't know. I mean, I can't say. I really can't. Morty is a . . ." Vivian searched her mind for the right word. "Friendly guy," she finally said. "He likes to chat about radio technology to anyone and everyone." *To me especially,* she thought. "I assume he did the same with Marjorie. But I really can't see them having any sort of friendship."

"Maybe it isn't a friendship we need to be

looking into," Charlie said to Sergeant Trask.

Vivian looked up, confused. "What are you suggesting?"

"I'm suggesting," Charlie said, "that they weren't friendly at all. I'm suggesting," he continued, removing his hand from her shoulder and flexing his fingers, "that perhaps they'd had a nasty fight."

Vivian's attention swiveled to Sergeant Trask. "Did Morty mention that he'd fought with Marjorie?"

Sergeant Trask quickly scanned his notes. "No, but that doesn't necessarily mean anything."

"Especially if he was the one who killed her," Charlie said.

Vivian shook her head, not wanting to believe the accusation. "I can't see Morty quarreling with anyone."

"He does have access to every area of the station, every studio . . ." Charlie argued.

"Every script," Vivian added in a small voice. "But so do a lot of people."

"We need to find out where these letters came from," Charlie said. He turned to the policeman. "Did the police find an envelope that may have come with Marjorie's letter? Postage marks? Things like that?"

Sergeant Trask shook his head. "Nothing."

"Mrs. Fox's home has been searched, I assume," Charlie said.

The sergeant shrugged. "I can't share that information with you, Mr. Haverman," he said firmly.

Charlie sighed and sat back in his chair, his expression unreadable. When the policeman got up to leave, Charlie leaned in to Vivian and murmured, "We'll figure this out on our own then, won't we? Who would know about Mrs. Fox's fan mail here at the station?"

"Imogene," she answered without hesitation. "Imogene would know."

Imogene was on the phone when Vivian and Charlie approached her desk, the receiver cradled in the nook between her chin and her shoulder, her hand cupped over the mouthpiece. Her eyes widened when she spotted them. She whispered something they couldn't hear and then hung up the phone.

"Viv!" she said, smiling broadly. "Felt like slumming, did you?"

Vivian smiled at the friendly jab. "How's George?" she asked, nodding toward the telephone. They weren't supposed to use the station telephones for personal calls, especially not for calls to boyfriends. "Did

164

you give him my regards?"

Furious red blotches appeared on Imogene's cheeks and crawled down her neck. Her eyes flicked to Charlie and then back to Vivian.

"You wouldn't get me in trouble, would you?" Imogene said.

"Oh, come on, Genie. It's me you're talking to. I was just kidding you." Imogene relaxed, and Vivian continued. "I'm . . . We're . . ." she corrected, gesturing to Charlie who stood by her side. "*We're* actually here in a sort of nonofficial investigative capacity."

Imogene glanced at Charlie again. "You're Mr. Haverman, I assume?" she said, extending her hand.

Charlie shook it. "And you're the Imogene that knows everything about everything at the station."

"Quite right," she answered with a nod of her head and a funny closed-lipped smile. "And I assume this 'nonofficial investigation' has to do with Marjorie Fox's death?"

"Yes," Vivian said, taking a seat in the one guest chair afforded to Imogene in her meager position.

"What can I do to help?"

Vivian glanced at the door to Mr. Lang-

165

ley's office, which was shut tight.

"Don't worry. Mr. Langley is in a very important lunch meeting that I expect to last well into the afternoon." Imogene made an almost imperceptible drinking motion with her hand and rolled her eyes.

"With Mr. Hart and Mrs. Gill-Davison?" Vivian asked.

Imogene nodded.

"Good," Charlie said. "We just have a few questions for you."

"Shoot."

"Who handles the fan mail at the station?"

"It depends. Sometimes a page, sometimes another secretary, but mostly yours truly." Imogene smiled ruefully and leaned back in her chair.

"So what happens with all of it? Do you read the mail and pass it on to the actors?" Charlie asked.

"Not usually," she said. "It has to be a really special letter to make it through to the actors."

"Did any ever make it through to Mrs. Fox?"

"I've never given her any. Mostly because I didn't want to have anything to do with her," Imogene murmured. "But I didn't say that," she added quickly.

"Did she receive a lot of fan mail?" Vivian asked.

"*She* didn't," Imogene responded. "But Evelyn did."

Imogene stood and walked to a door in the corner of the room. She swung the door open, and three canvas sacks slumped to the floor. Envelopes spilled from the top bag, which had fallen open.

"It was the Garretts' twentieth wedding anniversary last week," she said, bending to retrieve one of the letters. "We got three bags of mail congratulating them. I don't know if people think the Garretts are real, or if they know they're not and just can't help themselves." She sighed heavily and held a letter out to them so they could read the address. *To: Mrs. Roger Garrett, The Golden Years, WCHI Radio, Chicago.* "We get all sorts of things sent here for the characters on the serials: baby booties, condolence letters, flowers . . . you name it. The characters on these shows are real to people. They're like members of their family." She nodded at the bags of mail. "As far as I know, they are all very complimentary cards and letters. I haven't heard a word about anything threatening being received, ever, and I would know."

Still gazing at the mail, Vivian asked,

"Have you looked through all of those bags?"

"Those bags?" Imogene repeated, looking at the sacks of mail like they were covered in slime. She shook her head. "No time recently. Mr. Langley's got me hopping with the changes to the schedule."

"Did *anyone* look through them?" Charlie asked.

Imogene shrugged. "I doubt it."

"There could be more threatening letters in there," Vivian said quietly.

They all stared at the mailbags in silence for a moment. Suddenly, the inoffensive white envelopes and small brown-paper packages didn't seem quite so innocent.

"It'll take hours to go through all of those," Imogene said. She slumped back into her chair, discouraged by just the idea.

"It's actually more likely that the letter wasn't delivered here at all," Charlie said, lost in thought.

Vivian turned to him, one eyebrow raised. "What do you mean?"

"I think the letter was delivered directly to Mrs. Fox. How would she have received it otherwise? No one's even looked through these bags of mail, and Imogene has never given her letters before. It's safe to say none of the other secretaries have either."

Vivian nodded, thinking. "The killer would know that and would want to be sure she got it. And my letter was hand delivered." Vivian shuddered.

"*Your* letter? You got a letter?" Imogene asked, her hand at her throat.

"Yes," Vivian said. "I read it just before rehearsal for *Millicent Morris.* It was slipped into my script for *Love & Glory* this morning. I'd tucked it in my pocket and forgotten about it."

"Gosh . . ." Imogene said quietly, brown eyes wide.

"Do you know who would have access to the scripts like that, Miss . . . uh . . . ?"

"Crook," Imogene supplied.

"Miss Crook," Charlie repeated.

Imogene bit her lip. "Lots of people might have access," she said. Her brow suddenly wrinkled in concern as the information she'd received finally sunk in. "Viv, are you okay?"

"I'm fine," she said quickly. If Charlie hadn't been there, she would've told Imogene the truth: that she was terrified nearly out of her mind with worry.

"Say," Imogene said, "does this mean you won't be at the masquerade tonight?"

"Masquerade?" Vivian asked. She'd forgotten all about the station's annual Hal-

169

loween party. "They're going through with that?"

Imogene nodded and leaned forward. "They've sunk a lot of money into it. They can't really afford to cancel it now, despite what happened to Marjorie."

Vivian looked to Charlie. "I . . . Well, I don't think it's such a good idea for me to go to any parties right now, Imogene."

Charlie nodded. "I agree."

Imogene glanced at Charlie and then back to Vivian. She frowned. "I suppose I can understand that," she said, disappointment evident in her voice. "But you're going to miss my costume. It's a real corker."

"I'm sure," Vivian said.

"If you change your mind," Imogene said, sliding her top-left desk drawer open dramatically, "the key to the costume closet is right here."

Vivian looked at her friend doubtfully. "Thanks, Genie," she said.

"But now," Imogene said, glancing at the clock on the wall above the door, "I'm afraid we have a previous engagement." She looked pointedly at Vivian, and when Vivian didn't respond, she hinted in a singsong voice, "The photo shoot . . ."

Vivian blinked. Right. She and Graham were scheduled for a Halloween-themed photo shoot for *Radio Stars* today. She'd been looking forward to it for weeks. Had been. But now she found herself wondering how she could smile for the camera when a killer was on the loose.

CHAPTER FOURTEEN

Vivian and Graham had smiled broadly for the *Radio Stars* photographer over sweet scenes like carving a pumpkin and bobbing for apples under the guise that those were normal activities at the station this time of year. It had been difficult for Vivian to hide her agitation from the camera, as well as from Graham, but she'd done her best.

And now she found herself standing in front of the closed twelfth-floor lounge door, yellow police tape still stretched from one side of the frame to the other. It had been her idea to come up here. She'd thought it might be helpful to look at the room again. After all, a policeman who'd never been in the lounge before might miss something she would spot immediately. That is, if there were anything to notice at all.

"Are you sure this is such a great idea?" Charlie asked her. "Are you up to it?"

The truth was no. Vivian wasn't at all sure she was up to it. She could still see Marjorie's lifeless eyes in her mind. She swallowed, her fingertips resting lightly on the doorknob. She suddenly felt like she might be sick and whirled around, shaking her head.

Charlie placed his hand lightly on her arm and nodded. "Don't worry about it," he said in a soothing tone. "I don't think anything in this room is the answer anyway."

Vivian nodded and took a deep breath.

"Viv!"

She let the breath out slowly and turned to find little Sammy Evans rushing toward her.

He was just a slip of a man with round spectacles and thinning, light brown hair that clung to the sides of his head in tufts above each ear. His eyes were bloodshot behind his spectacles. Vivian wasn't sure he'd be in the station today with *The Golden Years* broadcast still up in the air, but here he was.

"Have you heard anything?" His pale green eyes were magnified behind the thick lenses of his glasses.

"About what?" Vivian asked, pressing her hand lightly to her stomach to staunch the queasiness.

"Anything about *The Golden Years.* What Mr. Hart's going to do."

Vivian shook her head. "Sorry, I haven't heard a thing."

"I know he's meeting with Mrs. Gill-Davison right now," Sammy said with a shake of his head. "Without Marjorie, well, I don't know if it will continue. And I got a wife and three kids to take care of . . ." He glanced at the police tape covering the door behind her.

"Sammy," Vivian said softly, "would you mind talking to us for a bit?"

Sammy turned his head sharply, his eyes focusing on Charlie. "Who's that?" he asked warily.

"Charlie Haverman," Charlie said, extending his hand. "Special consultant to *The Darkness Knows.*"

Sammy nodded and shook Charlie's hand. "The private detective," Sammy said. "I heard you were knocking about around here."

Vivian and Charlie exchanged glances.

"Sure. I already told the police everything I know," Sammy said. "What harm can it do?"

They found an empty rehearsal space. Sammy seemed eager to get his true feelings about Marjorie Fox off his chest, and he launched directly into his story without being prompted.

"I hate to speak ill of the dead," Sammy said solemnly, "but I hated Marjorie Fox. She talked down to me all the time like I was a mental deficient. I know she despised me for being . . . a midget." He looked down at his hands clasped in his lap. "But her drinking was really the worst of it. She would come into the studio for a broadcast three sheets to the wind sometimes. I complained about her to the director a few times in the beginning, but nothing ever happened, except that she got even more attention. Sometimes Mr. Hart himself would come in and watch the broadcast — he treated her with kid gloves. She was never reprimanded, from what I could tell. It was a sort of favoritism that I didn't understand. Of course, she hated me even more for tattling on her —"

"And for being popular with the listeners," Charlie added.

Sammy nodded. "But what could I do but accept the situation? This is — was — a good gig."

"What happened during the show yesterday, Sammy?" Charlie prompted.

Sammy hesitated and stole a quick glance at Vivian. She nodded her reassurance.

175

"She was her usual terrible self, sniping at everyone during rehearsal."

"Had she been drinking?" Charlie asked.

"I assume so," he said, then added in a whisper, "She was always drinking."

"Did you happen to see her with a letter?" Vivian asked.

"A letter?" Sammy's forehead creased in thought. "Yes, as a matter of fact, a page brought an envelope in for her between the rehearsal and the live broadcast."

Vivian looked at Charlie, and he nodded. So Marjorie's letter had also been hand delivered.

Charlie leaned forward, one elbow on his knee. "Did she read it there? In the studio?"

Sammy looked off into the distance. "She opened it, but I didn't see her read it. The writers had just given me some extra dialogue to review. Boy, she loved that," he said sarcastically.

"Sammy," Vivian said. "What did the letter look like?"

"Look like?"

"Yes, what did the paper look like?"

He thought for a few seconds and shrugged. "White, I suppose."

"All white?"

"No." Sammy wrinkled his brow in thought. "I think it had a stripe at the

176

top . . . blue or green . . . And a crest of some kind."

Vivian nodded. "The same letter I saw her with shortly before . . . well, you know." She fidgeted uncomfortably in her seat. "Did you see her talking with a man at any point?" she asked, thinking about the argument she'd overheard through the ladies' room door.

"A man?" He shook his head. "Just the men working on the show. Me, Lester Garvey . . ." He glanced toward Charlie. "That's her husband on the show," he explained. "The director, Morty . . ."

"Did she have an argument with one of them?" Charlie asked.

"One of them?" Sammy laughed. "How about *all* of them?"

Vivian and Charlie looked at each other.

"What did she argue with Morty about?" Charlie asked.

"Ah, the usual stuff. Morty wasn't getting the sound levels right. She thought he was making her microphone weaker than everyone else's." Sammy rolled his eyes behind the thick lenses.

"Did they argue often?" Charlie asked.

"Yeah, all the time, but Marjorie argued with everyone all the time." Sammy shrugged. "All I know is that she stormed

177

off the second we were off the air. I don't know where she went." He looked down at his hands again and hitched in an audible breath. "Viv, will you let me know . . ." Sammy continued, his voice trembling slightly. "If you hear anything about the show?" He looked up, his eyes watery with tears.

Vivian placed her hand over his and pressed down lightly. "Of course, Sammy," she said softly. "I'm sure everything will be fine."

He nodded and looked down at the floor.

As they were leaving the station, Charlie grasped Vivian's arm and pulled her into a small alcove near the elevators.

"Are you sure you're okay?" he asked, his eyes searching her face.

Vivian nodded. She did feel a little better after talking to Sammy. She wasn't sure he had told them anything helpful, but at least it had been something concrete to do.

"Good, because I think I may be on to something."

"What? Is it something that Sammy said?"

He nodded. "I think the letters were switched."

"Switched? Which letters?"

"I only saw it for a moment or two last

night, but I'm certain that the letter found with Marjorie's body was typed on plain white paper. No blue stripe. No crest."

"But both Sammy and I saw her with a letter with a blue or green stripe and a crest."

Charlie waited for Vivian to make the connection.

"The killer switched the letters?" she asked.

"Someone did, anyway."

"Why?"

"I can only assume there was something in the original letter that the killer didn't want anyone to see. The motive for Mrs. Fox's murder, maybe."

"But why bother to replace the letter with another? Why not just take the letter and leave it at that?"

Charlie shrugged. "To deflect attention, send the police on a wild-goose chase . . ."

"A wild-goose chase?"

"Buy some time by sending them after a man named Walter who probably doesn't exist. To keep the focus on preventing your murder instead of finding Mrs. Fox's killer . . ."

Vivian blinked, and a smile of relief spread slowly across her face. "So the threat letters are just red herrings then? There's no Walter? No one wants to kill me?"

"Now, now," Charlie said, holding both hands up. "I wouldn't jump to any conclusions."

"But it's a possibility?"

"I'd say so."

Vivian let out the breath she hadn't known she was holding in a long, slow rush of air. "Thank God," she said.

"Don't get too excited," Charlie said. "That's just my hunch. We need to find out what was in that original letter — the one the killer didn't want anyone to see."

"But wouldn't the killer have destroyed it?"

"Most likely," he answered, his jaw working in agitation. He cocked an eyebrow at her. "And let's not forget that someone's still threatened you, red herring or no."

"You're right," she said, her brow furrowed with renewed concern. "My letter may be a fake, but it was still placed in my script by the killer. So we're back to square one, aren't we? It's someone I see every day. And that means that anyone at the station who had a grudge against Marjorie . . ." she said, deep in thought.

"Is a suspect, yes," he finished.

"That's a lot of people," she said helplessly.

180

"It seems to be," Charlie agreed.

Vivian thought for a moment, watching people pass in the hallway. As luck would have it, Chet Whibley chose that moment to saunter by, along with a few of his *Country Cavalcade* girls, replete in their Western finery. Vivian turned back to Charlie.

"But there *is* some good news," Vivian announced brightly. "I know where everyone who worked directly with Marjorie will be between, oh, roughly eight and midnight tonight."

Charlie eyed her suspiciously.

"We just need to make a pit stop in wardrobe before we leave," she said, grabbing his sleeve and pulling him back out into the hustle and bustle of the hallway.

CHAPTER FIFTEEN

"I look ridiculous."

Vivian eyed Charlie's reflection in the full-length mirror in her mother's study and suppressed a smile. "Well, I think you make a marvelous cowpoke," she said. "Very Randolph Scott." He cocked an eyebrow in surprise at the compliment until she added, "If I squint my eyes and cock my head to the right."

"I knew there was a catch," he said dryly. "Are you sure this getup is strictly necessary?" He pulled at a piece of the red fringe hanging from his sleeve.

Thanks to Imogene's tip and the key she kept in her desk, Vivian and Charlie had had their pick of *Chet Whibley's Country Cavalcade* outfits from the station's costume closet. Charlie sported a Chet Whibley special, most likely last used while the wearer crooned a mournful country ballad. The costume consisted of a cowhide vest over a white-collared shirt replete with delicately embroidered red carnations that ran up the entire length of the placket. Silky red fringe extended down the seam of both sleeves and swayed like prairie grass with the slightest movement. Cowhide chaps matched the vest, and the same fringe appeared on the seam from hip to ankle. Vivian considered the overall effect. Everything fit Charlie remarkably well. In fact, she didn't know why she'd tempered her earlier compliment with a slight dig. He *did* resemble Randolph Scott.

"Of course it's necessary. You can't go barging into a masquerade in a suit and tie," she admonished. "You'd stick out like a sore thumb."

Charlie made a face at himself in the mirror. "I still look ridiculous."

"Yes, yes, but how do *I* look?" Vivian spun in a tight circle, allowing the fringe on her skirt to flare. Then she stopped and posed fetchingly, she hoped, with one hand on her hip. Her outfit matched Charlie's almost exactly, except that the hemline and neckline were both considerably more daring.

"I do declare, Miss Witchell," he said, hitching one thumb on the side of his vest and pretending to chew on a piece of straw. "You sure do look purdy."

"Oh, pshaw," she said, fanning herself with one red cowhide glove.

"May I have the pleasure of a dance later?" he asked. He reached to tip the brim of his hat toward her, but his fingers touched only air.

"Your hat!" Vivian cried in alarm. "It's key to the ensemble."

"No need to panic, missy," he said, pointing.

Vivian turned and spied the Stetson sitting atop a pile of papers on her mother's desk. As she lifted it, something caught her eye in the pile below.

A sheet of paper with a tantalizingly familiar blue stripe across the top lay half-hidden among her mother's correspondence. Vivian handed the hat to Charlie without turning away from the desk and pulled the letter farther from the pile with her thumb and index finger. The letter was upside down, so she tilted her head to the side in an effort to glean its contents without disturbing its placement further. Her mother didn't like her things bothered.

Vivian let out a little yip of triumph and snatched the letter from its spot on the desk — Mother be damned. She whirled around and held the paper mere inches from Charlie's nose.

"This," she said dramatically, shaking the piece of paper with excitement, "is what I saw Marjorie with just before she died."

Charlie settled the cowboy hat atop his head, then squinted to read the letterhead. *Chicago Foundlings Home.*

"My mother's on the board. Believe it or not, she has a soft spot for babies." Vivian smiled ruefully at Charlie. "But why would *Marjorie* be getting mail from the foundling home?"

Charlie shrugged and turned back to the mirror. "You're sure that's the same letterhead?"

"Positive," she said.

"Who knows?" he said over his shoulder. "Maybe she was on the board too."

Vivian shook her head. "Boards are for rich swells."

"Like your mother."

Vivian felt the heat rise in her face but said nothing. She flipped the letter over and kept reading. "This is about an upcoming fund-raiser," she said.

"Well, then Mrs. Fox was probably helping with fund-raising efforts," Charlie said.

"Using her stature for charity work?" Vivian considered the idea for a moment. "I guess it's possible . . ."

"Right," he said. "But Mrs. Fox wasn't

the charity type?"

"And the letter seemed to upset her so much . . ."

Charlie wrinkled his brow and yanked the knot of his scarlet kerchief loose. He began to retie it just under his Adam's apple.

"Of course!" Vivian exclaimed, slapping her forehead lightly with the tips of her fingers. "It was right in front of me all the time . . . Rich swells . . ."

Charlie slowly turned on his heel so that he faced her again. He raised his eyebrows in expectation.

"Mr. Hart is a board member too!" Vivian continued. "I used to type letters on this letterhead for him when I was his secretary. No wonder it looked so familiar. It would make sense for him to ask Marjorie to get involved, wouldn't it? The star of the biggest family serial in the country was at his disposal. Why wouldn't he take advantage of that to raise some money for his favorite charity?"

"Your mother is on the board of directors with Mr. Hart?"

Vivian nodded.

"Well, isn't that cozy," he said.

"I know what you're thinking," Vivian said. "But I didn't get my job as Mr. Hart's secretary through my mother's influence."

She declined to add that she'd gotten the job due more to her looks than her typing ability — although she'd never let Mr. Hart do anything but look, contrary to what Frances Barrow thought. She further declined to mention that her mother had abhorred her job as Mr. Hart's secretary only slightly less than she abhorred Vivian's current job as an actress.

"I was just teasing you," he responded. "It does make sense that Mr. Hart would have asked Mrs. Fox for help with fund-raising efforts." Charlie grimaced as the knot he'd spent the last few minutes carefully attempting came out decidedly lopsided. He yanked the kerchief free yet again and sighed. "I can ask him about it later. I need to update Mr. Hart on the recent developments anyway."

"That the fan letters are a red herring?"

"*Suspected* red herring," Charlie corrected.

"Of course." Vivian rolled her eyes and stepped over to him, squeezing herself between Charlie and the mirror. She reached up and tied a perfect knot in the troublesome kerchief with one deft movement. She patted her handiwork lightly as she spoke, not quite meeting his eyes. "And while you're doing that, I'll question the more suspicious members of the station's staff."

"Oh, no you won't."

"I won't what?" she asked, looking up at him, her eyes widening.

"You're not questioning anyone."

"Why not? Someone at the station has to know something about the letter from the foundling home — why Marjorie would have it and why someone would kill over it."

Charlie nodded. "True, but you're an amateur, for one. And for two" — Charlie held up the first two fingers of his right hand and wiggled them in front of her nose — "your life seems to no longer be directly in danger."

"So?"

"So I think you should just enjoy the party and keep yourself out of harm's way."

Vivian stepped to the side and crossed her arms. "I want to help."

"And I want you to keep that pretty little head of yours attached to your shoulders."

Vivian blushed and looked away.

"Look, Viv," he said, softening his tone. "It's likely that someone at the masquerade tonight is a murderer."

The idea ignited a rash of goose bumps on her forearms.

"And murderers don't take kindly to being found out," Charlie finished. "Why do you want to keep digging anyway? If the letters are indeed a red herring, then you aren't really involved in this. Why tempt fate?"

Vivian chewed on her lower lip for a moment. "Because this is hanging over my head like a black cloud. Whether I'm really in danger or not, someone is watching me and making me feel threatened. I can't concentrate. I flubbed my lines in front of the most important woman in radio today, Charlie. If I do that again, I won't even have a career to worry about. Besides," she added, "I thought it would be fun playing detective for a bit."

"You have a strange idea of fun, doll." Charlie smirked at her.

Vivian returned the smile. "You have no idea."

Charlie tilted his head to the side. But before Vivian could elaborate, the study door opened behind them with a protracted creak of its hinges. They both turned toward it as they moved ever so slightly apart.

"What's going on in here?" Vivian's mother stuck her head through the door. Her eyes flicked back and forth between her daughter and Charlie, the bit of forehead

189

between her eyes puckering disapprovingly. "What on earth are you wearing?"

Charlie flushed and eyed the floor as though he wanted to sink directly into it and disappear.

Vivian smiled sweetly at her mother and answered for both of them. "The station's Halloween masquerade, Mother. It's tonight."

Mrs. Witchell's head bobbed slightly, her eyes squinting. "You're not going," she said. "That's lunacy. With everything that's happened recently? I think it's in bad taste to even hold a party in such close proximity to a murder." She uttered the word "murder" in a hoarse stage whisper.

"It's happening. They've sunk a lot of money into it."

"That doesn't mean you should be attending, Vivian. Please, Mr. Haverman, *you* can see reason, can't you?"

"I can," he agreed without looking up.

She stared at him for a moment without speaking. Then she said, "Thank goodness for that," in a low voice and ducked back out the door.

"Oh, Mother!" Vivian called.

Her mother's head reappeared, a scowl already on her face.

"Did you ever hear of Marjorie Fox having a connection to the foundling home?"

The scowl was replaced with a look of surprise.

"Marjorie Fox and the foundling home? No. Never."

"She wasn't doing any fund-raising work or anything?"

"Not that I know of. I never met the woman."

"Thank you, Mother." Vivian returned her gaze to the mirror, inspecting the fringe hanging from one elbow-length glove.

"No masquerade," her mother warned before closing the door.

Vivian met Charlie's eyes in the mirror.

"Well, that settles that. Marjorie wasn't doing anything for the foundling home," she said, running the tip of an ungloved finger along her lower lip to smooth her lipstick. "Mother would know."

Charlie shrugged. "Mr. Hart may not have mentioned it to the rest of the board yet."

"Maybe," she said thoughtfully. Vivian pulled on the remaining glove and watched Charlie out of the corner of her eye. He plucked the hat from his head, smoothed his hair to the side, and returned the hat, trying a more rakish angle. He frowned at his reflection, and her face broke into a grin despite her best efforts to remain solemn. "I can't take you seriously in that outfit."

Charlie scowled, pulled the tin pistol from the holster slung around his hips, and aimed it at his reflection.

"Bang, bang," he said.

CHAPTER SIXTEEN

Vivian had been to the Empire Room of the Palmer House a few times before. She and Graham had danced to Hal Kemp and His Orchestra just last week, gliding under the massive crystal chandelier that hung directly over the dance floor. It had been a magical evening — until they'd posed for a few photos and he'd put her in the waiting cab to send her home, that is.

Tonight the room buzzed with electricity. The band was already in full swing on the dais across the room. Couples bounced across the dance floor dressed as knights, harlequins, and Indian princesses, and though she couldn't be sure, Vivian thought she saw Queen Victoria jitterbugging with the Red Baron.

"It must have cost a pretty penny to rent this place for the night," Charlie said, eyes running over the floor-to-ceiling gold brocade drapes.

"I imagine so."

"Is the station doing that well?"

Vivian shrugged. "I'm no longer privy to the financials. Strike that," she said after a moment. "I was *never* privy to the financials."

Vivian felt the crowd push in to her left and then an elbow to her ribs. She heard "Oh, pardon me, miss" in an over-the-top Southern twang somewhere just above her left ear.

She half turned and caught a glimpse of cowhide and an elaborately embroidered yellow shirt. Butterflies fluttered in her stomach. She didn't have to look up at the face to recognize that Chet Whibley was standing before her.

"Hello, Chet!" she said, turning to face the man with a huge smile that she hoped conveyed nothing of the utter mortification she was feeling inside.

"Oh, Vivian," he said gruffly. "I didn't even notice it was you."

"It is . . . me," she said, smile faltering. She noticed his eyes drawn to the white Stetson she wore. He regarded it for a moment but said nothing. Chet then turned his attention to Charlie, narrowing his eyes at the detective over Vivian's head.

"Oh, I'm sorry," Vivian said, flustered.

"How rude of me not to introduce you. Chet Whibley, this is Charlie Haverman."

Charlie held his hand out, but Chet ignored it. Instead, his eyes roamed slowly from the top of Charlie's Stetson, down his rawhide vest and matching chaps, all the way to the tips of his borrowed cowboy boots.

"Nice getup," Chet drawled, each syllable drawn out until Vivian thought the words themselves would crack.

"Thank you," Charlie answered.

"Seems a mite familiar," Chet added. He lowered his chin and nearly closed his left eye as he sized Charlie up.

"Does it, now? I guess great minds think alike." The words were casual, but the delivery was not.

The two men stared at each other, Charlie's right hand clenching and unclenching.

"Yes, you both look smashing," Vivian said stupidly, trying to defuse the tension.

"Mmm," Chet replied.

Chet's date joined them then, sidling up beside him and threading her arm through his. She was dressed as Cleopatra, a fake snake twisting its way through her jet-black wig.

"Chet, darling," she murmured, eyeing both Vivian and Charlie with disdain. "You simply must meet Mimi O'Herlihy . . ." And without a parting word to either of them, the couple sauntered off, Chet's spurs jangling against the polished wood of the dance floor.

"What a piece of work," Charlie mumbled, watching the radio cowboy walk away.

Vivian noticed that the flush blossoming from underneath Charlie's kerchief nearly matched the scarf's scarlet color. He was angry, and perhaps even worse, he was embarrassed.

"He's just a pretend cowboy, you know," Vivian said, her voice overly bright. "Actually, I hear he's from Peoria, and his real name is Milton Bronstein."

Charlie's eyes slid sideways, regarding her skeptically.

"Cross my heart. You're more of a cowboy than Chet Whibley is, and you wear that ridiculous outfit far better than he could ever hope to."

Charlie's lips twitched with the semblance of a smile, and he squinted off across the room. "Thank you, I guess."

"It's also terribly gauche of him to wear his work attire to a masquerade. He could have at least put a bit of effort into his costume. Very poor taste, if you ask me."

Their eyes met, and after a moment, they

both laughed.

"Ah, *this* is not my element." Charlie pulled on the knot in his kerchief uncomfortably as he surveyed the room.

Vivian's eyes roamed the room as well, taking in the opulence of it. The gold leaf on seemingly every surface glittered in the lights of the chandeliers. Even the chairs at the linen-draped tables gleamed gold in the mellow light. If you had to hold a masquerade, this was definitely the place to do it, she thought. And Mr. Hart didn't do anything by halves. The band ended the current song with a blare of trumpets, and the swirling couples on the dance floor broke apart as they erupted into applause.

Vivian's eyes traveled past the dance floor and landed on Frances. She stood near the refreshment table, dressed as Snow White, of course, and flirting outrageously with Mr. Langley, a squat, red-faced man dressed appropriately enough tonight in the regally flowing robes of Henry VIII. Frances rested one white-gloved hand on the poor man's shoulder and leaned daringly close to say something directly into his ear. Mr. Langley's face was so red with excitement that it looked like it might pop. Vivian turned away with a sigh.

"I appreciate you going along with this

scatterbrained idea," she said, looping her arm through Charlie's. "I owe you one."

Vivian's attention shifted to a couple approaching from the dance floor, and her face broke into a wide grin.

"Well, if it isn't Maid Marian and her dashing Robin Hood!" she exclaimed. "You two look marvelous!"

Imogene beamed and curtsied to them, pulling out the sides of her skirt. She wore a fitted silver-white bodice attached to a full periwinkle-blue skirt with a sparkling silver overlay. A matching periwinkle headdress was held in place by a shimmery silver crown.

"I'm so glad you decided to come! Chet Whibley and his cavalcade never wore it better." Imogene nodded approvingly at the matched pair of cowboys in front of her.

Vivian clasped Imogene's hands warmly in her own and turned to Imogene's boyfriend, George. "And my, if it isn't Errol Flynn himself!"

George's face blushed three shades of crimson. Even he knew nothing could be further from the truth. "Naw," he sputtered. "*He* looks like Errol Flynn." George cocked a thumb toward the edge of the dance floor, where Graham stood chatting up a small woman dressed as a nun. Graham happened to be wearing the same Robin Hood outfit as George, right down to the dusky-green tights and penciled-in mustache.

Imogene said in a dreamy voice, "More Robert Taylor than Errol Flynn, if you ask me."

George shot her a withering look, and Imogene shrugged an apology.

"Well, I, for one, think you look dashing," Vivian said quickly, tearing her eyes away from Graham with some effort. "Swash-buckling even."

Charlie leaned down and whispered into her ear, "You're thinking of Captain Blood."

Vivian followed Charlie's raised index finger to a man on the far side of the room dressed as a pirate, complete with over-the-knee boots and a paper sword drawn from its scabbard. It was Mr. Hart, and he was brandishing the sword in lazy circles as he spoke to a man Vivian didn't recognize.

"Posh," Vivian said in exasperation. "I'm getting my Errol Flynns mixed up. Sorry, George — about your costume twin, I mean."

"Don't worry about it, Viv. It's demoral-izing, but I'll cope." His expression turned sober. "Speaking of coping, how are you doing? I heard about the letter."

"I'm fine," she answered automatically.

George touched her arm. "Really," she said. "Completely fine. And I have Charlie here." She patted Charlie's arm. "He's looking after me."

"Ah, so *this* is Mr. Haverman," George said with an exaggerated wink. "George Pfeffer," he announced to Charlie, extending his hand.

Charlie shook it. "Charlie Haverman. I take it my reputation precedes me."

"I've heard good things," George said, nodding toward Imogene, who widened her eyes at them with feigned innocence. "Take care of my Viv, Mr. Haverman. She's one of a kind."

Imogene slapped her boyfriend playfully on the shoulder.

"I mean, one of a kind after my Genie, of course."

They all laughed, and George's face burned anew at his latest gaffe.

"Don't worry," Charlie said. "She's in good hands."

The orchestra launched into a lively version of "Bei Mir Bist du Schön," and both Imogene and George turned their heads toward the dais.

"Ooh, I just love this song!" Imogene squealed.

"Go dance, you two," Vivian said, laughing. "Don't let us hold you back."

"If you're sure," Imogene said over her shoulder as they hurried to find an empty spot on the crowded dance floor.

"I guess I didn't have to twist her arm." Vivian turned to Charlie, but he wasn't listening. She followed his gaze and saw that Mr. Hart had resheathed his paper sword and ended his conversation. He was now leaning down to whisper into the ear of a Little Orphan Annie, who blushed brilliantly at his comment and gazed up at him in rapt attention. Vivian squinted at the girl. It was his secretary, she realized. And by the way she was smiling up at Mr. Hart, Vivian could see that *she* had not been one to turn down Mr. Hart's clumsy advances.

"You should go speak with him," she said, nudging Charlie with her elbow.

Charlie's face was tense. "You're sure you'll be all right?"

"Safe as a kitten."

"No questioning anyone while I'm gone," he warned as he backed away from her, his index finger wagging. "Have a drink. Have a dance. Have a nice, bland chat with someone about the unseasonably warm weather."

Vivian rolled her eyes and smiled. "I promise to behave, Marshal."

201

Charlie ducked his head to glance at the tin badge pinned to his vest and then back up at Vivian, his finger still raised in admonition. He pointed it at her one last time, eyebrows raised, and warned in a low tone, "I'm serious." Then Charlie turned on his heel, spurs jingling, and disappeared in the throng of costumed partygoers.

CHAPTER SEVENTEEN

It took five full minutes for Vivian to make her way through the throng to the refreshment table. She walked with a slight smile on her face, nodding whenever she met someone's eyes. It was so hard to tell if she was supposed to recognize these people, especially the ones with face-covering masks or complete body-covering costumes like the man in the furry head-to-toe gorilla getup. At least, she assumed it was a man.

She finally made it to the table and was lifting a ladle of punch to her glass when a voice behind her announced, "The punch is spiked, I presume."

Vivian half turned from the bowl, ladle in hand.

The Lone Ranger stood just behind her. His voice was distinct and decidedly familiar, but the mask threw her off, and the eyes peering out from underneath it were an unhelpful shade of nondescript gray. She watched them twinkle with amusement as she failed in her attempt to identify the speaker.

"I'm sorry . . ." she began, shrugging her shoulders in apology.

"Oh, Viv." The man laughed. "It's me." He flipped the mask up with two fingers and smiled at her.

Vivian smiled back at Bill Purdy, the announcer for *The Darkness Knows* and other shows too numerous to count.

"Great costume," she said. She turned her wrist and watched the red liquid cascade into her waiting glass.

"Hi-yo, Silver!" he exclaimed in a perfect imitation of the Lone Ranger's signature call. "So is it? Spiked, I mean."

Vivian brought the glass to her lips and sipped. "Appears so," she said. "Wouldn't be a party without a little rum."

Vivian stepped away from the punch bowl, and Bill slid into her place at the crowded table. He picked up the ladle.

"I'm actually surprised this party was still a go," he said over his shoulder. "You know, with Marjorie and everything . . ." He raised his eyebrows significantly at her.

"And you're especially surprised to see me here?" Vivian asked, picking up on the implication.

"Well, yes." He filled his own glass and turned back to face her. "I'm not sure I'd risk it if I were you."

"Risk it?"

"Someone's out to get you, Viv," he said.

"Oh, really? I'd forgotten." She'd meant it to come out lighthearted, but instead, it sounded flat and mean.

Bill's face lost all traces of good humor under the black mask. His mouth drew into a tight line, the lips pinched almost white.

"Do the police have any leads?" he asked, his voice low.

Vivian shook her head.

"They think it's a crazed fan?"

Vivian nodded.

"I'm not surprised Marjorie ended up this way, you know." Vivian was taken slightly aback by the abrupt proclamation. "You knew, didn't you?" he continued. His voice was so low that she could barely make it out over the din of the party. "About her drinking?"

"Yes, but if it was a crazed fan —"

"It wasn't," Bill said, his melodious voice trembling ever so slightly.

Vivian felt the hairs on her arms bristle.

"How do you know?"

"I just do," he said vaguely. "She'd been getting letters for weeks. The 'I know what

205

you've done' kind." He lowered his chin and looked directly into Vivian's eyes for a few long seconds.

"She was being blackmailed?"

He nodded.

"By whom? About what?"

Bill shrugged. "I would think you'd know that better than me. After all, you're next, aren't you?" he said ominously. He raised his glass to his lips and took a long swallow, wincing as the punch went down.

"Too strong for you, Purdy?" Superman — or rather, Dave Chapman dressed as Superman — pushed his way into their circle. He led with his own nearly empty glass, his face flushed, eyes watery. He stepped on the toe of Vivian's boot and muttered an apology before grabbing her arm to steady himself.

"It's seems like you've had plenty, Dave," Vivian said, shaking his sweaty fingers off her forearm.

"Oh, just a few glasses," he said. "Having a nice time, Viv?"

"Yes, actually."

"You have a lot of gumption, showing up here," Dave said. "Or maybe you're just rattlebrained." He smiled too widely at his own joke, and she felt her stomach turn over.

Vivian glanced around, hoping to catch a glimpse of a familiar white Stetson near her in the crowd, but Charlie was nowhere to be seen.

"I don't know who'd want to do in a pretty thing like you . . ." Dave continued, eyes lingering over the beaded vest of her costume for a second too long. Vivian glared at him, and his hand flew to cover his open mouth. "I'm sorry, Viv," he said through his fingers. "I guess I've had too much to drink."

"I guess you have," she replied coldly, pointedly eyeing the gold band on his left ring finger.

"Dave, tell me about that vacation you're taking with the family," Bill interjected suddenly. "Planning to play much golf?"

In the pause that it took Dave to switch gears and come up with a reply, Vivian made her exit, shooting a grateful look at Bill's worried face as she slipped away.

So Marjorie was being blackmailed, she thought. *About what? Her drinking? No, that's an open secret.* She scanned the crowd for Charlie, but she didn't see him. She did, however, catch sight of the unmistakable brown feather in Graham's Robin Hood cap bobbing above the throng ten feet in front of her. She attempted to push her way toward him but couldn't get through the crowd. Then she stumbled on something and heard a small *oomph* from somewhere below, followed by, "Hey, up there! Watch where you're walking!"

Vivian looked down to find Sammy Evans, dressed as a court jester, standing directly in front of her. Another step and they both would have gone tumbling to the floor in a heap.

"Hello, Sammy," she said with a sigh. "Having a nice time?" She craned her neck in an attempt to see over the crowd. This was one time she didn't appreciate being so short. Then she glanced down at Sammy and realized it could be worse.

"I'm having a wonderful time. You?"

"I was," she answered truthfully.

"Well, what happened?"

Charlie's warning voice echoed in her head. *Just chat about the weather,* she told herself. *It's unseasonably warm.*

"It's not important," she said, waving her hand.

Sammy watched the fringe on her glove sway. "I'm glad this little soiree wasn't canceled because of Marjorie. I'm having a wonderful time." Sammy nodded his head vigorously, and the bells on his hat tinkled.

You already said that, Vivian thought irritably.

He leaned in toward her. "Have you heard any more about what may have happened?"

Vivian shook her head.

"What was that letter all about then?" he asked.

Vivian shrugged, afraid that if she spoke, she'd say something she shouldn't.

"That woman had skeletons in her closet," he said, shaking his head. A strange half smile formed on his lips. "I suppose I just assumed she'd been horrible to someone she shouldn't have and it came back to bite her. She was always being horrible to people," he said cryptically. He gazed off into the crowd, his eyes glassy. Then his head snapped toward her again. "By the way, did you hear?"

"Hear what?"

Sammy's chest puffed inside the colorful jester's tunic. "You're looking at the new regularly appearing character on the *Carlton Coffee Variety Hour!*" He hoisted his glass and tipped it toward her in a toast to himself.

"Congratulations," she said. "Does that mean *The Golden Years* is no more?"

Sammy nodded solemnly and leaned toward her, the back of his hand held to his mouth. "You know I shouldn't say it was a good thing that Marjorie was murdered," he said in a hushed tone, "but I never would have gotten this role if she hadn't been." He looked meaningfully into Vivian's eyes until she nodded uncomfortably.

"I've got to go, Sammy. Did you happen to see where Graham went?"

Sammy lifted his drink and pointed. Some of the punch sloshed over the side and splashed on the floor at his feet. He stifled a giggle with his free hand.

She scanned the crowed, but it was no good. Graham had slipped out of sight while she'd been talking to Sammy. She hurried off anyway before Sammy could attempt to drunkenly unburden his soul to her again. She glanced over her shoulder and saw him making his way unsteadily through the dancing throng. He'd be lucky to not be trampled by this lot.

She slid into a chair at an empty table near the dance floor. Couples floated past her in a blur as her mind raced. Who could have been blackmailing Marjorie, and about what? Her alcoholism was an open secret. Certainly, a threat to expose that would have gone over like a lead balloon. It had to be something else, she thought absently. Something in Marjorie's past . . . but what?

Perhaps information about the illusive Mr. Fox? There had been speculation about him but no solid leads.

Who would benefit from Marjorie being gone? Certainly not Mr. Hart or Edith Gill-Davison or the sponsor of *The Golden Years.* Marjorie's death could only complicate all of their business ambitions. The only person so far who had truly benefited had been Sammy. But that didn't figure, because he'd been beside himself with worry because of her death only hours earlier, terrified that he was about to lose his job.

Vivian sat for a few minutes, watching the dancers and trying to sort everything out in her head. It was no use. Everyone was a suspect, and no one was. Vivian sighed in exasperation as a flash of red appeared to her right. She glanced over and smiled absently at Red Riding Hood, who'd just taken the seat next to her.

A female voice floated up from beneath the hood. "Hello, Viv." Then two hands appeared from underneath the cape to pull the sides of the hood back.

"Oh, hi, Peggy," Vivian said with a sigh.

"Something wrong?" Peggy asked.

"Just, well, you know . . . frayed nerves," Vivian answered honestly.

"I can imagine," the girl said. She stirred

a swizzle stick around in her glass of punch. Then she lifted it to her mouth and took a tiny sip. "Do the police know any more about this mysterious Walter person?"

Vivian snorted. "The police don't know a thing."

Peggy nodded.

Vivian glanced sidelong at the girl. "I'm sure you saw Marjorie quite a lot around the station," she said.

Peggy sighed as if the topic of Marjorie bored her. "I rarely had anything to do with *The Golden Years,* but I saw her fairly often, yes."

"What did you think of her?"

Peggy blinked. "Think of her?" she repeated, as if the answer were obvious. "She wasn't very nice."

"Do you know of anyone at the station who had it in for her?"

Peggy smirked. "Who didn't?" The girl thought for a moment and then leaned toward Vivian conspiratorially, as if she were going to tell her a juicy bit of gossip. "Marjorie Fox clawed her way into the business tooth and nail," she said. "I'm sure she did plenty of unsavory things on her way to the top."

True, Vivian thought, but hardly a revelation. There had been a strange lilt to Peggy's voice, as if she'd intended Vivian to take something she'd just said at more than face value. Vivian shook her head. She was probably just tired and imagining things. "Have you seen Charlie, by any chance?" she asked.

The girl shook her head.

"Well, how about Graham — have you seen him lately?"

"Yes," Peggy answered, her expression turning quickly into one of disgust. She seemed to lose her train of thought for a moment, then said, "They looked like two bugs in a rug."

"Who did?" Vivian asked. For some reason, she immediately thought of Mr. Hart and his secretary and scanned the ballroom for them. Had Peggy stumbled upon them somewhere? Did she know of her father's dalliances?

"Graham and Frances," Peggy said quietly.

"Graham and Frances," Vivian repeated. "Where?"

"Not that I hadn't heard the rumors," Peggy continued, as if she hadn't heard Vivian's question. "But I didn't want to believe them." She glanced sidelong at Vivian, eyes peeking out from beneath her large, red hood. The sour look on Peggy's face broadcast that Vivian was not the only one disappointed at this turn of events.

"Rumors," Vivian repeated. Of course she'd heard them, but she wouldn't believe it until she saw it for herself. "Where were they?"

Peggy looked straight ahead, her face invisible behind the red curtain of her hood, and replied, "I just passed them in the coat-room —"

If there was more to Peggy's sentence, Vivian didn't hear it. She jumped from her chair and rushed off, pushing aside court jesters, dairy maids, and anyone else who dared to get in her way.

CHAPTER EIGHTEEN

They were still there standing just inside
the door to the coatroom. Frances's back
was to Vivian, but she could see Graham's
face clearly over the red velvet bow perched
on the crown of Frances's head. He was
smiling at Frances, the kind of knowing,
flirtatious smile men flashed to women they
knew very well, or wanted to know very
well. Vivian watched as Frances placed her
white-gloved hands on Graham's broad
chest, and then he leaned down toward her,
the brown feather in his cap bobbing jaun-
tily.

Vivian whirled on her heel and hurried
off, head down in embarrassment and
indignation. She should have known. She'd
heard the talk — everyone had. Of course,
Frances would make a play for Graham.
Why wouldn't she? Vivian's head was still
down, her mind still swirling, when she
smashed headlong into someone. She felt a

stinging icy coldness dribble down her front and heard the distinct crash of glass hitting floor. Strong hands grabbed her forearms, fingers digging into her flesh to keep her from falling backward from the impact.

Morty's freckled face came into focus above her.

"Viv! What on earth?"

"I'm sorry," she muttered, straightening and brushing Morty's hands away. "I'm just . . . I'm just . . ." She couldn't find any more words.

"Are you hurt?" he asked.

"Of course not," she said angrily. The last thing she wanted right now was to be covered in punch and chatting with Morty Nickerson.

"You aren't leaving, are you?" Morty looked stricken at the thought.

"No," she assured him. She resisted glancing behind her. Graham wouldn't be following. He hadn't seen her. And why would he come after her when he had Frances in his arms and at the ready?

"I'm sorry about . . ." Morty gestured helplessly to the bright red punch stain spreading across the front of her previously pristine costume.

Vivian waved his apology away.

"It's a really nice costume," he said feebly.

"Is it —"

"Ruined, yes," she finished. "Don't worry about it. It's from the costume closet — *Country Cavalcade*." She appraised his attire. "What are you dressed as?"

"Isn't it obvious?" he asked, straightening his spine and smoothing the blue velvet tunic over his chest. "I'm Prince Charming, of course," he said seriously.

"Of course," she replied without enthusiasm.

"Maybe I should go find Frances . . . You know, the Snow White to my Prince Charming." He chuckled.

Vivian narrowed her eyes in irritation at hearing the woman's name.

Morty took a step toward her and leaned down to look directly into her face. "Look, Viv," he began, his voice soft. "I want you to know that I don't blame you for putting the police on my trail."

Vivian blinked. "What?"

"The police," he repeated. "Sergeant Trask came at me with all sorts of questions this afternoon. I just want you to know that I don't blame you."

Vivian's body went cold. A thousand questions formed in her mind, but her mouth couldn't grasp on to any of them.

"I . . . Well . . . I don't know how he got

217

that impression," she said stupidly.

"From you," Morty answered simply. "I know you told Sergeant Trask that I asked you about your letter."

"I . . . Well . . ."

"It's okay," he said calmly. "Really. I would've done the same thing." He leaned even closer to her, and Vivian shrank away from the smell of rum-laced punch on his breath and the manic look in his wide blue eyes. "But I want you to know that I didn't do it. Marjorie was a horrible person, but I didn't kill her."

"Oh."

"And I didn't send you any letter."

Vivian didn't respond.

"Be sure to tell Sergeant Trask that," he said, staring at her intently.

"I have to go, Morty," she said, taking one wide step to the left.

"You'll tell him?"

"Of course."

Vivian had no intention of telling Sergeant Trask anything. Everyone was the bogeyman, or so it seemed tonight. Any one of ten people could have killed Marjorie without batting an eye, and someone in this room most certainly had.

Vivian needed to find Charlie, but she

couldn't see him anywhere. She scoured the dance floor, sifting through the musketeers and Cleopatras, bouncing on her toes in the middle of the throng in a vain attempt to see over plumed hats and powdered wigs. At the edge of the crowd, she did spot a familiar and welcome face — Imogene. Her friend's eyes widened as she approached.

"Have you seen Charlie?" Vivian asked, ignoring the distress on her friend's face.

Imogene shook her head, the glittery silver veil sending out sparks of light. She pointed to Vivian's chest. "What on earth happened to you?"

Vivian glanced down at the stain turning a nasty mottled brownish-red on the pristine white of the cowhide vest.

"Morty happened to me."

"Please tell me that's not from the costume closet," Imogene said.

"I'm sorry, Genie. It was an accident." Vivian brushed at the stain. "It's fine. It'll come out with a little club soda."

Imogene made a face. "Not likely." She took a sip of her punch, regarding Vivian carefully over the lip of her glass. "What's wrong? You have that pinched look to your face that tells me things aren't going as planned."

Vivian turned and glanced quickly around

219

the room. She still didn't spot Charlie's white Stetson in the crowd. She looked at Imogene. "Frances," she said in an exasperated exhale.

"What's she done now?"

"What she always does, I guess. Make trouble." Vivian watched her fingers pull at the fringe on her vest as she spoke. "I just saw her with Graham in the coat closet. They were very close." She looked up and locked eyes with her friend. "Very."

Imogene shook her head in sympathy. "I hate to say it, but that's not really a surprise. I've been hearing for months that she wanted to get her hooks into him."

"Well, it looked a few minutes ago like she got her wish."

Imogene touched Vivian's arm lightly. "Are you going to call off your date tomorrow night?"

Vivian shrugged. She had no claim on Graham Yarborough. She'd be a fool to think that those thousand-watt smiles were reserved just for her. Graham was a flirt, and Frances was an attractive girl. It was just biology. Still, it hurt Vivian's pride to see them together like that — so cozy.

"I don't know," Vivian said, distracted. She didn't have time for this drama right now. "I need to find Charlie."

Imogene took another sip of her drink. "Is that really all that's bothering you?"

"Yes," Vivian said. She'd turned and gazed over the dancing crowd so that she wouldn't have to look her best friend in the eye as she lied to her. She felt terrible, but she couldn't tell Imogene about the blackmail. She couldn't tell anyone but Charlie, and he was the only person she hadn't run into since she found out. She turned back to her friend. "Sorry, Genie. I've got to go."

She could tell from the look on Imogene's face that she didn't believe her. Genie knew her too well for secrets. "Try the balcony," she said. "Maybe he needed some air."

Vivian nodded, turned on her heel, and headed toward the balcony on the opposite side of the room. She fought her way across the dance floor again, getting a painful shot to the ribs from an overzealous jitterbugger on the way. She was within steps of the doorway when a shout stopped her in her tracks.

"Viv!"

She turned to find Graham bearing down on her, his path appearing in the throng of bodies as if he were Moses parting the Red Sea. He did make a terribly dashing Robin Hood, she thought, watching him approach. He might be the only man in the Western

Hemisphere, besides Errol Flynn himself, who could pull off that ridiculous penciled-in mustache. He reached her and smiled. "There you are. I've been looking all over for you."

"Have you?" Vivian asked, her face the picture of innocence. *Looking for me in the coat closet,* she thought, *as you pressed yourself against Frances Barrow?*

Graham nodded and held his hand out to her, palm up. "How about a dance?"

"I'm afraid I'm not much in the mood for dancing." She rubbed her sore ribs.

Graham's sparkling smile faded a bit. "A rain check then?"

Vivian nodded, her eyes darting over Graham's shoulder and around the room. Still no Charlie.

"Later it is, my lady." Graham doffed his Robin Hood cap and bent at the waist with a flourish in an exaggerated impression of a courtly bow. As he did, Vivian's eyes wandered above him over the dance floor. Frances stood on the opposite side of the room directly in her line of vision. As their eyes met, Frances's lips curled into a syrupy, taunting smile.

Vivian watched Graham disappear into the crowd on the dance floor, then turned and stepped through the doorway and onto the balcony. She needed some air herself. The balcony was a long, thin strip running the length of the ballroom. It was unlit and quiet. The only noises were the sounds of traffic three stories below and the ever-present rumble of the El trains. She'd expected to come across at least a few amorous couples out here in the darkness, but she seemed to be alone. Maybe it was too early for those kinds of shenanigans. She walked to the edge of the balcony and placed her hands on the railing with a sigh.

She heard a rustling in the far corner, feet shifting on the concrete. She squinted into the shadows, her pulse quickening. "Who —" She'd meant to sound authoritative, but the word had come out in a whisper inaudible to anyone but herself.

Then a white Stetson became visible in the gloom. *Charlie, thank God.* She took a deep breath to slow her racing heart. He walked toward her, and she said, in what she hoped was a casual tone, "Oh, I didn't see you there."

He smirked and turned away from her again, elbows on the balustrade. "So I gathered," he said.

"Have you been enjoying the party?" Vivian asked.

"Not really," he said, squinting into the alley below. "You?"

"I've had better evenings," she answered. She walked over next to him and rested her hands on the railing.

"Trouble in paradise?"

"I don't know what you mean," she answered, trying to keep her tone neutral. Vivian clutched the railing a little tighter and then released it. She tugged impatiently at the cuff of one glove.

"How long have you being seeing Yarborough?" Charlie asked, tilting his head toward the ballroom door. His tone was matter-of-fact, and Vivian couldn't tell if he was asking for personal reasons or if he was merely inquiring as part of his investigation.

"I'm not *seeing* him," she said automatically. "Well, I mean . . ." She sighed. "I don't know what I mean . . ."

"You're going out with him tomorrow night."

"How did —" She cut her question short. Charlie was a detective after all. It was his job to know things. "I'm not so sure about tomorrow night anymore." *I'm not sure about Graham anymore,* she thought. She followed Charlie's gaze and squinted into the darkness of the alley below. She couldn't see anything except shades of gray and tiny pools of yellowed pavement where the lights of the streetlamps reached into the dark.

"Maybe that's for the best," Charlie said.

Vivian glanced sharply at him. "What do you mean by that?" she asked.

"No one's above suspicion, you know." He turned to favor her with a long, meaningful look.

"You can't be serious. Graham? He wouldn't hurt a fly."

The detective just shrugged.

"That's ridiculous," she said, a puff of impatient air exiting her nostrils. "Besides, Graham couldn't be the killer. He and I were together in the coffee shop when Marjorie was murdered. Dozens of people saw us there."

"Of course," he answered. "I'm just trying to impress upon you that you shouldn't trust anyone." She could only see Charlie's profile in the light from the ballroom. He looked like the cover of a pulp comic, his expression cold, impassive.

"You think Graham used me as his alibi?"

"I'm saying it's possible, that's all." He paused before adding, "Anything's possible."

"So you've said," she replied curtly. Vivian studied Charlie's profile for a moment longer. His mood had changed drastically since he'd gone to talk to Mr. Hart. "I don't know what's happened," she began. "But this conversation is —"

Charlie's hand darted toward her, and he held one finger up to her lips, his eyes focused over her head. After a beat he pointed over her right shoulder toward the end of the alley.

Vivian twisted her upper body and squinted into the darkness but saw nothing. She turned back to Charlie, exasperated. "What's the meaning of all —"

In a flash, Charlie clamped one hand over her mouth and pulled her toward him with the other. He squeezed her so tightly that she could scarcely breathe. He'd knocked the hat from her head as he pulled her to his chest; she could feel it hanging down the middle of her back, pulling at the strap around her neck. The smell of cowhide filled her nostrils, and one tip of Charlie's tin sheriff's badge scraped against her cheek. She struggled frantically, but he held her arms in a viselike grip.

Almost instantaneously, a bang and an explosion came from beyond her line of vision. Vivian let loose a scream, but the sound was muffled under Charlie's hand. She twisted to look up at him, panicked, but he was focused on something in the alley below. He tossed her roughly to the floor of the balcony and threw himself on top of her. "Don't move," he whispered, his lips brushing her ear.

"What's going on?" she asked, her voice squeaky with alarm. She squirmed, but he must have outweighed her by fifty pounds. After a moment, Charlie jumped up to crouch near the railing. He popped his head over the top and then quickly back down. She began to sit up with some difficulty.

"Stay where you are!" Charlie hissed.

"What's going on?" she repeated as she lowered herself back to the floor. In her peripheral vision she could see hundreds of tiny pottery shards scattered across the balcony floor, the remains of the potted fern that had been sitting on the railing next to her.

"Someone's taken a shot at you," he said. "Now stay down!" Then he sprang from his crouched position and sprinted off through the doorway back into the ballroom.

Vivian gaped after him, openmouthed. She turned to stare at the remains of the pot and realized, with embarrassing clarity, how right Dave Chapman had been. She'd been a fool for coming here tonight. Someone really did want her dead.

CHAPTER NINETEEN

Vivian felt like Charlie had left her alone in a heap on the balcony floor only seconds before, but already he was back. Flushed from exertion, he helped her to her feet. When she tried to speak, he silently put a finger to her lips. Then he grabbed her roughly by both shoulders and steered her back through the melee of the ballroom, deftly dodging swirling couples, and into a small room just to the right of the bandstand. The music and laughter must have drowned out the echoing bang of the gunshot, because the party was continuing as if nothing had happened. Charlie shut the door quickly behind them. When he finally spoke, his voice was urgent.

"Are you all right?" he asked.

The band struck up again: "Begin the Beguine." Instead of answering, Vivian looked wistfully at the closed door, picturing the carefree time being had beyond. She found herself deeply regretting her refusal of Graham's earlier offer of a dance. This wouldn't have happened if she'd just danced with him.

Charlie placed his knuckles under her chin and tilted her face back toward him. His own eyes were hard and narrowed, his features now pale. He searched her face for a moment before his eyes shifted down to the front of her costume. His gaze focused sharply, and his eyes widened with alarm.

"You're hurt!" he said.

Vivian shook her head, but before she could explain, Charlie had swept her up into his arms and carried her to an armchair in the middle of the room. He lowered her gently into it and fell to his knees in front of her, his hands passing lightly over her midriff, poking here, prodding there, concentrating on the task at hand. Vivian could only watch, her mouth agape. It was only when Charlie began to unbutton her blouse from the bottom up, fingers sliding under the fabric to inspect her "wound" further, that she finally regained her senses and smacked his curious hands.

Charlie looked up, confused, his hands still hovering over her stomach.

"It's just punch," she said wearily, rubbing her stinging palm.

"Punch?"

"You know," she answered, her voice flat. "The drink in the big bowl out there?"

Charlie's face was blank. "You're not bleeding?"

"No."

He pulled his hands away from her and rocked back on his heels. The color rushed back into his face in an instant, and he muttered his apologies. He straightened to his full height. "What happened?" he asked.

"Morty," she said, glancing down at the stain, which had dried to an unsightly maroon.

Charlie looked at her and blinked several times. "Morty threw a drink on you?"

Vivian would've laughed if the situation hadn't been so dire. Instead, she exhaled slowly through her nose. "I ran into him. Literally. And the punch he'd been carrying spilled on me." She smiled then, mouth tightly closed, but the smile faded when she recalled the conversation she'd had with the engineer afterward. "He knows I told Sergeant Trask about his strange behavior yesterday," she said.

Charlie scowled at the information. "And?"

"And he was very adamant about me rectifying the situation with the police."

"Was he angry?"

"Angry enough to shoot me, you mean?" As Vivian considered the idea, she raised her hand to brush an errant wisp of hair from her forehead. She sat mesmerized by the trembling of her fingers for a few seconds before finally answering "I don't know" and letting her hand fall back onto her lap.

Charlie grunted thoughtfully.

The door flew open, emitting a blast of sound from the orchestra. Mr. Hart strode in, the heels of his pirate boots clacking on the wooden floor. He looked so livid that Vivian thought he might draw his paper sword from its scabbard and threaten to flay both of them.

"What happened?" he shouted over the din. His eyes darted wildly back and forth between Vivian and Charlie, then were drawn like a magnet to the stain on the front of Vivian's costume. "Oh my God!" he cried, taking a stride toward her.

Vivian held up both hands palms flat out to stop Mr. Hart from advancing on her further in a panic. "I'm fine," she said firmly. "Really."

Mr. Hart's eyes darted warily from the stain to Charlie, who nodded to confirm that Vivian was unharmed. Then he nodded toward the open door, and Mr. Hart rushed to close it.

Charlie moved behind Vivian and rested his hands on the back of her chair. Vivian felt him clutch the upholstered chair back, then release several times. He waited until the door was securely latched, then said in a clear voice, "We were standing on the balcony a few minutes ago, and someone shot at Miss Witchell from the alley below."

"Shot at her?" Mr. Hart's expression remained calm, but a telltale redness crept out from under his pirate's cravat.

Neither Charlie nor Vivian responded.

"Well, did you see who it was?" Mr. Hart asked.

"No," Charlie answered. "I gave chase, but the alley was empty when I reached it."

"You informed the police?" Mr. Hart asked.

Charlie nodded. "Sergeant Trask is on his way here now."

"The papers will have a field day," Mr. Hart growled. He looked down at the floor, deep in thought.

"I don't understand any of this," Vivian said, holding Charlie's gaze. "The letters were supposed to be a red herring."

Mr. Hart looked up sharply. "Red herring?" he asked.

Vivian narrowed her eyes at Charlie. "You didn't tell him?"

Charlie shook his head and looked away.

"What's all this about red herrings?" Mr. Hart asked, his voice rising in irritation.

Charlie glanced down at Vivian, his jaw clenched, and addressed Mr. Hart. "I had thought that the letters to Mrs. Fox and Miss Witchell were fabricated to send the police down the wrong path."

"*Had* thought," Mr. Hart repeated. He glared at Charlie. Vivian thought he seemed much angrier than the situation warranted. He wasn't just alarmed that an attempt had been made on her life. He was angry at Charlie for not seeing it coming, and perhaps for something more.

"Until someone took a shot at Miss Witchell, yes." Charlie briefly met Vivian's eyes before he looked away again.

"What made you think a fool thing like that?" Mr. Hart asked. The anger in his voice was unmistakable.

Vivian rose from her chair, stepping between the two men. She said to Mr. Hart, "I had seen Marjorie with a letter from the foundling home earlier in the evening, and then her body was found with that fan letter. The letter from the foundling home was missing. *We* assumed," she said, locking eyes with Charlie, "that the killer had switched the letters after Marjorie was dead."

Mr. Hart's face blanched.

"Was Marjorie doing something for the foundling home?" Vivian asked. She watched unreadable emotions pass over the older man's face. When he didn't respond, she added in a tentative voice, "Fund-raising perhaps?"

Mr. Hart continued to gaze at something on the far side of the room for a few seconds after the question had left her lips. After a moment, his eyes focused on Vivian, and he smiled weakly. "I was trying to talk her into doing some fund-raising, yes," he admitted.

"She didn't want to?" Charlie asked.

Mr. Hart shook his head. "She was a stubborn woman," he said. "We argued."

A puzzle piece clicked into place in Vivian's mind.

"You argued with her outside the ladies' washroom on the twelfth floor just before she was killed," she said.

Mr. Hart turned his head sharply in Vivian's direction. Something flickered behind his eyes and then was gone.

"Yes," he said in a faltering voice. He sat down heavily in the chair Vivian had vacated. "Of course, you know about her drinking? Everyone did," he added, quietly answering his own question. He looked from Charlie to Vivian and back to Charlie. Some of the color was returning to his face. "Well, it was really starting to come to a head, and that was part of it: a large part."

"Her drinking," Charlie confirmed.

Mr. Hart sighed and rubbed his temples with his fingertips. "Yes. She was making a shambles of things. I tried to talk her into getting some help."

"But she disagreed," Charlie said, starting to pace at the back of the room, distancing himself from Mr. Hart and Vivian.

"Of course she did." Mr. Hart's mouth turned down at the corners, and he seemed to be lost briefly in some internal reverie. Then he said, "I was too soft on her, I know. I wish I could've helped her." He glanced over the back of the chair at Charlie and offered a small shrug of his shoulders.

"Did you know that Marjorie was being blackmailed?" Vivian asked before she could lose her nerve.

Both Mr. Hart's and Charlie's heads snapped toward her.

"Where did you hear that?" Charlie asked, his tone accusing.

Vivian shrugged. "Gossip," she said. "You can't stop people from talking." She focused her attention back on Mr. Hart. "Did you know she was being blackmailed?" she repeated.

Mr. Hart looked down at his hands, which were clasped tightly in front of him. "No," he said in a flat voice without looking up.

The door opened behind Vivian, admitting Sergeant Trask, two more police officers, and another blast of dance music. The two officers headed toward Mr. Hart while Sergeant Trask strode straight toward Vivian. The whole maneuver seemed strangely choreographed, like they were all playing parts in a well-rehearsed drama.

Sergeant Trask stopped abruptly in front of Vivian and said rather than asked, "Miss Witchell, you're unhurt."

"Yes," she confirmed. "Just shaken up a bit."

"Glad to hear it," the policeman said, glancing briefly at the punch stain and then back up at her face. "I need to talk to both of you," he announced, addressing Charlie over Vivian's head. "What can you tell me about what just happened?"

"Not much," Vivian said. She recounted the events of their last few minutes on the balcony.

Sergeant Trask made a few quick notes as she spoke. Then he turned his attention to the detective who'd moved to stand protectively at her side.

"Anything to add?" he asked, glancing at Charlie.

"I didn't see much either," Charlie answered. "I noticed some movement in the alley below as Miss Witchell and I were talking. I was just suspicious enough to pull her out of the way before the shot was fired. By the time I'd made my way down to the alley, the shooter was long gone."

"Sounds like you're a lucky woman, Miss Witchell," Sergeant Trask said drily.

"Don't I know it." Vivian shot a meaningful look at Charlie and mouthed the word "Thanks."

Charlie nodded quickly at her, then said to them, "I need to go speak with Mr. Hart. Please excuse me."

Sergeant Trask finished his notes with a few quick flicks of his pencil. Then he snapped his notebook shut and placed it in the breast pocket of his shirt.

"I'm sorry I can't be of more help," Vivian said with an apologetic lift of her shoulders. Her head was suddenly muddled, her thoughts foggy.

The policeman nodded, then studied her in silence. "You got here quickly," she observed, more to cover the awkward silence than to make an actual point. Silence was a tactic she'd heard policemen and therapists used to get people so nervous that they spilled their guts. Unfortunately for Sergeant Trask, she had nothing to spill.

The policeman nodded again, a quick up-and-down jerk of his jaw. "We were in the building. We're keeping a close eye," he said.

"On . . . ?"

"On everyone."

She glanced at the group of men on the other side of the room. Charlie had joined them, and they were deep in conference. Then she turned back to focus on Sergeant Trask's round, earnest face. "You have someone in particular in mind," she said.

"I wish," he answered. "But we have nothing concrete to go on yet. It's just likely that the killer was someone from the station."

"If you're keeping such a close eye," she said in a whisper, "you must have seen something outside, something of the person who took a shot at me."

Sergeant Trask's lips pursed. "We didn't, I'm afraid," he said.

Vivian felt the blood rush to her face. "I was nearly killed!" she blurted out. As soon as the words were out of her mouth, she regretted them. She glanced back over at the group of men, but none of them turned in her direction.

Sergeant Trask's eyes widened a bit, but otherwise, his face registered no surprise at her outburst. "We're doing our best, Miss Witchell," he said.

She stared into his pale blue eyes, looking for some sign of sympathy. He'd offered no explanation, no theories. The police either had no new information, or they didn't want to share what they had discovered.

Then the policeman leaned in toward her and said in a low voice, "Try to keep your head, Miss Witchell. You're in good hands." He looked over at the quorum of men and then winked at her.

Vivian narrowed her eyes. He was patronizing her. She'd run across this attitude before; she was a woman and therefore a simpleton. She forced a smile to her lips. Keep her head indeed. Despite the sergeant's attitude, this was not a game, and she was not a damsel in distress.

"I'll keep —" the policeman began.

"Me informed," Vivian finished for him. "Yes, I know."

Then Sergeant Trask excused himself to join the group of men on the other side of the room.

"I'm not a fan of your friend," she said to Charlie as he approached.

"My friend?"

"The diminutive Sergeant Trask," she said, her voice full of venom. She eyed the policemen from across the room as she spoke.

"What makes you think he's my friend?" Charlie asked.

Vivian shrugged. "You seemed friendly, that's all."

Charlie regarded her for a moment, his expression remote. "I'm friendly with everyone, Viv. It helps in my line of work."

"I suppose," she agreed with a sigh. She nodded toward Charlie's bare head. "You lost your hat," she said.

Charlie's eyebrows came together over the bridge of his nose, and he frowned. "In the chase, I'm afraid. Come on, it's time to get you home," he said.

"Home?"

"Where I can keep a close eye on you."

Vivian sighed. Home was the last place she wanted to be right now. "I'd like to stay and have a dance," she pleaded. "I haven't had one all night." She gazed up at Charlie, but his face was set.

"We're going," he said, taking her arm.

"Okay, okay, no need to manhandle me."

He muttered a curse under his breath and steered her toward the door.

"Hey there!" one of the policemen shouted. "Where do you think you're going?"

"I'm taking Miss Witchell home where she belongs." Charlie tossed the words over his shoulder without slowing his gait.

"Mr. Haverman, wait!" Mr. Hart shouted.

Charlie stopped in his tracks and turned toward the older man, face grim, head cocked toward Mr. Hart expectantly.

There was a pause before Mr. Hart said, "Let the police escort you."

Charlie let his breath out in a long, slow hiss. "Come on then," he said to the policemen. "I don't have all night."

CHAPTER TWENTY

She glanced over her shoulder at Charlie and then back out the kitchen window. As she watched, one of the policemen assigned to guard the house came into view, tapping the bushes near the window with his nightstick. Forget her mother, she thought; the neighbors would have a field day with this. Armed policemen rustling through the bushes while trying to flush out any armed gunmen lying in wait?

"Mother's going to flip her wig when she sees those two," she said, finding herself slightly pleased at the idea despite everything.

The officers had insisted on escorting her and Charlie out of the ballroom and all the way to Charlie's car. One good thing about attempted murder at a masquerade was that no one blinked at seeing three men dressed as police officers follow a couple of cowboys across the dance floor. Plus, the punch was flowing freely, and the crowd was in such high spirits by then that no one even batted an eyelash. Most likely not even the person who had attempted to kill her.

"Someone at that masquerade tonight wanted me dead," Vivian said. Despite her best efforts to keep her voice steady, it quavered on the word "dead."

"It would seem so," Charlie agreed simply.

She let the curtain drop back into place and returned to her seat at the table. They'd come back with the police escort to find her house blessedly dark and silent, with both her mother and Mrs. Graves already in bed. The latter had left a freshly baked coffee cake on the kitchen table with a note that read *For all your hard work, Mr. Haverman.* Now Charlie sat tucking into a large piece of that cake with a napkin inserted into the collar of his embroidered cowboy shirt.

Vivian watched him shovel a forkful of cake into his mouth and sighed. She couldn't sit still. Her body thrummed with nervous energy. She wanted to talk about what had happened and, at the same time, wanted to pretend nothing had occurred. She jumped up to fill the kettle and light the stove, then stared at the blue gas flame for a long time, biting her lower lip.

Charlie broke the silence. "I still think you

know something," he said almost casually.

Vivian whirled to face him. "I swear I don't!" she protested. "I already told you I don't!"

Charlie's brow wrinkled at her sudden outburst of emotion. "I need you to stay calm and think now, Viv," he said. "Really think. Anything you can remember helps, no matter how small or unimportant it may seem."

"I can't think of anything," Vivian insisted. "I can't think of anything I did, or anything I know, that would make someone want to kill me. Why don't you believe me?" She leaned back against the counter and hitched in a long, shaky breath, and then the torrent started, and she was helpless to stop it. She tried to weep quietly into her hands, but it was hopeless. Racking sobs overtook her, and all of the frustration and stress and pent-up emotion of the last two days was released despite her best intentions to keep a stiff upper lip.

After a moment, she felt Charlie's strong arms envelop her. He pushed her face to his chest and held it there, his hand resting lightly on the back of her head. He held her in silence until she'd stopped sobbing. When the tears had slowed to an inconsistent soft hiccup, he pushed her out to arm's length and bent down to look into her eyes.

"Come on now," he said in a soft voice. "What's all this?"

Vivian let her breath out in a hiss. "I'm scared," she said.

Charlie snorted softly and brushed the wet strands of hair from her cheeks. "Someone tried to kill you, Viv. You *should* be scared."

"Gee, thanks for the reminder," she said. She felt her lower lip tremble as she fought back a fresh onslaught of tears. Despite his intentions, Charlie's concern was less than reassuring. Wasn't he supposed to be telling her there was nothing to worry about?

Charlie reached into the breast pocket of the flowery cowboy shirt and pulled out a handkerchief, dabbing at her tearstained cheeks before handing it to her.

"Thanks," she said quietly. She blew her nose and looked up at him with red-rimmed eyes. "I just don't understand who would want to kill me. I mean, why me? What have I done?" She looked away, ashamed of the state she was in. She must look a mess — bloodshot eyes, puffy, pink tearstained cheeks . . .

Charlie turned her chin gently with his fingertips until she met his gaze again. "I'm not going to let anything happen to you," he said in a low voice. "Ever. You understand that?"

She swallowed and nodded, unable to look away. His fingers slid up along her jawline to lightly stroke her cheek. Without his eyes ever leaving hers, he leaned down and brushed his lips against hers. It was a soft kiss, almost chaste, but Vivian felt herself responding automatically, leaning into him. She slid her hands slowly up his broad chest, the silky fringe of his borrowed cowboy shirt tickling her palms. Charlie touched her hair, cupping the back of her head and pulling her deeper into the kiss. As her mouth opened against his, the kettle began to whistle directly behind her, and Vivian jerked away, startled out of the moment.

Charlie pulled back too, but only slightly. "I'm sorry," he said, brushing his thumb across her chin as he let his hand fall back to his side. "That wasn't very professional of me."

"You're right," she said, sounding strangely prim. "It wasn't." She met his eyes for an instant before looking away again. Every bit of her tingled, and she knew that despite what she'd just said, the only thing she wanted right now was to feel his arms around her again, to feel his lips on hers.

Instead, he stepped away and sat back down at the kitchen table, picking up his fork again. Vivian watched him for a moment as the kettle still whistled behind her. Irritated, she finally turned and twisted the gas knob to the off position.

"Who told you that Mrs. Fox was being blackmailed?" he asked casually, as if the last few minutes had never happened.

Vivian blinked and looked down at the handkerchief still clutched in her hands. Her knees were shaky, and she knew it wasn't because of the threat of imminent death. "Bill Purdy," she said.

"Blackmailed," Charlie said quietly to himself, absorbing the word. He chewed thoughtfully for a moment before adding, "So what was our Mrs. Fox being black-mailed about?"

Vivian dabbed at her nose with a corner of the handkerchief and shrugged again. "All Bill said was that I should know because I was next."

"Was Mr. Purdy threatening you with this information?"

"Threatening me? Bill?" Vivian smiled at the idea, but the smile slipped from her face as quickly as it had appeared. "No, he seemed frightened for me . . . and maybe himself."

"How did he know Mrs. Fox was being blackmailed?"

"I don't know," she said, crinkling her forehead. "He just said he knew."

Charlie grunted. "Does anyone else know about the blackmail?"

Vivian shook head.

"Not even Imogene? Or Yarborough?"

Vivian turned her face away, embarrassed about Charlie bringing Graham's name up at a time like this. "I did not mention it to Graham," she said curtly.

Vivian heard the chair scrape against the linoleum as Charlie pushed his chair back from the table. Instead of standing up as she expected, he leaned back precariously on the back two legs of the chair.

"Mrs. Graves will have your hide," she said, pointing to the chair legs straining under the man's weight.

"I don't give one fig about Mrs. Graves right now," Charlie answered coldly. "What did Sammy Evans have to say?"

"He said he just assumed Marjorie was murdered because she'd been horrible to someone she shouldn't have."

"She'd been horrible to Sammy," Charlie said thoughtfully.

Vivian shook her head at the idea. "Sammy had nothing to gain from killing

Marjorie — or even blackmailing her, for that matter. He needed her to keep it together for the sake of the show."

"True," Charlie agreed, letting the front legs of the chair return to the floor with a thump. "And now that Mrs. Fox is dead, they've canceled *The Golden Years*?"

Vivian nodded, but then a new thought struck her. "But . . ." she began, then paused.

"But what?"

"Thanks to her death," Vivian said slowly, the thought still forming in her head, "Sammy's got a new gig."

"Right," Charlie said, putting the last forkful of coffee cake into his mouth. "What kind of gig?"

"Recurring character on the *Carlton Coffee Variety Hour,*" she said, deep in thought.

"So he killed her to be able to move on."

"No, killing Marjorie would have been a horrible gamble." Vivian shook her head furiously. "He had no way of knowing it would work out in his best interest."

"Plus, there's the physical aspect," Charlie added almost as an afterthought.

"Physical aspect?"

"Mrs. Fox was a full foot taller than *little* Sammy Evans." Charlie held one hand high over his head. "How could he strike her over the head with a whiskey bottle? Logistically, it doesn't work."

"He could've stood on a chair," Vivian said.

"Yes, but that takes both the passion and the element of surprise out of the whole thing, doesn't it?"

Vivian bit her lip, trying to imagine Sammy putting his murderous rage on pause long enough to drag a chair behind Marjorie Fox and clamber aboard, whiskey bottle in hand.

"I think you're right," she admitted. "It doesn't work. Sammy certainly hasn't been the only one to seem unfazed by Marjorie's murder. It's been really difficult to find anyone who is even remorseful over her death. Most people treat it as either a juicy piece of gossip or a simple inconvenience."

Vivian took the teakettle from the stove, filled both of their cups, and sat back down at the table.

"Charlie," she began. "I've been thinking. Do you think it's possible that the shooter tonight only wanted to scare me?"

"I suppose."

That was a relief, but a minor one.

"But who would want to scare you like that?"

"It's just that . . . what if I got so scared

by all this murder business that I left? Went to that cabin in the woods that my mother's been harping about?"

"Who would profit from that?"

"Frances," Vivian answered immediately. "She'd love me to just drop everything and leave." The more she let the idea stew, the more plausible it seemed. "Yes, she'd do anything to get her mitts on Lorna Lafferty," she said.

"Do you think Frances is capable of taking a shot at you?" he asked.

Vivian sat back in her chair. She thought of Frances's taunting smile over Graham's bowing form in the ballroom doorway. There had been jealousy in that smile, certainly, but had there been malice in it as well? But Frances would have only had a few minutes to leave the ballroom and set herself up in the alley below while Vivian spoke with Charlie. It was possible, but only just.

"I think she might be," Vivian finally said. "What about Marjorie? Do you think Frances could have killed Marjorie?"

Charlie bit his lower lip, then released it with a sigh. "Would she have profited from Mrs. Fox's death?"

Vivian thought for a minute. "I can't see how she would have. They weren't exactly competing for the same parts. Getting Marjorie out of the way doesn't do much for Frances's career."

"Are there any personal reasons Frances might want Mrs. Fox dead?"

Vivian shrugged. "I don't think so. I hadn't heard anything at the station about them quarreling."

"Then we're looking at a more complicated scenario," Charlie said. "The killer, and Frances piggybacking on top of that murder to scare you and get you out of the way."

Vivian sighed. "I don't know," she said. "It is awfully complicated. And I'm not sure that even Frances could be that conniving and underhanded. I mean, *shooting* at a person?"

"It's just a hunch," Charlie said. He paused and continued, his voice soft, "And you recall where my last hunch got us." He smiled weakly at Vivian. "You know, it's also still a possibility that there really is a lunatic named Walter."

Vivian frowned at that idea but said nothing. She picked absently at the oilcloth covering the table. She'd worried a tiny hole in one of the strawberries in the pattern during the conversation, and she hoped Mrs. Graves wouldn't notice. "Charlie, what did you really talk about with Mr. Hart earlier this evening?" she asked, keeping her tone light and hoping to catch Charlie off guard.

"The case," he said, carefully sweeping the crumbs from the table into his open palm. He turned to deposit the crumbs in the waste bin under the sink behind him.

"No, really," she said to his back. "I know you weren't discussing Marjorie's murder."

He turned slowly, looked at her through narrowed lids for a long moment, and then said, "It's been a long night, Viv. I think you need to get some sleep."

Chapter Twenty-One

"Cops Hunt Crazed Fan!" screamed the headline from the front page of the newspaper on the dining room table. Dual photos were centered directly under the thick, black letters. Marjorie Fox and Vivian stared up from the page.

Vivian groaned as she took a seat opposite Charlie at the table. She pulled the *Tribune* toward her and scanned it quickly.

"So the —"

Mrs. Graves entered, and Vivian snapped her mouth shut, flipping the newspaper over on the table to hide her photo. She watched the housekeeper carefully as she made her way behind Charlie to place a fresh scoop of scrambled eggs onto his plate. Mrs. Graves was utterly incapable of hiding her emotions, and clearly she'd already seen the papers. She didn't so much as glance in Vivian's direction, and that alone told Vivian all she needed to know. Mrs. Graves moved on to Vivian's side of the table and scooped eggs onto her plate without a word. Vivian touched the older woman's arm, stopping her as she turned to go.

"Has Mother seen them?" Vivian asked.

"She hasn't come down yet."

"Give me a chance to speak to her, please," Vivian said in a quiet voice.

Mrs. Graves nodded, her forehead puckered with worry, and then left the room.

"So the letter's finally made the paper," Vivian said as the dining room door swung shut.

Charlie paused in scooping eggs into his mouth long enough to nod. "The original one, yes, where you were only mentioned in passing." Then he added, "The *Tribune* also mentions that you found the body."

Frankly, it was surprising none of this had come out earlier. The station's employees were like sieves — none of them capable of holding any information, no matter how trivial, close to the vest. Mr. Hart's power to keep this story contained as long as he had amazed her. Vivian stared down at her own face on the front of the *Tribune.* She could hardly believe what she was seeing. There she was, Vivian Witchell, on the front of one of the largest and most widely read newspapers in the country. Thankfully, they'd picked the publicity photo in which she wore the black crepe dress with the lovely white lace collar. Her freckles were barely even visible in that one. It was fantastic exposure, for sure, but she could hardly be pleased.

"And the shooting last night?" she asked, her eyes sliding from the photo to skim the contents of the article.

"Not a word about that or the second letter directed specifically at you," Charlie said.

"Well, that's a relief anyway." Vivian plucked a piece of toast from the holder next to her plate and clutched it in both hands as she read. "The *Tribune* doesn't seem to know much of anything," she said after a moment.

"Don't bother to read it," Charlie said. He scooped up the other paper on the table and held it up. "Now *this,*" he said tapping the front page. "This one is interesting."

He held the morning edition of the *Chicago Patriot.* The headline screamed "Marked for Murder!" with the same publicity photo of Vivian centered underneath. Marjorie's face was absent.

Vivian sucked in her breath and then let it out in a slow curse. "Jesus, Mary, and Joseph," she said, her eyes wide in horror, but also wide with the thrill of seeing her photo gracing the front page of not one, but two major newspapers.

"Now, don't get too excited," Charlie said. Fortunately, he saw only horror on her face. "It's a bunch of malarkey, really. Most of it about some diary Mrs. Fox was supposed to have kept about her secret life away from *The Golden Years.*" He set the paper down on the table and laughed uncomfortably. "But some of it is eerily close to the mark. They're either excellent at grasping at straws or they've got a source on the inside who's feeding them information."

"What do you mean?"

"I mean this." He slid the paper over to her side of the table, marking a particular passage with the tip of his index finger. Vivian read aloud:

Sources say that Mrs. Fox had been receiving threatening letters for quite some time previous to her murder and that the letter writer may be targeting others within the WCHI family. One actress in particular, a rising star at the station, has been threatened further and provided police protection until the matter is resolved.

She looked up at Charlie. "It doesn't mention me by name."

"But with your photo plastered above the article stating Lorna Lafferty was mentioned in the original fan letter, it implies pretty heavily that the star actress under police protection is you," he said matter-of-factly. He took a bite of a jam-laden piece of toast, chewing thoughtfully as he studied her reaction.

"Wonderful," Vivian said, sighing heavily. Things seemed more real in the light of morning. Someone had shot at her. Someone wanted her dead. And yet she had to pull herself together before her mother came downstairs. Her mother couldn't find out about this latest turn of events. No one could know. Vivian had to pretend everything was fine, and so she would. She was an actress, wasn't she? It might turn out to be the performance of her life.

Vivian pushed the paper away, refusing to think about it anymore. She stirred some cream into the cup of fresh coffee awaiting her and tapped the silver spoon on the side of the china cup.

"How are you feeling today?" Charlie asked.

"Tired," she said. She touched the puffy skin under one eye. Her pancake makeup was getting a workout this week. What she didn't say was that she had been up half the night thinking about that kiss in the kitchen, not worrying about whether some crazed person really wanted her dead.

Vivian met Charlie's eyes briefly, then let her gaze drift out the dining room window and across the manicured side lawn. Leaves skittered across the dying grass. Vivian took a bite of her toast and considered the events of the previous evening — everything up to the kiss, that is.

"Charlie?" she said. "Why do you think Mr. Hart lied to us last night?"

Charlie's head snapped up. His eyes narrowed, but he leisurely finished chewing the bite of eggs in his mouth before replying, "What makes you think he lied to us?"

"I heard that argument he had with Marjorie outside the ladies' room," Vivian said, lowering her voice to a whisper even though they were alone in the room. "They weren't talking about fund-raising or Marjorie's drinking."

"What were they talking about then?"

"Mr. Hart said he'd take care of something, and I suspect since Marjorie was still holding the letter from the foundling home that it had something to do with that. She was very angry . . . and he seemed fed up with her . . ." She realized her case wasn't as strong as she'd thought.

259

"I don't know, Viv," Charlie said, his eyes fixed on the newspaper in front of him. "Mr. Hart was fed up. That matches what he said last night, doesn't it? He was fed up with Marjorie's drinking and her attitude. It also explains that letter from the foundling home and why it made her so upset. She didn't want to do any fund-raising, and she argued with Mr. Hart about it."

"Well, yes and no," Vivian responded, her confidence faltering. Charlie was technically right. Mr. Hart's explanation did make some sense, but there was still something out of place. She just couldn't put her finger on what. "I just think there's something else about the foundling home," Vivian said. "Some connection we're not making."

Charlie took a sip of his coffee.

"Charlie, what do you think?" Vivian prodded, dropping her toast back on the plate and fixing him with a stare.

"I think you're looking for connections that don't exist," he said.

"Well, what else do we have right now? Everyone wanted her dead, Charlie. This is the only thing that seems to lead us in a direction, any direction. The killer switched those letters. Why would the killer do that unless there was something in that foundling home letter he or she didn't want to be seen?"

"The switch is just a red herring," he said irritably. "We've discussed this."

"Yes," she answered, irritated herself. "But what if it's not? What if the red herring *is* the red herring?"

Charlie raised one eyebrow.

"I know," Vivian said, reddening. She waved a hand in front of her face. "It doesn't make much sense, but what harm could it do to ask a few questions? And I think we both know that Mr. Hart isn't going to be forthcoming with any definitive answers. If anything, it would serve to rule out the foundling home angle. Isn't that worth something?"

Charlie seemed to consider this information as he chewed and swallowed the last of his eggs.

"You're right," he said finally with some reluctance. "It couldn't hurt to rule the foundling home out. I can run by there this morning."

"And you're going to take me with you," Vivian added.

"No," he said.

"Aren't you supposed to be watching me night and day? You're going to shirk your duty? Let some madman have full access to me?"

Charlie didn't take the bait. "You'll be fine right here surrounded by patrolling police-men."

Vivian slumped back in her chair. "Well, I'm not sitting here all day twiddling my thumbs."

"I don't care what you do as long as you don't leave this house," Charlie said, match-ing her steely gaze with his own.

"You're not going without me."

"Like hell I'm not," he said, setting his fork down a bit harder than necessary.

The telephone rang in the foyer. Vivian and Charlie glared at each other as they listened to Mrs. Graves making her way to it. She answered in a muffled voice and then came the soft thump of the receiver being laid to rest on the foyer table. After a mo-ment, the door to the dining room swung open a crack.

"Vivian, telephone for you," Mrs. Graves said.

Vivian plucked the napkin from her lap and placed it next to her plate on the table. "For me?" she asked. "Who's calling at this hour?"

"It's a Mr. Yarborough," Mrs. Graves an-swered.

262

"Oh," Vivian said. Graham.

What on earth would she say to him? She caught Charlie's eye and shrugged.

Vivian paused for a moment to steady herself before picking up the receiver. She didn't want to seem in too much of a hurry to answer Graham's call. And she wasn't really. After all, it was her first performance of the day, and there was no script. She took a slow, deep breath, counted to fifteen, and only then reached for the receiver.

"Hello, Graham," she said smoothly.

"Hello, Viv," he replied. "How are you this morning?"

"Oh, I'm fine, thanks," she answered. "You?"

"Not bad," he said. He paused. "I've just been sitting here wondering what happened to you last night. You promised me a dance, and then you just disappeared."

Vivian's stomach twisted into a knot. She had a split second of panic when she feared she would just blurt out the truth: *Oh, someone attempted to kill me, Graham, so I thought it best to hurry off.*

"I had an awful headache," she lied. "It must have been the punch. Rum doesn't agree with me sometimes."

There was a beat of silence, and then Graham replied, "Oh. Well, that's too bad." There was skepticism in his voice. "You could have at least said good-bye."

"I'm sorry," she said. "I'm afraid it came upon me rather suddenly. I wasn't thinking clearly."

Graham "mmm-hmm'd" into the phone. "Feeling better this morning then?"

"Right as rain," she answered.

"Good," Graham said. "Anyway, I called so early to arrange our date for this evening. I was hoping to catch you before you could run out on me again."

He was teasing her, but Vivian detected an edge to his voice.

"Yes," she said. "Our date." Her stomach turned — and not in an I-have-a-date-with-a-charming-man kind of way. She shouldn't be going out on the town when someone was trying their level best to do her in. Then again, she was supposed to be pretending that nothing had happened last night. If she declined, made up some silly excuse, Graham would see right through that. She pinched the bridge of her nose with her fingertips, trying to decide what to tell him.

Charlie appeared in the doorway, and Vivian forced a smile at the detective. *Nothing to concern yourself with here,* she tried to convey with her eyes.

Charlie didn't buy it. He waved his hands in front of his face and mouthed "Cancel."

"I'll pick you up at eight?" Graham asked.

Vivian turned away from Charlie and leaned back against the telephone stand. She couldn't cancel on Graham. What excuse could she use? She'd already said she felt right as rain. So she'd go, but she didn't want Graham to pick her up at home — not with Charlie here. Besides, Charlie would insist on trailing along if she went through with this, and it would best if Graham didn't know from the get-go that there would be a third party at their assignation. She resisted the urge to glance back at the detective.

"Why don't we meet somewhere instead? I think that would be easier." She wound the telephone cord around and around the index finger of her right hand and studied the floor. She could see Charlie waving frantically out of the corner of her eye, but she ignored him.

"If you'd rather," Graham agreed. "Let's meet at Chez Paree at eight o'clock then."

"Chez Paree. Eight o'clock," she repeated. "I'll be there."

"Vivian?"

"Yes?"

"I'm looking forward to it."

The smile formed like a reflex, and she was incapable of stopping its spread across her face. "Me too, Graham," she said. "Good-bye." She ducked her head to avoid meeting Charlie's eyes and fumbled the receiver back into its cradle. When she'd gathered her wits enough to form a coherent sentence, she looked up to see Charlie turn on his heel without a word and retreat through the door to the dining room. Vivian followed.

"Charlie, I don't see why —" She stopped short.

Vivian's mother stood openmouthed over the copy of the *Tribune*. She picked up the paper, unfolded it, and laid it back down on the table, smoothing the middle crease with her fingertips. She continued reading for a few more seconds in silence before finally looking up at her daughter. The shock was still evident on her face, but her voice rang out like a bell.

"What's all this?" she asked.

Vivian glanced at Charlie, noticing that he'd had enough time to flip the copy of the far-more-incriminating *Patriot* open to an inside page, a double spread on fall fashions.

"Oh, it's nothing," Vivian said, trying to sound breezy. She sauntered over to her chair and sat down, making an elaborate show of unfolding her napkin and letting it float gracefully into her lap.

"It looks like something to me," her mother said. She looked from Vivian to Charlie.

"A lot of claptrap, Mrs. Witchell, that's all," Charlie said. "Trumped-up stories to sell papers."

"Don't double-talk me," Mrs. Witchell sniffed.

"They found out about the fan letter is all," Vivian said, holding a heaping forkful of eggs she had no intention of eating. "It was only a matter of time. Everything's fine. Well, not exactly fine, but no worse than yesterday." Vivian's eyes flicked over to Charlie.

"Who phoned just now?" Vivian's mother asked.

"Oh, that was Graham," Vivian said.

"Graham Yarborough?"

"Yes, he's taking me out to Chez Paree tonight," Vivian said. She made the mistake of looking at Charlie again. The scowl seemed to have taken up permanent residence on his face.

"Well, well," Mrs. Witchell said. She finally took a seat at the table. "That's a brave man. But are you sure that's wise — going out at a time like this?"

"I'll be with her, Mrs. Witchell," Charlie said. "I won't let anything happen."

Vivian sighed and set the fork down on her plate.

Vivian's mother lowered her chin to her chest, glancing from Charlie to Vivian and back to Charlie. "You have something suitable to wear?" she asked, turning to Vivian.

"Well, that's just it. I don't think I have anything suitable," Vivian said, jutting her lower lip out ever so slightly. Then a deliciously perfect idea struck her. "But Charlie's just agreed to accompany me downtown for a little shopping trip this morning to remedy that problem. Haven't you, Mr. Haverman?" Vivian smiled brightly at the detective.

Charlie looked at her with narrowed eyes. He opened his mouth, closed it, then opened it again. "Yes," he said, never taking his eyes from Vivian's. "That's right."

CHAPTER TWENTY-TWO

The foundling home was on the Near West Side of Chicago, roughly two miles directly west of where Vivian spent most of her days at WCHI. Instead of driving through downtown, however, Charlie had skirted the city, driving west on Division through the industrial area by the Chicago River. There had been nothing but stony silence from the driver's seat for the first ten minutes of the drive. Vivian studied Charlie's profile against the backdrop of the sullen warehouses and smoke-belching factories. Brows lowered, chin jutting forward ever so slightly — he was angry, no doubt about it. When Charlie finally spoke, it was as if he'd been following her train of thought.

"You're a piece of work, you know that?" he said, taking his eyes from the road to fix her with an icy stare.

Vivian stared right back. "*I'm* a piece of work? You're the one trying to cut me out of all of this."

"For good reason."

"And that is . . . ?"

"You're a distraction."

Vivian turned her face to the window to hide her smile. She couldn't mistake that particular lilt in his voice on the word "distraction." A distraction was something you couldn't stop thinking about. Something your mind returned to again and again — like that kiss last night. Maybe he'd been thinking about it too?

"You're always twisting ankles and getting shot at . . ."

Vivian's smile faltered. He was teasing her, of course, but now she understood that what he'd really meant to call her just now was not a distraction but a nuisance. A nuisance was never endearing. A nuisance wasn't something you *wanted* to think about. She turned back to face him.

"Well, you can't cut me out. This involves me too. The foundling home was my idea, you know, and I'd find my way there with or without you."

Charlie sighed, but there was a smile at the corner of his mouth. "You always get your way, don't you?"

"Yes."

"Well, you didn't have to resort to cheap tricks."

"How do you think I always get my way?"

He snorted softly and stopped the Packard at a red light with a shuddering jerk. He drummed his fingers on the steering wheel and stared straight ahead for a moment and then glanced at her out of the corner of his eye.

"What happens when you come home without a new dress?" he finally asked.

Vivian waved the question off. "Mother couldn't care less about that. She just wants to make sure I put on a good show for the eligible young man. By the way," she added, thinking back to the scene at breakfast. "What did you do with that copy of the *Patriot*?"

"Left it on the dining room table for your mother," he answered smoothly, shifting the car into gear and pressing on the accelerator. The engine made a satisfying roar, and he nodded slightly to himself at hearing it.

"You didn't." Vivian gripped his arm, panicked.

Charlie turned to her with the merest suggestion of a smirk on his lips. "If you must know, I snuck it out under my coat and threw it in a garbage can on the way to the car," he said.

Vivian let go of his arm and sat back in her seat. She was thankful for the subterfuge, but it wouldn't matter in the long run. Her mother would find another copy. She would see the article.

Vivian paused a moment to let the tension ease a bit more before asking, "Do you suppose my mother's in any danger?"

"I don't think so. She's been instructed to stay home where the policemen can protect her," he said. But then he turned suddenly, thick brows knit together in accusation. "Why in the hell didn't you cancel your date with Yarborough like I told you to do?" he asked.

Vivian looked down at her hands, unwilling to meet Charlie's accusatory glare, and shrugged. "Graham was already suspicious of me leaving the masquerade early," she said. "I couldn't cancel our date on such short notice. He'd be even more suspicious."

"So let him be suspicious," Charlie said.

"I can't do that." She crossed her arms over her chest. "If I gave him any excuse, he'd just . . ."

"He'd just what?" Charlie asked impatiently.

He'd just take Frances out instead, she thought. Then she shook her head. It was

272

silly. Why did she even care? Graham could have Frances Barrow if that's what he wanted. Perhaps the real reason she'd agreed to go out with him tonight had more to do with sticking it to Frances than anything else. Perhaps with this date Vivian could win, if not the war, then at least one small battle. Her unfinished sentence hung there in the silence between them.

Charlie glanced at her, brow wrinkled. "He's really got you dangling on a line, hasn't he?"

"Dangling on a line?" she repeated.

Charlie fixed her with a stare. "How can you not see that?"

Vivian turned to look out the window. She exhaled heavily and watched her breath fog the glass. He was right, of course. She'd suspected the same thing since she'd spied Graham in the coat closet with Frances, but she wasn't about to give Charlie the satisfaction of letting him know that. Who did he think he was — her own personal agony aunt? "What do you know about it anyway?" she said into the glass.

"I know more than you think I do," he said almost under his breath.

Vivian pursed her lips together in irritation.

"No, I'm not at all happy about this little

rendezvous tonight," Charlie continued.

"Oh?" She couldn't help but glance at his mouth again. She couldn't seem to help herself.

Charlie's eyes met hers for an instant before he turned his attention back to the road.

"Your life is in danger," he said, pulling the car to a stop in front of a large Victorian building of mellow cream brick. He put the car in park, and the engine died with a cough and a rumble. He turned to her, expression deadly serious. "You should be staying home where I can protect you."

Vivian let her breath out in another long sigh. "Oh," she said.

"But barring drugging you and tying you to a chair like a villain in your radio show, I don't think I can stop you from poking your nose into this investigation." Charlie stared intently at her for a few seconds.

"You're right," Vivian said, meeting his steely gaze with one of her own and lifting her chin defiantly. "You can't stop me."

CHAPTER TWENTY-THREE

The building was larger than Vivian had expected and better maintained. It was a substantial, light-brick structure built near the end of the last century, the peaked dormer windows at the roofline speaking to its Victorian pedigree. There were four floors housing abandoned children, as well as a hospital for impoverished expectant mothers who would likely leave their babies at the orphanage.

She and Charlie were ushered briskly into a sterile waiting area outside the head matron's office. Charlie stood at the window, gazing out onto the lawn and the small group of children that played there, supervised by several nurses. Vivian sat in a hard, stiff-backed chair surveying a brochure that spoke in sweepingly bland terms of the charity's history and the services it currently provided to the community.

"Honestly, I didn't know places like this

existed anymore," Vivian said, setting the thin pamphlet aside. "It's not at all what I expected."

"What did you expect?" Charlie asked from his station at the window.

Vivian glanced around the spotless white room. "Something darker, more Dickensian. You know, *Oliver Twist:* dirty urchins in ragged clothing . . ."

She stood and joined Charlie at the window. The children on the lawn were in the midst of a spirited game of blindman's bluff. The "blind man" was a boy of about eight. An unruly mop of auburn hair tumbled over the blindfold covering his eyes. As Vivian watched, he lurched unsteadily toward a young girl. The girl dodged the boy's hand at the very last moment, and she laughed as his fingertips brushed one of her long, dark braids.

"This isn't a story," Charlie said, his profile stern. "These are real children."

"I know," Vivian said quietly.

The boy jerked to the right, catching a much smaller boy squarely around the middle. He pulled him off his feet in a jovial bear hug while the smaller boy shrieked with surprise and pleasure.

Charlie opened his mouth to say something more but shut it again and remained silent.

"You've been here before?" she asked after a long moment.

Charlie glanced at her, then back out the window before he answered. "Yes," he said.

"It seems like a nice place," Vivian continued. "Clean anyway." She smiled as a tiny boy came into view, toddling across the lawn toward the group of children. His chubby fingers clutched those of a petite nurse in a crisp, white uniform, and he smiled broadly as he came into earshot of the happy shouts of the playing children. Vivian's heart twisted in empathy as the little boy struggled to pull away from the nurse, eager to join the group. "Are all of these children really just abandoned?" she asked.

"Yes," Charlie answered simply. "Most handed over by mothers who've been widowed, parents who can't provide any longer, things like that."

Charlie had made it clear that there was nothing romantic about children being in an orphanage, but Vivian couldn't help visualizing the scene as etched in a Victorian melodrama: a sleeping baby swaddled against the cold of a long, dark night lying in a basket on the back stoop of this building.

"They really must be desperate to give up their children," she said.

Charlie sighed and turned away from the window. "That's what I want to believe too."

Vivian supposed the hard economic times had kept the place not only in business, but also thriving. The Depression had forced terrible choices on desperate parents. She knew that much, even if her only exposure to their plight was of the secondhand newsreel variety. She had seen the photo of the migrant mother and watched the dust cut a swath of choking black across the Oklahoma Panhandle, but nothing had brought it home to her like actually seeing the children who had lived this tragedy, all of these little souls alone in the world.

It was quite fashionable these days for celebrity couples to adopt from an orphanage. She'd read about it nearly every week in the gossip magazines. Jack Benny and Mary Livingstone, George Burns and Gracie Allen, Bob Hope, and Al Jolson had all adopted children from an orphanage in the suburb of Chicago, as a matter of fact. She eyed the children outside, who were now being gently herded into a line. Would she do something like that when she became a bona fide star? She imagined a posed portrait of herself with the small, pudgy, dark-haired boy from outside and a tall man, his face a blank. Was that what she wanted, she wondered. Then she heard purposeful footfalls approaching from down the hall.

A tall woman, perhaps fifty years of age, entered the room dressed in a severe black habit. Her bare face was encased in a white wimple, her papery skin wrinkled at the corners of her eyes and mouth. She nodded to Charlie and then Vivian and ushered them to an oak door with a large frosted window with *Matron* stenciled on it in thick, black letters. The nun motioned to two chairs in the room before taking a seat behind an enormous wooden desk.

"Mr. Haverman," she said. "Nice to see you again. I trust you're well?" She smiled serenely at him.

"Yes, Sister Bernadine, quite well. Thank you." He extended an arm toward Vivian. "This is my friend, Vivian Witchell."

"Miss Witchell," the nun said, turning her gaze to Vivian. Her eyes were a brilliant blue and stood out in stark contrast to the drabness of her habit.

"Hello," Vivian said, unsure of how to address a nun.

The nun placed her hands on top of the desk and knit her fingers together. "Now," she said. "What can I do for you two?"

"Did you know a Marjorie Fox, Sister?" Charlie asked.

The woman tented her fingers together under her chin. "No, I don't believe so. Should I?"

"I'm not sure," Charlie said. "She is — was — a radio actress."

"I'm sorry, Mr. Haverman." The nun smiled kindly at him. "I haven't much time for radio."

Charlie leaned forward in his chair. "Sister, Mrs. Fox was murdered two days ago."

"Good heavens." Sister Bernadine crossed herself and looked up at the ceiling. She mumbled a quick prayer under her breath, then fixed her gaze on Charlie. "How can I be of help?"

"We have reason to believe that Mrs. Fox had ties to the foundling home."

The nun caught her lower lip between her teeth as she thought. "Marjorie Fox, you said?" She shook her head slowly back and forth. "I don't recognize that name."

"She's never been here? Never met with you? Isn't on any sort of mailing list?" Charlie's questions were rapid-fire, but the nun's calm expression never changed.

"Not to my knowledge," she said.

"Mr. Hart had never discussed a benefit

for the home involving Mrs. Fox?"

"A benefit?" Her face brightened. "Oh yes, Mr. Hart *had* mentioned organizing a benefit the last time I spoke with him, but he didn't offer any particulars."

"Do you speak with Mr. Hart often?" Vivian asked.

"Not that much anymore, really. Once or twice a year. He used to be much more actively involved." Sister Bernadine pulled out a pocket watch from within the folds of her habit. She frowned as if the time was not at all what she expected it to be.

"How well do you know Mr. Hart?" Vivian asked, ignoring the obvious hint that their time for questions was quickly drawing to a close.

Sister Bernadine glanced up at Vivian, then slipped the watch back into her robes.

"He's been on the board since I started here," she said, furrowing her brow. "That was over twenty years ago now, but I know he was also here some time before I arrived."

Something niggled at Vivian's brain, but she couldn't put a finger on what it was.

"Sister," Vivian began. "I'm curious why someone like Mr. Hart would be so involved with a foundling home. Did he ever explain to you over those twenty years, even mention in passing, why he was so passionate about the home?"

Sister Bernadine sat back in her chair. "Only vaguely. He'd mentioned that he'd had a rough childhood. That led him to wanting to take care of the children that no one wanted. He hoped to help find them loving homes, if he could."

"Had he adopted from the home himself?"

Sister Bernadine's kindly smile faded entirely.

"Those records are confidential, Miss Witchell. And as I've told Mr. Haverman before, any records prior to 1930 were lost in a fire several years ago."

Vivian glanced at Charlie. Before? He'd been here to inquire about adoption records before?

The nun pushed herself out of her chair and stood, her back ramrod straight, the severe black and white of the habit giving her a somewhat regal bearing. "Now, if you'll excuse me, I have another appointment."

"Yes, of course." Charlie stood too. His eyes darted to Vivian and then back to Sister Bernadine. "Thank you for your time, Sister," he said.

Sister Bernadine held one hand in front of her chest, fingers together and pointed up. "May God save and keep you," she said before sweeping out of the room.

CHAPTER TWENTY-FOUR

"So Mr. Hart seems to be arranging a benefit," Vivian said, trying to keep up with Charlie's long-legged strides as they made their way back to the car. She'd fallen several paces behind, and he showed no signs of slowing. Vivian winced with pain with every jarring step on the uneven concrete. She'd have to remember to wear more sensible shoes if Charlie insisted on more of these nature hikes.

Charlie strode ahead without slowing his gait.

"Charlie," Vivian said. "What do you think?"

He finally turned to her as he reached the driver's side door, the car keys already in his hand. "I think this is a dead end," he said.

"A dead end? But the letter that I saw Marjorie with, the one that disappeared, was from the foundling home." She followed him to the driver's side and stood staring up at him, hands on hips. "There's something to that. You said so yourself."

"You heard Sister Bernadine. She doesn't know a thing about it." He glanced off into the distance.

"And you don't think she could be lying?"

His head snapped back to her. "Lying?"

"She's a nun, but she's also a human being." Vivian raised her eyebrows, and she could tell by the incredulous look on his face that he may be a detective that saw the worst of human nature, but he was likely also a good Catholic boy who simply couldn't fathom such a terrible thing as a nun telling untruths. "People lie, Charlie. All the time. Especially if it's in their best interest to do so."

Charlie stared at her. He looked about to say something but then just grunted noncommittally. He opened the driver's side door and slid in. She stood outside for a few moments, staring at him through the glass. He looked straight ahead, drumming impatient fingers on the steering wheel.

"Stubborn mule," Vivian muttered and grudgingly made her way to the other side of the car.

"We only came here to rule this angle out," he said after she'd slid into the passenger's seat and slammed the door. "And we've done that."

Vivian nodded, deep in thought. Something still niggled at the back of her mind. Something told her they shouldn't disregard the foundling home, not entirely. "But that letter I saw Marjorie with was from the foundling home," Vivian insisted again. "If Sister Bernadine wasn't lying outright, then at the very least she knows more than she told us."

Charlie shrugged. "It must have been a fund-raising letter," he said. "Or maybe it was something else entirely, written on stationery that only resembled that of the foundling home."

Vivian shook her head but had no evidence to back up her conviction. The orphaned children had left the yard, and the large building seemed suddenly lifeless. She watched leaves rustle about the lawn in the slight breeze. It was another brilliant late October day, the sky blue, the sun bright and warm on her skin.

"You've been to see Sister Bernadine before," Vivian said. "She said that she had told you about the records being confidential. Why?"

He didn't answer immediately. Vivian could tell by the set of his jaw that he was angry with her. She was a nuisance. She was complicating the investigation.

"Another case," he said, his voice clipped.

"Involving what?"

"A client who had been adopted from the home as an infant and was looking for their birth parents." She watched his jaw clench and unclench as he looked off into the distance.

He was trying to keep that stony, I-don't-care-about-anyone-or-anything expression, and he was almost succeeding, but she could see him struggle with some emotion. It wasn't anger exactly, but perhaps anger tinged with something else. Sadness? Charlie fidgeted in his seat, gripping the steering wheel with both hands before letting it go and refusing to meet her gaze.

She should let the matter drop, Vivian thought. Change the subject. He clearly didn't want to talk about it. But there was something to this. She knew it. She could feel it in the marrow of her bones, and she had to press just a little harder before giving up. Her life may depend on it. "It wasn't just *any* client, was it?" Vivian asked, probing for anything that might make Charlie share what he knew.

He glanced at her and then immediately back out the windshield. "Client files are confidential," he said shortly, mimicking Sister Bernadine.

"Was it Peggy Hart?" Vivian asked.

He looked at her, one eyebrow raised quizzically. "Peggy Hart?"

Vivian shrugged. "She doesn't look anything like either of her parents. Mr. Hart is on the board of the foundling home, which you have to admit is a strange choice of charity affiliation for someone like him." She realized that her reasons for harboring this theory were woefully thin.

Charlie frowned at her theory. "It wasn't Peggy Hart," he said, a note of finality in his voice. "We really shouldn't have come here, Vivian. This was a wild-goose chase."

"Well, we have to do something to try to figure out what happened to Marjorie."

"No, *we* don't."

Vivian rolled her eyes. "My life is in danger, remember? I'm not just going to stay home and darn my socks — not when I can go out and *do* something."

Charlie sighed, removed his hat, and ran a hand through his thick, blond hair. A wave flopped over his forehead, and he impatiently pushed it back into place. "I'm the private investigator here. I'm the one with the experience."

Vivian crossed her arms across her chest.

It sounded to her like he was trying to convince himself of that fact as much as her. "So that's why you're angry? I'm horning in on your territory, and you feel threatened?" she asked.

"Don't be ridiculous," he said. "This is a dangerous business. If someone's going to get hurt, it's going to be me."

"I'm not going to get hurt," she said under her breath.

Charlie turned to her suddenly, eyes blazing. "Someone's been murdered," he said. "Murdered with a capital *M,* as Harvey Diamond would say. You've already been threatened . . . shot at, for God's sake. What makes you think that whoever it was won't want to finish the job?"

Vivian lowered her head. He was right, of course. She was being impetuous and reckless. She wasn't qualified to do this kind of work.

"I just want this to be over with," she said and felt her lower lip tremble.

Charlie put his hands on her shoulders and forced her to look him in the eye.

"I promise you, this will be over soon," he said softly. "I know what I'm doing."

"I know," she whispered.

"You have to trust me."

"I know," she repeated.

He looked into her eyes for a few seconds longer, then released his grip. He turned back to the wheel and put the key in the ignition, and the car's engine roared to life.

"I'm taking you home," he announced.

"Home? Why?" Vivian couldn't hide the disappointment in her voice. The last place she wanted to be right now was home, cooped up with her mother and her thoughts all day.

"I have things to take care of," he answered.

Vivian sighed. "You're angry with me," she said in a small voice.

"Yes," he agreed without looking at her.

Vivian looked down at her hands. "Well, I'm not sorry for tricking you into taking me along," she said.

"What a surprise," he said, putting the car into gear.

Vivian bit her lip and watched the unappealing neighborhood float by outside the window.

"You're going to Marjorie's apartment," she ventured.

"Yes," he said.

"Then I'm going with you."

"You most certainly are not," he replied firmly.

They drove on in silence, but only for a

moment. Charlie hadn't bothered to skirt the worst of the Near West Side this time. Too distracted, too angry with her to bother with her delicate female sensibilities, she thought. The area had always been rough, but its population had swelled significantly during the Depression. Chicago was slowly recovering from those terrible times, but the streets in this part of town still swarmed with the drunken, the hapless, those who had lost everything — or never had anything to begin with. The car rolled past a dollar-a-day flophouse optimistically called the Starr Hotel, and Vivian eyed a man passed out on the curb in front, mouth open in a snore and an empty bottle lolling from his hand. Vivian looked away and crossed her arms.

"My mother will be suspicious if I come back without a dress. She knows how excited I am about this date with Graham."

Charlie's eyes narrowed. "I thought you said she wouldn't care," he said.

"I lied. People lie." Vivian sighed dramatically and looked wistfully out the side window. The scenery was grim: gray concrete, gray factories belching gray smoke. Definitely not the Chicago she knew and loved.

"If you're suggesting I take you the ladies'

department of Marshall Field's right now —"

"I'm not suggesting anything," Vivian said, letting an edge creep into her voice. "I was just wondering what I'd tell her if she asked about it."

"You'll think of something. You're a bright girl," Charlie said, the tone of his voice making it clear he wasn't paying her a compliment.

Vivian turned and fixed Charlie with a determined stare. "I can help you, you know," she said, willing him to see her sincerity. "I can help you look for clues at Marjorie's apartment. I was the one that knew her, remember?"

"What you can do is get in my way," he said.

Charlie turned the wheel abruptly and steered the car to the curb, shoving the gearshift into neutral. For one terrifying moment, Vivian thought he meant for her to get out and walk home. She glanced at the sidewalk outside — gray concrete, its surface zigzagged with cracks, trash strewn about. Two men ambled slowly down the sidewalk in their direction, both looking considerably down at the heels. One carried a liquor bottle, and as Vivian watched, he brought it to his lips and took a long swig without breaking stride. She swallowed and opened her mouth to begin her mea culpa to Charlie. There was no way she'd leave the car in this neighborhood, even if that meant she would have to apologize and let Charlie have his way.

"I'll be right back." Charlie leaped from the car before Vivian could respond. She sat back in her seat, arms crossed over her chest. Charlie jogged across the street to a telephone booth. So he was making a call, she thought. To whom? Maybe he was ratting her out to her mother. *Mrs. Witchell, your daughter is not playing nicely. She needs to come home now.* Vivian smiled to herself. Her mother had certainly gotten a few of those calls when Vivian was small. She had never been a fan of playing nicely.

The call was brief, only a few moments. She watched Charlie stride across the deserted street back toward the Packard, his face grim.

"It's your lucky day," he announced, sliding in the driver's seat.

"My lucky day?" she asked, eyeing the men on the sidewalk. They were still approaching and were so close now that she could see that the smaller one had blue eyes.

Charlie didn't respond. He put the car into gear and drove off, tires squealing.

CHAPTER TWENTY-FIVE

Marjorie Fox had lived in an apartment on the second floor of a solid brick duplex on the North Side right behind Wrigley Field. So close, in fact, that if she'd stood on her roof (something Vivian could not picture the woman doing), she could have reached up and caught a home run ball as it soared over the left field bleachers. Vivian gazed at the rear of the structure as they turned from Clark onto Waveland. There were no cheers now; the season was over.

She glanced up at the back of the large wooden scoreboard, having a sudden, clear memory of a hand materializing from one of the little doors built within to change the numbers when a team scored. She'd thought it was magic. Then again, she'd been ten years old at the time. She'd been inside Wrigley Field only that once, when her father had taken her. She could still feel the salty stickiness of Cracker Jack between her molars.

". . . thought maybe this was their year. Then they went and got themselves swept in four."

"Hmm?"

Charlie pointed to the large brick building beside them. "Wrigley Field, home of the Cubs." When she didn't respond he added, "Baseball. The World Series."

"Right," she said, rolling her eyes at his condescension. She didn't care much for baseball, but she'd heard about the Cubs' dismal showing in the Series this year. They'd been swept twice by the Yankees in the past decade — once in '32 and again a few weeks ago. She'd glanced over the somber headlines when it had happened. Everyone had been in an uproar over a couple of lost baseball games.

"I guess there's just no stopping that Gehrig. He's a force of nature."

"Uh-huh," she said automatically, unable to add much to a conversation about baseball but glad to see that Charlie's mood had improved. He was talking to her again at least. That was something after another thirty minutes of unyielding silence on the way here. She glanced at him as he parked the car directly across from Marjorie's building.

"This isn't where I pictured someone like Marjorie Fox would live," Vivian said.

Charlie considered the building for a moment and then turned back to her. "Maybe she was a fan."

He pulled open the front door of the building with ease, his eyebrows rising in surprise at finding it unlocked. Vivian was disappointed — she'd been looking forward to seeing how he would manage to talk their way into the building. They crept past the doors of the first floor apartments, the floorboards squeaking under their feet. Vivian could make out the mumble of a radio in the apartment to the right. The distinct smell of boiled cabbage assaulted her nostrils, and she thought with some amusement that perhaps the building wasn't as posh as she'd first assumed. She glanced at Charlie, and he motioned her silently up the staircase.

"How are we going to get in?" Vivian whispered, eyeing the locked front door of Marjorie's apartment and terrified that everyone in the building had heard them ascend the creaky staircase. But there hadn't been a sound from the other tenants. The radio still murmured reassuringly from the apartment on the floor below. Ill-matching wallpaper covered the holes on the wall where the gaslights had once been installed, she noted.

In lieu of an answer, Charlie pulled a small metal cylinder out of his inside jacket pocket and bent at the waist, pulling a long, thin pin out of the cylinder. He inserted it into the lock and smoothly flicked his wrist clockwise. After an audible click in the mechanism, Charlie glanced up at her and smirked. "Like this."

Vivian glanced around the hallway. "Very nice," she whispered. "But I meant, how are we going to get in without getting caught?" She trained a wary eye on the closed door opposite Marjorie's apartment, certain that it would swing open at any second to produce a put-out neighbor.

"Don't worry about that," Charlie said. He turned the doorknob and tapped the door open with the toe of his shoe, gesturing for Vivian to enter the apartment ahead of him. "Ladies first."

Vivian hesitated. Through the open door she could see the remnants of a life that had ended abruptly. Feeble, gray daylight filtered through the heavy blue damask curtains in Marjorie's sitting room. A teacup perched on a doily on a side table next to a fussy, high-backed chair, and a magazine lay open next to the teacup, upside down, spine splayed wide. The apartment was relatively neat, except for a few dirty dishes stacked in the sink and an overflowing ashtray near the telephone in the nook a short distance down the hall. Marjorie had just left home one morning and never come back, Vivian thought. It had been as simple as that.

She shook away a sudden chill and stepped across the threshold. She turned to see Charlie quietly close the door and flick the bolt to relock it.

"So where do we start?" she asked, glancing about the room. "What are we looking for?"

Charlie shrugged. "You'll know it when you see it. Right? Isn't that why you're here to help?"

Vivian nodded, but now that they were here, she wasn't so sure that she would.

She walked over to the side table where the teacup sat and bent to pull the cord on the Tiffany-esque green-shaded lamp that rested there. Black smudges covered the beaded brass pull cord. She glanced down at the table. There were matching black smudges on the handle of the teacup "What's that?" she asked, pointing.

"The police dusted for fingerprints," Charlie said from somewhere behind her.

"Do you think they found anything suspicious?"

"I doubt it," he said. Vivian turned and saw Charlie absently pick up a magazine from the top of the expensive-looking floor-model radio in the corner, leaf through the publication, and drop it unceremoniously back down. It was this week's *Radio Guide* with the blurb about her and Graham being Radioland's newest couple.

"Why not?" she asked.

Charlie crouched in front of the radio and opened the walnut-paneled door, riffling through the contents with a practiced hand as he spoke. "Fingerprints are generally only useful if you know who you're looking for." He held up a piece of paper and studied it before tossing back into the cabinet and closing the door.

"Couldn't they match the fingerprints they found here against people from the station? Just to rule suspects out?" she asked.

"They could and they might, but finding a matching fingerprint here really doesn't rule out anyone she already knows."

"Why not?" she asked again, feeling stupid at her ignorance of police procedure.

"Mrs. Fox might have invited any acquaintance from the station over at any time. They may have left fingerprints here from a purely innocent tea, for example." Charlie pointed at the cup on the table in front of Vivian.

Vivian grasped the handle of the teacup with the tips of her thumb and index finger. She brought the cup to her nose and sniffed it. "Innocent tea," she repeated as the faint odor of alcohol reached her nostrils. "Right. Did the police dust the murder weapon — the whiskey bottle?" she asked, setting the teacup down again.

"Yes, and most of the discernible prints belonged to Marjorie."

"Most of them?" Vivian asked, looking back over her shoulder at Charlie. "So there were others?"

"Partials, yes." Charlie shook his head. "But those could belong to anyone, especially if Marjorie shared her drinks."

"Oh, Marjorie never shared," Vivian answered with certainty. She paused for a second, then primly added, "Or so I've heard."

The apartment was cramped and the furnishings fussy, full of doilies and antimacassars. Vivian wondered what Marjorie had been like outside work. No one at the station seemed to know a thing about Marjorie, the real Marjorie. And that suddenly struck Vivian as incredibly sad.

She wandered over to the far side of the room and brushed one of the heavy curtains aside. The view was completely obscured by the hulking brick building next door, the only place to look over the dim alley below. As Vivian watched, a cat jumped from a garbage bin and scurried down the street, hot on the heels of something small and quick. Vivian wished she could open the window and get a bit of fresh air. It was stuffy in the apartment, the air cloying and dusty. Her stomach was starting to turn at the task of rifling through a dead woman's things — especially since it felt like the woman had only stepped out briefly and was going to burst through the front door at any moment and catch them.

A loud clang rang out behind her, and Vivian jumped. She turned to see Charlie bending to retrieve something from the floor in the kitchen. He stood upright again, the handle of a saucepan clutched tightly in one hand.

"Sorry," he said with a shrug. "I opened the cupboard door, and it just slid out."

"Be quiet," Vivian admonished, finger to her lips. "We're going to get caught."

He nodded and worked the pan back into the cupboard in perfect silence. The ticking of the hall clock was almost deafening to

301

Vivian's ears. She made her way to the magazine rack on the other side of the chair, brushing the intricately crocheted antimacassar on the arm with her fingertips as she bent down to retrieve a handful of magazines. Had Marjorie crocheted this herself? Vivian shook her head. That seemed highly unlikely.

Charlie disappeared down the short hallway, and now his hushed voice carried back to her.

"I don't see any signs of a family," he said. "No photos."

"No," Vivian agreed. "Nothing." There were no photos or identifying personal possessions in plain sight at all. It was odd but not unheard of. A lot of people in the city had distanced themselves from their families for one reason or another, and it was especially true among those in show business.

"Wait," Charlie called from the hall. "I may have something here." His voice was calm but insistent, and Vivian rushed to the hall, the magazines still clutched in her hands.

He was holding up a small notepad.

"It's blank," Vivian said, staring at the clean, white sheet of paper.

Charlie smiled. "Yes, but there are still the indentations of the pencil on the pad under-

302

neath. If I rub the pencil across the paper like this . . ." He set the pad on the surface of the telephone nook and hunched over it, lightly brushing the side of the graphite tip against the paper. Vivian began to see white marks pop against the swath of gray. "We may be able to see what the last note she made said."

"What is it?" she asked, excitement welling inside her. "What does it say?"

The excitement on Charlie's face peaked and then dimmed, the corners of his mouth drawing down after only a few strokes of the pencil. His brow furrowed, and he held the notepad up so that Vivian could see it.

"What's that?" she asked, considering the muddle of swirls and angles on the paper's surface.

"It's a doodle," Charlie answered, unable to hide the disappointment in his voice. "Looks to be a shark," he said, squinting at the drawing. "Or one of those fish with teeth. What do you call them?"

"A piranha," Vivian said. "Couldn't that mean something? A nickname or something?" Vivian imagined a swarthy character named the Piranha sending Marjorie threatening letters.

"I doubt it," Charlie said. "I've never

heard of anyone like that, but make a note of it."

Vivian nodded thoughtfully. Charlie wandered off down the hall, poking his head into Marjorie's bedroom. Vivian looked down at the magazines still clutched tightly in her hands, relaxing her grip and glancing at the titles. *Ladies' Home Journal, Pictorial Weekly, Popular Mechanics, Ladies' Home Journal* again . . . Vivian blinked. *Popular Mechanics?* She walked back into the sitting room and dropped the rest of the magazines into the magazine rack. One missed and fell to the floor, but she didn't bother to pick it up.

Vivian scanned the pages of the incongruous periodical as each flicked past her thumb, looking for any type of clue. *Popular Mechanics* was undoubtedly a strange magazine for Marjorie to have, but Vivian noticed nothing out of the ordinary — until something caught her eye on the bottom of page 93. More precisely, it was the lack of something that caught her attention. Three neat squares had been cut out of an ad for radial tires — three squares that directly corresponded to what should have been an *S*, a *G*, and a *T* in the ad's copy. Vivian's stomach fluttered. This was the "something" she would know when she saw it. Quickly, she flipped through the rest of the magazine and found two more pages that looked as though they'd been chewed on by very precise, literate moths.

Charlie didn't look up as Vivian entered the bedroom. His head was bent over a little black leather-bound book, his brow furrowed in concentration.

"Did you find something?" she asked.

Charlie didn't answer.

"What's that?" Vivian nudged his elbow.

Charlie looked up, slowly focused his eyes on her, and said, "No, it's nothing." Then he shut the book and shoved it unceremoniously back into the nightstand drawer, shutting it with a thump and turning back to her.

"Well, I did," Vivian said, giddy with excitement. "At least, I think I did." She held up the magazine, open to page 93, and peered at him through one of holes. "I would never have guessed that Marjorie was the *Popular Mechanics* type."

Charlie snatched the magazine from her hands and flipped through it. "Did you find any other magazines like this? With letters cut out?"

Vivian shook her head. "This one was wedged between two *Ladies' Home Journal,*" she said. "Why would she cut the letters out like that? I mean, I've seen in the movies that people do that for ransom notes or . . ." Vivian gasped. "Do you think Marjorie was blackmailing someone?"

Charlie eyed her, his face expressionless. "I think that may be *exactly* what she was doing."

Vivian furrowed her brow. "But I thought Marjorie was the one being blackmailed. That's what Bill Purdy said last night anyway."

"Maybe he got things confused," Charlie said. "Or maybe he was intentionally misleading you."

"Misleading me? Why would he do that?"

Charlie shrugged. "To throw you off the scent if he was somehow involved," he said. "This is quite a turn of events. Any ideas who Mrs. Fox would be blackmailing?" He riffled through the rest of the issue as he spoke, noting the two other pages with missing letters.

"I haven't a clue," Vivian said. "Do you think the police missed this?" She smiled, pleased with herself. She'd found something important. She *had* been helpful after all — even Charlie had to recognize that.

"I think they did," he said. Then he rolled the magazine into a tight cylinder and tucked it inside his suit jacket.

"You're taking it?"

"Of course," he answered.

"But that's evidence," she said. "Shouldn't we give it to the police?"

"So you're a Goody Two-Shoes all of a sudden?" Charlie raised his eyebrows at her.

"I'm getting nervous about being in here," Vivian said, rubbing the goose bumps on her forearms. Charlie remained still, deep in thought. "Charlie," she tried again. "I think —"

"You're right," he said suddenly, head snapping up. "Let's go."

"Really?" she said, relieved. She hadn't expected him to give in so easily.

"I think we found what we needed," he said, avoiding her gaze. He stepped out into the apartment's hallway, and she heard his footfalls heading toward the front door. Instead of following, Vivian hurried to the bedside table and snatched up the little black book Charlie had been so engrossed in when she entered the room. She considered it for a moment and felt the unexpected heft of it in her hands.

It was a pocket-sized Bible — the kind little girls get at their first communion. She had just stuffed it safely into her jacket pocket when she heard Charlie's steps grow louder again. He was coming back into the bedroom — and quickly. He rushed in, stopping just inside the doorway. His eyes darted around until they lit on the closet in the far corner.

"Come on," he said, taking her hand and jerking her along with him.

"What's going on?" She tried to yank her hand free, but Charlie held it fast.

Without answering, he disappeared into the darkness of the bedroom closet and pulled Vivian in behind him. He pulled the door almost completely shut, leaving only a crack of gray light.

"Someone's coming, but Trask said there wouldn't be police here for an hour," he said, his voice low.

"Trask?" she repeated, but Charlie just widened his eyes and held a finger to his lips. The closet was tiny, the air stifling. Vivian found herself pressed against Charlie, his holster pressing uncomfortably into her arm. She tried to shift her stance, but that only brought them closer together.

"What do you mean Trask told you the police wouldn't be here?" she whispered into his chest. "What's going on?"

Then Vivian heard the *click-thump* of the front door unlocking and felt the hair stand up on the back of her neck. Someone *was* coming. The front door swung open with an ominous creak. Vivian sucked in her breath and held it. She heard nothing for a long moment except the pounding of blood in her ears, then the floor creaking under shuffling footsteps. Someone lingered just inside the front door. Her mind flitted over what Charlie had just said. The police weren't due for an hour. So if they weren't in the front room, who was?

Her mind ticked over the short list of possibilities and settled on the most unwelcome. Who else but the murderer who'd tried to kill her at the masquerade the evening before? Bile rose in her throat. Oh God, it was Walter. Walter was real. Walter was here. Walter would find them in this closet, and it would be curtains for both of them — like shooting fish in a barrel. She pressed her cheek into Charlie's chest and shut her eyes. If she had to die, she didn't want to see it coming.

Then there was another set of footsteps — these quicker and lighter. Two other people were in the apartment now. Walter had a friend? Could there be a pair of murderers?

The intruders didn't speak, but Vivian heard the floorboards creak under their weight as they moved about the front room, and then the sound of one body falling heavily into the stiff chair near the radio. Vivian waited, anxiety twisting her guts, for them to notice that someone had been in the apartment. Then with something akin to horror, Vivian remembered the magazine she'd dropped next to the magazine rack. Panicked, she looked up. "I left —"

Charlie placed his free hand over her open mouth. Vivian's eyes had yet to adjust to the dim light of the closet. She tried to glare at him, but he was just a featureless shape in the darkness, even at this close range. How dare he shush her like a child? She placed her palms on his chest to push him away. But then a floorboard creaked in protest near the bedroom door, and they both froze, listening.

There was a long, agonizing silence. Vivian's back was to the closet door, but she could tell from Charlie's pinched expression that he could see the man in the bedroom doorway. There was another creak, and then the footfalls receded toward the sitting room.

"What did Trask want us to pick up again?" The man's voice was slightly muffled as he moved away from them.

Trask? Had she heard right? Vivian sighed in relief against Charlie's palm still clamped over her mouth. She and Charlie were not

310

about to be murdered. Arrested for breaking and entering possibly, but not murdered.

Vivian heard the click of the radio's power knob. The muffled roar of a crowd floated toward them as the announcer welcomed them to a live broadcast of the football game between Northwestern and Minnesota.

"Some letters or something," the other man replied.

"Shouldn't we get to it? Probably just in the bedroom back there."

Vivian felt Charlie's body tense under her palms.

"What's your hurry? We don't need to be back for a couple hours. We could listen to the whole first half."

There was a pause and then the scraping of wood on wood as the formerly reluctant policeman pulled another chair up to the radio.

"What do ya think Northwestern's chances are?" one of the policemen asked the other.

Charlie gave Vivian a warning look and took his hand away from her face. She hitched in a great gulp of air, immediately regretting it as she gagged on the thick scent of mothballs. Her hands still rested on Charlie's broad chest, but she didn't move away. There was nowhere to go inside the

311

tiny closet. Besides, his solid nearness was comforting.

Vivian glanced up, but Charlie's eyes were still trained on the crack in the doorway. Her eyes traveled down to stop almost involuntarily on his lips. That kiss — she'd been thinking about it all day, despite her every resolve not to. But now, being in such close quarters, she couldn't help but think of how easy it would be to pop up on her toes right now and repeat it. She was acutely aware that there wasn't an inch of her body not in contact with his.

She shifted uncomfortably and realized she could feel the solid lump of the little Bible in her front jacket pocket pressing against Charlie's hip. She moved again before he had a chance to notice it too. He looked down on her with a frown of disapproval, and she scowled back. A fur coat tickled the back of her neck, and she brushed it away with an irritated flick of her hand.

Vivian raised her eyebrows at Charlie in a question: *So what now?* They were stuck. Trapped in a dead woman's closet by a pair of policemen.

Charlie sighed. He glanced at the door and then back to her. Vivian's eyes had adjusted now, and she could see the reality of the situation dawn on him as well. He raised one eyebrow in response, his shoulders rising in a halfhearted shrug. She clenched her fists against his chest in frustration. Charlie's eyes narrowed. He glanced down at her hands, and then his eyes slid slowly back up, pausing at her mouth before locking with hers again. One corner of his mouth quirked up as his hand brushed down her side, his palm coming to rest on her hip.

It was a subtle move, but its effect was immediate on Vivian. She melted into him and lowered her forehead to his chest. She hitched in a breath, taking in the smell of him — a hint of spearmint chewing gum under the musky citrus of his aftershave. She slipped her hands higher over the woolen lapels of his jacket, her head still bowed. Then she brushed the tip of one index finger lightly against the side of his neck. He started slightly at her touch, as if it had surprised him, and then she felt his other hand glide around her waist to rest at the small of her back.

Vivian didn't move, didn't breathe. She was almost glad for this ridiculous predicament, because it meant she couldn't talk. And if she couldn't talk, she couldn't say anything to ruin the moment. His warm breath ruffled the hair at the top of her head, and she shivered — all of her nerves on fire. His hands moved lower to cup her bottom, pressing her into him. She lifted her head at the urgency in his touch to find Charlie's face, his mouth, was inches from hers.

She slid both hands up to clasp together at the base of his neck and held his gaze, stroking his neck with her thumbs until his mouth twitched into a smile. There was a clank from the hall, and Charlie's head jerked toward the sound. He tensed, automatically alert. His grasp tightened, his fingertips digging into Vivian's flesh. They stood silently, not breathing for a long moment, listening for any sign that they were about to be discovered.

Vivian waited for the closet door to be flung open behind her, for the policemen to be standing there, guns drawn. But there was nothing except the announcer barking excitedly from the radio: "Wildcats recover the fumble!" The crowd roared, and the policemen grunted approval. The radiator in the hall clanged fully into life with a screech, and Vivian let her breath out in a long exhale of relief. She smiled and used her fingertips to gently nudge Charlie's chin back in her direction. She raised her eyebrows again in a silent question: *Well?*

Charlie's half-closed eyes flicked down to her mouth again, the smirk returning to his lips. He leaned down until his forehead touched hers and rested it there a moment. Then he inched forward and nudged her nose with his. Vivian lifted her chin and nuzzled into him, the sandpaper of his cheek stinging her lips. She stood on tiptoe to reach the soft spot where his neck met his ear and breathed him in again. Now she smelled the soapy clean scent of the pomade in his hair. Her lips wandered and found his earlobe. Impulsively, she pulled it quickly into her mouth and released it. He sucked in his breath sharply in a mixture of surprise and pleasure. She dragged her lips back down his cheek and then finally, decisively, caught his mouth with hers.

They fumbled silently in the darkness of the closet, mouths hungrily searching, hands roaming. Then Charlie lifted her up, and Vivian squeaked in surprise as her feet lost contact with the floor. She leaned too hard against him, making both of them lose their balance. They stumbled, and Charlie's back hit the wall of the closet with a thump. He dropped Vivian to the floor, and she had to grasp a handful of mink coat to stay upright. Charlie held one finger to his lips and cocked his head to listen. Vivian held her breath, heart pounding.

But there was no sound from the other room except the roaring crowd from the radio speakers. The policemen hadn't heard anything. Thank God for ninety-yard touchdown runs, Vivian thought.

Charlie blinked and shook his head as if to clear it. He leaned down again, grim-faced and businesslike this time, positioning his lips next to her ear. He whispered so quietly that she almost couldn't make out the words: "We have to get out of here."

Vivian paused, panting slightly and trying to put the words into a context that she felt fit the moment, but they didn't jibe with the butterflies still swirling in her stomach. "Now?" she whispered.

He nodded and, without giving her a chance to protest, pushed the closet door open slowly with his fingertips. Charlie glanced out into the room and then back at her as he stepped through the door into the bedroom.

He held out his hand to help her out of the closet. She took it and very carefully stepped over the threshold. The floor creaked under her weight, and they both froze. Again, the policemen seemed oblivious to their presence. A roar from the cheering crowd miles to the north had masked the sound.

"How?" she mouthed, cocking a thumb toward the living room, but then she followed Charlie's gaze to the window.

"Oh no," she whispered. "I'm not climbing out of any windows."

"I thought you were a fan of shimmying down drainpipes," he hissed.

Vivian glared at him.

"Well, that's the way I'm going," he said. "Follow me or spend the evening among the mothballs." He dropped her hand and pulled away.

Vivian waited only a split second before following him.

Charlie turned to her from the window, hands resting on the sill. "We're in luck," he said. "There's a fire escape."

CHAPTER TWENTY-SIX

Despite Vivian's protestations that she needed to arrive at Chez Paree no earlier than fifteen minutes late for her date with Graham, Charlie had deposited her in the elaborately decorated lobby-cum-lounge at precisely 7:50 p.m. He then took his leave of her to "make his rounds" of the establishment, making sure no assassins were lurking among the potted plants, Vivian supposed. She stood awkwardly against the wall and tried to look discreet and completely unconcerned with her solitude.

She tried not to meet the questioning gazes of the couples sauntering past — all of whom she imagined pitied her for her lack of an escort. She glanced at the coat check and ran one freshly manicured hand down the soft ermine of the coat she'd borrowed from her mother's closet. She was overly warm in the crowded room, but if she checked the coat before Graham arrived, he wouldn't see it. And Graham seeing it — and being impressed by it — was precisely why she'd snuck it out of her mother's closet in the first place.

She'd been trying not to think of the passionate scrabbling in Marjorie's closet earlier in the day, but her mind kept returning to it over and over. She felt Charlie's palms on the small of her back and running over her hips, his lips hungrily parting hers, and she smiled involuntarily. The man certainly knew his way around a kiss. But the incident had gone unmentioned in the hours since.

On the drive here, Vivian had felt Charlie stealing glances at her out of the corner of his eye, and she had done the same when he hadn't been looking at her. What was it about that detective that got under her skin? He was handsome and charming, but he was also a man who earned his living by skulking in alleyways and taking photos of illicit lovers outside hotel rooms — hardly respectable. But her life was certainly more exciting with him around, and damn if that didn't make her pulse quicken.

The nightclub lobby was made to look like a Parisian street scene, complete with black, wrought iron accents, like those that might be found at an outdoor café, and a small Eiffel Tower painted on the back wall. Tiny lightbulbs were strung along the midnight-blue plaster walls. As Vivian watched, they all came alight, and she gasped at the simple beauty of it.

"Pretty swanky place, right?" a voice whispered close to Vivian's right ear.

She jerked her head around in surprise to find Morty Nickerson smiling shyly down at her, hands rooted deeply in the pockets of his trousers.

"Morty," she said, letting her breath out in a rush. "You're always lurking around."

Morty's blue eyes grew wide at the accusation. "I'm sorry," he said, immediately on the defensive. "I didn't mean to frighten you."

Vivian pressed a hand to her chest, her heart still hammering from the sudden shock. She waved her other hand dismissively. "It's all right," she said in a lighter tone. "What are you doing here?"

Morty smiled, a small dimple appearing in his freckled right cheek. He might be attractive with a few more years — and a few more pounds — on him, Vivian thought. "I'm working," he said with no small amount of pride. He cocked a thumb toward the open door to the ballroom. "Live remote for Abe Lyman tonight."

"Oh," Vivian answered, relieved. Abe Lyman was one of the top bandleaders in the country, and Morty was here to set up the remote equipment that enabled the band's set to be broadcast live over WCHI. That was a perfectly reasonable reason for his presence here. Vivian was almost embarrassed to admit, even to herself, that she'd suspected Morty had come to Chez Paree specifically for her, that he'd been following her.

"You look nice," he said, gaze traveling down from her face to her soft silk dress. "All in white. Like an angel."

Vivian registered the earnestness in the boy's eyes and glanced quickly away, studying the nearest illuminated yellow bulb.

"Say," he began in a small, timid voice. "Do you think . . . I mean, would you mind . . ."

Vivian's eyes swiveled back to meet Morty's, and his gaze immediately shifted to the floor. "Yes?" she asked impatiently. She glanced down at her wristwatch. Graham was now officially late.

She saw a flush of embarrassment work its way up under his collar to his cheeks. "Would you mind saving a dance for me?"

Vivian sighed. She opened her mouth,

unsure of what she would answer until she heard it herself. Just then she saw someone approach in her peripheral vision — someone tall and dark. Vivian sighed audibly with relief.

"Graham!" she said, her voice overly bright. "You're here!" She smiled at him so hard that her cheeks strained from the effort.

"Of course I'm here," Graham said. His eyebrows lifted, and Vivian watched his appraising gaze travel from her hair to her shoes in one long, slow movement. Then he smiled at her and pronounced, "You look wonderful."

Vivian felt her smile grow wider. "You really think so?" she asked.

Graham winked at her and leaned in ever so slightly. "Don't pretend you don't know it," he said with a smirk.

Vivian laughed.

"Shall we?" Graham asked, offering one arm.

"Good luck with the remote," she said, smiling at Morty.

Graham glanced over and exclaimed, "Well now, Morty! I didn't see you there!"

Morty's face was a mottled reddish purple. "Graham," he said in a strangled voice, with a stiff nod of acknowledgment.

"Working tonight, eh?"

Morty nodded.

"Poor sap," Graham responded happily and led Vivian into the waiting ballroom.

They had a fantastic table, so near the bandstand that Vivian thought she might be able to reach out and play the piano herself if she wanted. The musicians hadn't arrived, but the buzz in the room was growing, the excitement palpable.

Each woman who passed was more glamorous than the last. Sequin-covered dresses, some daringly backless. Red lips, rouged cheeks, every other coiffure dyed a platinum blond. Vivian felt that her appearance paled in comparison. She glanced self-consciously down at her own gown, which had a daringly low neckline but fully covered every other inch of her. She regretted checking the white ermine coat she'd worn to the club. It lent her an air of sophistication that she felt she sorely lacked on her own. She looked up at Graham and caught his eyes on her.

As if reading her thoughts, he said, "You do look fantastic, Viv. That dress really suits you."

As if on cue, a swarm of photographers descended on the table, their voices a jumble of compliments and questions. Gra-

323

ham leaned into Vivian and snaked an arm around her shoulder. She'd expected photographers, of course. What was a date with Graham without them? Still, she found it hard to muster a smile. It all seemed so manufactured, so forced.

"Closer!" One photographer shouted. Graham's chest pressed roughly into Vivian's shoulder as he squeezed in toward her.

"Give us a smile, doll," another said.

Vivian obliged. She'd been to Chez Paree before, of course. It was the hottest nightclub in town. But no one had clamored for her photo then. Now she was with Graham, and the photographers couldn't get enough of her — or rather, of them together. She was somebody now — because of the *The Darkness Knows,* because of Graham.

The flashes popped in rapid succession until Vivian's world was a blur of white.

"How do you feel about Marjorie Fox's murder? Are you next?" the photographers shouted.

She had been expecting those questions. Still, she rose half-way from her chair and gave the reporter a dark look. A flash from one of the cameras blinded her again, and she turned back toward Graham, who had risen from his seat after her. "That's enough," Vivian said. She closed her eyes and burrowed her face into Graham's expansive shoulder. She saw nothing but the mottled green-and-yellow remains of the flashbulbs behind her eyes.

She felt Graham's arm around her, pushing her gently back down into her seat. "No comment," he said to the photographers as he flicked his fingers at two burly men watching the action from the entrance. The men glanced at each other and moved toward their table.

"Sorry about that," Graham said, watching the reporters and photographers being led away by nightclub security. She noticed with disappointment that they weren't escorted off the premises, just to the opposite end of the room where they descended on another table like a ravenous flock of vultures.

"It's not your fault," she said automatically, but as soon as the words were out of her mouth, she started to wonder. This had happened every time she'd been out with Graham — reporters showing up, taking photographs. Tonight was supposed to be different, a real date. She didn't like being made a fool of. "Graham, were those photographers tipped off that we'd be here tonight?" she asked.

"There are always photographers in a

place like this," Graham said dismissively. "A lot of famous faces around. Look, there's Gabby Hartnett from the Cubs right there." Graham lifted his chin at a man at a table across the dance floor. "Too bad they got swept in the Series," Graham said with a shake of his head. "I really thought they'd get the Yanks this time around. He seems to be holding up though."

What was it with men and baseball? She turned and glanced at the smiling man across the room who was flanked on all sides by beautiful women. She recognized him. He'd been in all the papers — the hero that led them to the Series, in fact. He'd hit a home run to get them there that the papers liked to call the "Homer in the Gloamin'," whatever that meant. She turned and scanned the crowd for Charlie. And there he was, not far away, watching her with Graham. She smiled slightly at him and quickly returned her attention to Graham.

"Is this a setup?" she asked, trying to keep her voice even.

"A setup?"

She took a deep breath, speaking slowly and clearly so there could be no mistaking her intent. She thought of Graham's face as he'd looked down at Frances the evening before. She wasn't jealous, not exactly, but if all of this was just part of some attention grab, she wanted to know. "Is this just another date for publicity?"

Graham eyed her for a long moment.

"Of course not, Viv," he said finally. He leaned toward her, and the intensity in his dark eyes made her a little uncomfortable. "I asked you to have dinner with me because I like you." He held her gaze until Vivian turned away to look out over the dance floor. She gathered her courage and turned to face him again.

"It's just that this has happened so many times before . . ." she said, her voice getting lost in the buzz of the voices in the room.

Graham nodded, then said, "But *I* asked you this time. This was not set up by publicity."

Vivian shrugged noncommittally.

Graham sighed. "Look, I hate it as much as you do. I don't have any control over the guys in the publicity department. They dictate what they think is good for the show and the station. They seem to think we're good together." He tapped the cigarettes on the table and tore the box open. Another brand of cigarettes was concealed within the distinctive Sultan's Gold box. Graham even let the station control the illusion of which cigarettes he preferred. "And I'm inclined to agree," he finished, glancing at her as he fished a cigarette from the pack.

"You do?" she asked quietly.

"Of course I do," he answered firmly, slipping the cigarette into the corner of his mouth. He tipped the box toward Vivian and raised his eyebrows. She waved it away. "Speaking of setups," Graham continued, "I assume your shadow is lurking around here somewhere?"

"Charlie?"

"Oh," Graham said, eyebrows raised. "It's *Charlie* now, is it?" His voice was cool, detached. He plucked one of the matchbooks out of the ashtray on the table, pulled a match from the row, and lit it in one fluid motion. He touched the flame to his cigarette and puffed slowly, eyeing her over the smoke curling out of his nostrils.

Vivian's eyes strayed over toward the control table, where she caught a glimpse of Charlie's dark blond head. He seemed to be in earnest discussion with Morty. It made her feel better, more relaxed, to have spotted him, to know he was keeping watch.

"He's being paid by *Mr. Hart* to keep an eye on me, as you know," Vivian said. "I've been threatened."

"So I've heard," Graham answered with

more than a hint of sarcasm in his tone.

"You don't believe me?"

"Of course I believe you, Viv." He sighed and leaned back in his chair in resignation. "You know, this date isn't going at all like I'd hoped it would."

"I know," Vivian agreed. "I think we're both on edge."

Graham squinted at the stage, where the musicians were taking their places, and took a deep drag from his cigarette.

"So he *is* here somewhere?" he asked with his exhale.

"Of course."

Graham nodded. "As much as I hate the idea of Chick hanging around you all the time, it does make me feel better to know you're being looked after — especially after what I read in the papers." His eyebrows lifted almost imperceptibly. "Speaking of, why didn't you tell me all that when I phoned you this morning?"

"I didn't want to worry you," she lied.

"So I have to read that your life's been threatened over my morning coffee?" he asked. "You didn't think I would worry about that?"

"Mr. Hart told me not to tell anyone," she said.

"Mr. Hart doesn't know —" Graham

began and then abruptly snapped his mouth shut, as if he had thought better of what he was about to say.

The waiter appeared at their table with their drinks. Vivian took a small sip of her sidecar, licking the sugar that had transferred from the rim of the glass off her lips, then placed the glass gingerly on the table.

"I'm glad you asked me to come tonight," she said, moving toward more neutral territory.

"I'm glad you accepted," Graham replied, turning to her with a smile. "You look lovely."

"Thank you," she said, smoothing the tiny pleats of the gown over her thighs. "But you already told me that."

"Well, it bears repeating."

Vivian smiled and met his gaze only briefly before glancing away again. Her eyes landed on the production table. Charlie had his back to her now. She could just see the top of Morty's head over Charlie's left shoulder. He seemed agitated, even angry, as he spoke to Charlie, his head bobbing.

"Things have been crazy," Graham continued with a sigh. "I can't believe what happened to Marjorie . . . but I can't say I didn't see something like that coming. Maybe not murder, but she'd been heading toward a bad end for some time."

"Mmm-hmm," Vivian answered, distracted by Charlie and Morty.

". . . you know, a drunk," Graham said, his voice nearly inaudible.

Vivian watched Morty for a few more seconds, then turned to Graham, confused.

"What was that?" she asked.

Graham gazed at her through a thin stream of cigarette smoke. "I just said that it's a shame about Marjorie, because she hadn't always been such a drunk."

"You knew her . . . before?" Vivian asked.

Graham paused and looked over at the stage. "We had something of a history," he said.

"What kind of a history?" Vivian lifted her glass to her lips and took a sip.

"Well . . ." He glanced down a bit sheepishly. "A romantic history." He nearly swallowed the word "romantic," as if the word itself were too much to say.

Vivian's eyes widened, and she somehow struggled not to choke on the mouthful of liquor.

"You and Marjorie?" she whispered. She couldn't hide the surprise in her voice. She tried to picture the two of them together, but it was impossible. Dried-up old Marjorie and Graham? It didn't make any sense.

"I didn't kill her, if that's what you're thinking," Graham said. He glanced around them and leaned toward her, the cigarette balanced precariously between the first and second fingers of his right hand. "You know I didn't kill her, don't you?" His voice was panicked. "I was with you at the time, if you recall."

"Of course I don't think you killed her," Vivian answered. "For God's sake, Graham, would I be having dinner with you if I thought you killed someone?" Her stomach fluttered uncomfortably. The truth was, she hadn't even considered the idea that Graham had killed Marjorie or had anything to do with Marjorie — until he brought it up himself. Graham made a shushing motion with his hand and glanced both right and left to make sure no one had overheard them. She glanced around at the other tables, but no one seemed interested in them or their conversation.

Then her eyes darted surreptitiously over Graham's shoulder to the control table, but it was empty. Both Charlie and Morty were gone. Vivian felt her stomach knot.

"I'm sorry, Viv." Graham leaned back in his chair again.

Vivian watched the end of the cigarette flare orange as he inhaled. He blew the

332

smoke out slowly as he composed himself. "Look, it's a bit of an embarrassing story for me."

He paused, regarding her intently, as if looking for permission to continue.

Vivian said nothing, merely held his gaze and nodded.

He leaned forward and lowered his voice. "It's not that there's anything disreputable in it," he began. "Don't misunderstand me. I just don't like people to know because . . . well . . . because my star is on the rise . . . and Marjorie's . . . wasn't." He paused again and tapped ash into the glass dish on the table. He stared abstractedly at the table-cloth for a moment, as if trying to conjure up a distant and long-buried memory.

"I was young," he said with a shrug of his shoulders. "We suffered through a summer-stock production of *Hamlet* together. I was Hamlet; she was my mother. I know, I know, the cliché." He looked at Vivian out of the corner of his eye and smiled ruefully. "She was older, more experienced, somewhat of a minor star in the theater world. So I hitched my wagon to her star. I used her, and I'm not proud of it, but she used me too. It was the right thing to do for both of our careers at the time.

"I gave her a certain . . . vitality . . . by

being seen with her. Even then she was somewhat past her prime. She took me to Broadway briefly, and when she decided to move to radio, she took me to WCHI. And then, well . . ." Graham seemed momentarily at a loss for words. He took a long drag on his cigarette, then stubbed it out. "Once we were here, our lives started going down different paths. She started drinking more and more. She was an unpleasant drunk. We barely spoke toward the end. We were like strangers to each other." He glanced at Vivian, then looked off wistfully into the middle distance.

Vivian realized her mouth was hanging open and closed it slowly. She tried to keep her face blank, but Graham wasn't looking at her. His mind was far away in another time with Marjorie Fox. Vivian took a swig of her drink and let the fiery liquid swish around in her mouth before swallowing.

"I never would have guessed that you had been *together*," she finally said, feeling a little silly. She couldn't bring herself to say something as intimate as "lovers." She felt her neck grow warm at the very idea.

"It was more of a business arrangement," he said. "I did what I had to do to get ahead. I'm sure you can relate." He fixed his deep brown eyes on her.

Vivian felt herself flush more deeply and glanced back down at her hands. Of course he would have heard the rumors about how she'd gotten the Lorna Lafferty part.

Graham continued with a slight shrug of his shoulders. "Things fell apart for us pretty quickly after getting to Chicago. As I said, we didn't even talk anymore. Still, it was rough hearing that she'd been *murdered.*"

"I can imagine," Vivian said. She looked up, scanning his strong-jawed profile as she mulled over his choice of phrasing. Rough, certainly, but was hearing that a former lover was murdered simply "rough"? It was nearly the same phrasing that Dave Chapman had used the day before to describe his own reaction to Marjorie's murder — more of a slight inconvenience than the tragic end to a person's life.

She felt the question form on her lips: *Am I just a business arrangement to you too?* But she didn't ask. It would hurt her pride too much to hear the truth. Instead, she swallowed, mimicking Graham's nonchalant attitude.

"Do the police know about this?" she asked. "You and Marjorie?"

Graham shook his head.

335

"You didn't tell them?" She blinked. "Why not?"

Graham looked sharply at her and narrowed his eyes. "Why should I? I didn't do it, and telling them of my past — *very* past — relationship with the deceased would have made me a suspect in her murder. I don't want to be a suspect," he said.

Vivian ducked her head and leaned in closer to Graham. "But what if they find out some other way?" she said. "Won't you look more suspicious for not having told them in the first place?"

Graham leaned back in his chair, seeming to weigh what she'd said and considering his response. He finally leaned toward her, elbows on the table. "You're the only one who knows, Viv," he said in a low voice. "Are you going to tell them?"

Vivian forced herself to meet his gaze. She searched his dark eyes for any sign that he might be joking and found only cold calculation. She swallowed the lump that had risen to her throat. Was this a threat? "No," she said quietly. "I won't tell."

Graham's smile was wide and immediate. "Good," he said with a slight nod, and in an instant his entire demeanor changed. He was back to the affable Graham Yarborough she knew. Vivian blinked, almost wondering if the past few minutes had really happened or whether she'd imagined it all.

The band had taken the stage, and the musicians, in white dinner jackets and black ties, were rustling their music sheets and running scales on their instruments. They would begin playing soon, and then the chance for any serious discussion would be lost among the din.

"You're not angry with me for telling you about my *sordid* past?" Graham asked, running his fingers across the rim of his glass.

She shook her head.

"Mildly put off, perhaps?" he teased. He reached out and rubbed the top of her hand with his thumb. Then he smiled at her, a full-on, knee-buckling Graham Yarborough special. It was the same smile he'd been flashing at her — and every woman around the station, probably — for weeks, but this time its effect on Vivian was decidedly muted. There was no thrill down her spine, no fluttering in her stomach. She recognized that smile for what it was this time, maybe what it had always been: smoke and mirrors.

"Of course not," she said. "We all have our secrets."

Graham arched one dark eyebrow. "Do tell."

She winked and gave his hand a playful squeeze in an attempt to deflect the question.

The orchestra launched into its first song. The tune was jumpy, a real dance number inviting everyone to get up from their seats and hit the floor.

"You know, I'll take a dance in lieu of secrets," Graham said, lifting their clasped hands and gesturing to the dance floor.

"I'd love to," Vivian said.

Graham was a good dancer, though he paid little actual attention to her on the floor. The room was crowded, and his hand rested lightly on the small of her back as they danced in place, making a tight circle to avoid bumping into any other couples. Vivian glanced up at his face every few seconds, hoping to think of a topic of conversation that might interest him. There was always Harvey Diamond, she thought ruefully, but she wasn't that desperate — not yet.

Her mind returned to the revelations Graham had let her in on just a few moments ago. He'd known Marjorie very well (just *how* well Vivian would rather not think about) and hadn't told the police about it. She thought of her and Charlie's trip to Marjorie's apartment and the missing letters from the magazine.

"Did you know that Marjorie was being blackmailed?" Vivian asked before she lost her nerve. She looked up quickly to catch Graham's expression.

Graham grimaced and pulled her a little closer.

"Yes, I knew that," he said, his expression unreadable.

"About what? By whom?" she asked. She knew he hadn't said one word to the police about blackmail. But he only shook his head mournfully, and when he finally looked down at her, his deep brown eyes were filled with sadness.

"I don't know," he said. "On either count. God only knows what she got up to when she was on the sauce," he added.

"How did you know?"

Graham narrowed his eyes at her. "There's been talk."

"Talk?" she repeated. Certainly if there had been talk at the station about Marjorie Fox being blackmailed, she would have heard it. Imogene hadn't mentioned a thing. Yet Bill Purdy had said the same thing at the masquerade the night before.

"So then you knew that Marjorie was dabbling in blackmail herself?" she asked.

Graham stopped dancing right there in

the middle of the floor. A couple bumped into them, forcing Vivian to rock on her heels, and she tightened her grip on Graham's shoulder. Graham's face was pale, and he simply stared down at her for one long moment.

"I guess not," Vivian said.

Graham studied her face as if trying to read the intent behind the question. "Well, it wasn't me that she was blackmailing, if that's what you're implying," he said, a flush washing his cheeks.

"I'm not implying anything," Vivian said. She hadn't mentioned anything about him, and she certainly hadn't implied anything either. She narrowed her eyes at him. To his credit, he seemed genuinely surprised and offended at the idea of him being black-mailed, but then again Graham was an actor. Maybe he had more than tough-talking Harvey Diamond in his repertoire after all. She had a feeling she'd hit a little too close to the truth. Maybe Marjorie *had* been blackmailing Graham. But why? What else was he hiding? Graham was silent for another long moment.

"I just don't like you acting like a detective, Viv," he said suddenly. "I don't like the idea of you creeping around in dark alleys, digging into things that could get you in trouble . . . get you hurt." Graham glanced meaningfully across the room to where Charlie and Morty were now standing by the control table. Graham looked down at Vivian, his jaw firmly set. The song ended with a crash of cymbals and a rattle of drums.

They stared at each other in the middle of the dance floor, applause erupting around them.

"Excuse me."

They turned to find a thin, bespectacled man with a receding hairline looking earnestly at Graham. "Might I cut in?" the man asked. He looked at Vivian, and his lips curled upward.

Graham lowered his eyebrows in irritation but passed Vivian's hand to the newcomer and smiled coldly at them both.

"I have a telephone call to make. I'll be right back," he said. He turned on his heel and walked off in the dimness toward the round, black lacquer deco bar.

CHAPTER TWENTY-SEVEN

Vivian glanced at her new dance partner's face, registering small, blinking eyes behind wire-rimmed glasses and a well-trimmed mustache under a prominent nose. She smiled weakly at him. She didn't really want to dance with this man, but she felt as though she couldn't refuse.

"You look familiar. Are you in the pictures or something?" the man asked as he led her deftly back into the dancing throng.

Vivian looked over her shoulder to see Graham's back receding into the crowd. He hadn't turned back to make sure she was all right or even give her a reassuring nod before he disappeared from sight.

"No," she said.

"Well, you oughta be," the man said earnestly. "You're gorgeous." His breath ruffled her hair, and she cringed.

"Thank you," she said tersely, unwillingly to give the man a larger opening to further conversation. She glanced up at his face and tried to gauge whether he was on the level.

"The name's Mack," he said, smiling down at her. She noticed that the smile didn't touch his pale eyes.

"Mack," she repeated.

He spun her suddenly in a quick turn, and Vivian gasped. Immediately, he righted them and continued dancing smoothly. He hadn't missed a step. Now they were in the thick of the dancing throng. Bodies pressed in on every side.

"And you're Vivian Witchell," he said, his voice low.

Vivian tensed and her feet stopped moving, but Mack and the crowd on the floor propelled her forward. Her eyes darted to the side of the stage, but Charlie had disappeared again.

"I didn't mean to startle you," the man continued. "I just recognized you from the paper. You *were* on the front page . . ."

"Oh," she said quietly. There was something odd about this man. His manner, his tone. He was too knowing. She wasn't sure she believed him about recognizing her only from the newspaper.

"I'm surprised to see you here," he continued. "You being marked for murder and everything . . ."

A tingle crawled up Vivian's spine at his slow, deliberate drawl. He'd stressed "marked for murder" like he was reading an announcer's script.

"You shouldn't believe everything you read, Mack," she said, searching the crowd for Charlie.

"You mean there isn't a crazed fan after you?" he asked, feigning innocence.

Vivian swallowed the lump in her throat and didn't answer.

"Aren't you afraid to be out in public?" Mack persisted, his voice hard.

"I'm not afraid of anything," Vivian blurted out. She winced at her trembling voice. She looked up at Mack, trying to keep her expression impassive. "Look, thank you for the dance, but Graham's going to be back at any moment," she said. "I'd like to sit down, please."

"And *I'd* like to keep dancing," he said, lips pursed into a thin white line. He pressed his fingers insistently into the soft flesh of her side.

Vivian swiveled her head to the place she'd last seen Charlie, but he still had not materialized.

"Looking for someone?" the man asked. His grip tightened, and Vivian found herself fighting panic.

Vivian's voice caught in her throat. Maybe this man was really Walter. Maybe he'd been following her all along, and now he'd seen his chance to make a move. She glanced up at the man's face, horrified at the idea. She found herself wondering if he would make his move right here on the dance floor. Would he press a knife to her side and force her out of the nightclub — make her disappear into the night? What would she do? What *could* she do?

"What do you want, Mack?" she asked finally.

"Just your story," the man said. His sudden smile was brilliant, his large, even teeth glowing in the dim light.

"My story?" she repeated.

"I'll make it worth your while," he said smoothly.

Vivian blinked, her mind whirling. She did a few revolutions around the floor in the stranger's arms: quick, quick, slow, quick, quick, slow. The white lights of the bandstand dazzled her. She caught part of the garbled conversation of a passing couple, "But Janet, that's what they're for!" the man said in an irritated tone. Then it dawned on Vivian that this man spinning her menacingly around the dance floor was a reporter. He didn't want to stick a knife in her ribs.

He wanted the scoop on Marjorie's murder.

She nearly laughed with relief. "My story," she repeated, releasing her breath in a heavy sigh. "What paper are you with?" she asked.

"The *Patriot.*"

Vivian considered that for a moment. She'd have preferred the *Tribune.* It was more respectable. "And just what do you have to offer that would be worth my while?"

"Publicity," he said, whirling her around in a tight spin. "All the publicity you can stand."

Vivian smiled. She could stand a lot of publicity. "A feature story?" she asked.

The man nodded. "For starters." He leaned toward her and added in a low, conspiratorial voice, "And how about a fashion spread in the Sunday supplement, huh?"

She could already see herself blazoned across the fold of the Sunday paper, looking stunning in an array of delicious outfits. "In color," she said. It wasn't a request. It was a demand.

"I'll see what I can do. Now," Mack said, "tell me about this letter you got."

Vivian bit her lip. "My letter?" Her pulse quickened. "How do you know about that?"

"Everyone knows," he said.

Vivian nodded, thinking. After all, information about the letter found with Marjorie's body had been in the papers this morning. She wrinkled her brow, trying to recall exactly what the articles had said. It was quite possible that the press knew about her own poison pen letter by now. But exactly how much did they know? She entertained the idea of how much she could tell this reporter without giving the game away and getting her into hot water with Mr. Hart. She shook her head and got ahold of herself. She wanted to be a star, but not this way.

Vivian frowned. "No deal."

The reporter pulled back from her, incredulous. "You'd give up that kind of publicity? You don't have to tell me anything, doll. All you have to do is confirm the things I already know."

She shook her head. If Mr. Hart caught her talking to the press, he would snuff out her fledgling career with the snap of his fingers.

Then their progress on the dance floor was met with an immovable object in the form of a large, unhappy detective standing stock still with hands on hips like the Colossus of Rhodes. She smiled hopefully at Charlie.

"What's the idea?" Mack said. He glared at Charlie, eyes small through the reverse magnification of his lenses.

"I'd like to cut in. If the lady doesn't mind," Charlie said, not looking at Vivian. His eyes narrowed at the reporter, and he made a show of rubbing the knuckles of his right hand, highlighting his heavy gold signet ring by twisting it slowly around on his finger.

Mack paused for only the briefest of moments before unceremoniously dropping Vivian's hand and taking a large step backward.

Though he was several inches taller than Vivian, Mack was not a big man. He glanced from Charlie to Vivian, then shrugged his shoulders at her with regret. "She's all yours, pal," he said over his shoulder as he retreated through the crowd.

Vivian watched him go, then turned back to Charlie, eyes flashing. "What's all this about?"

"Just saving you from the brink of disaster again."

Vivian rolled her eyes. "That man was no crazed fan, if that's what you're worried about."

"I wasn't worried for your safety." He stared down at her, a deep vertical crease appearing at the bridge of his nose. "I was worried about your reputation."

"My reputation?" She laughed. "That's rich."

Charlie glanced in the direction of Mack's retreat. "That guy is a hack."

Vivian crossed her arms over her chest and glared at the detective.

"Let me guess," Charlie continued, unfazed. "He offered you a two-page spread if you just answered a few little questions about Mrs. Fox's murder."

Vivian looked quickly. "So what if he did?"

Charlie narrowed his eyes. "You didn't tell him anything, did you?"

She shook her head.

"Thank God for small favors," he said. He shoved his hands into his pockets. "Where is Yarborough?"

Vivian shrugged. "He said he had to make a phone call."

"And he left you with some stranger? That weasel." The band struck up again, this time with a Cole Porter tune that had Vivian's toes tapping despite her annoyance. Charlie held out his hand to Vivian and raised his eyebrows in invitation. When Vivian didn't respond, he said in a lighter, cajoling tone, "Well, we can't just stand here in everyone's way." Just then, a man bumped sideways into Vivian, knocking her off balance. She grabbed Charlie's hand, and he pulled her in close. He was surprisingly light on his feet and steered her confidently around the floor in a quick fox-trot as the singers began, "And that's why birds do it, bees do it, even educated fleas do it . . . ."

"I said it was okay that Graham make his call, you know. I agreed to dance with that man," she said, her hand clasped tightly in Charlie's.

"That doesn't make it all right for him to leave you alone with a perfect stranger," he answered.

Vivian recalled the brief moment of terror she'd felt when she'd thought the reporter really was the Walter of the threatening letters. If Mack had been out to get her, she could have been in real trouble. She looked up at Charlie, towering above her.

"Well, what about you? Where were you while I was fox-trotting with oh-so-dangerous reporter types?" She thought about how helpless she'd felt without Charlie around, and she gripped his hand a little tighter.

"Following Morty Nickerson," he said, his face serious.

Vivian glanced sharply up at him. "Morty? Why?"

"He was acting strangely."

"Strangely how?" she asked, not sure she really wanted to know.

"He was watching you and Graham a little . . ." Charlie paused, searching for the right word. "Intensely," he finished.

"Watching us . . ." Vivian repeated quietly. She could feel the panic rising within her again.

"Yes, and after a few minutes he jumped up from his chair and hurried off. I had a bad feeling about it, so I followed him." He paused before adding, "You were rather close with Yarborough at the time, mind you. I assumed you were reasonably safe for a few minutes."

"Well?" she asked, impatient to hear the rest of the story.

Charlie frowned. "Well, nothing," he said. "Morty'd forgotten a wire or something for the remote broadcast. He just ran off to get it."

"That's it?" Vivian managed somehow to be both relieved and annoyed by the news at the same time.

"That's it," he answered. A wry smile came to his lips. "I think he's just lovesick, poor guy. Can't say I blame him."

Vivian met Charlie's eyes for an instant. Then she looked back down at their feet, still moving elegantly in synch over the parquet dance floor.

"But I tried to help him out," Charlie continued. "Take his mind off you." When Vivian glanced up at Charlie this time, he was smiling. Vivian followed Charlie's look over to the control table, confused that he could find anything funny in the situation.

Vivian couldn't help but smile herself when she caught sight of Morty, although it was difficult to recognize him since he was nearly obscured by the long, yellow and green feathers atop the enormous headpiece of one of Chez Paree Adorables, what the club called their showgirls. The lovely, limber brunette was perched on Morty's lap, her long legs curled effortlessly around him.

As Vivian watched, the showgirl ran one slim finger flirtatiously down Morty's cheek, then touched the tip of his nose. She laughed at his baffled response of wide-eyed shock. Morty looked simultaneously mortified and excited by this unexpected turn of events, his hands raised as if in surrender, seemingly terrified of touching the girl's bare flesh — of which there was plenty.

Vivian smiled in spite of herself. "Poor Morty," she said in all sincerity. "He has no idea what to do with her."

Her eyes flicked up to meet Charlie's. One corner of his mouth curled up in mild amusement, just barely cracking his tough-as-nails facade. Vivian had an intense flash of memory of what it had been like to be stuck in Marjorie's closet with him, his thigh pressed against hers. They were nearly that close now. She could feel the heat of his body through the thin satin of her gown, and her eyes were drawn to his mouth like a magnet.

He was no longer smiling, and his face once again held an expression of slight disapproval as he looked down on her. What about her made him scowl at her like that? She fought the insistent urge to rise on her toes and kiss that frown right off his face. With some effort she focused her gaze back up to meet his. She heard the elegant female singer coo the chorus for the last time, "Let's do it, let's fall in love."

"I hate to interrupt such a cozy scene."

Vivian started, pulling away from Charlie. She turned to find Graham, arms crossed over his immaculate white dinner jacket, irritation marking his handsome features. "You two seem to be having a wonderful time," he said.

"Oh, Graham!" She dropped Charlie's hand.

"Your phone call go through all right?" Charlie asked, any remaining trace of good humor wiped from his face.

Graham furrowed his brow. "Yes," he said. Then he held his bent arm out to Vivian and simply said, "Shall we?"

Vivian glanced at Charlie before taking Graham's arm. He met her eyes only briefly before looking away again. If there had been any disappointment in his stony expression at being interrupted, she hadn't seen it.

The cab ride home was silent. Both Vivian and Graham were reluctant to say much of anything in front of the driver besides, "Nice night." When they arrived at her house, Graham helped Vivian out of the cab and then frowned at her as they stood facing each other on the sidewalk just below the front steps.

"I'm sorry I've been so cross this evening," Graham said. "I guess it was all the talk of Marjorie. It put me in a foul mood."

Vivian said nothing. "Cross" wasn't the half of it. His mood had turned on a dime when discussing Marjorie, and it had frightened her a bit in the moment, but even more so now that she'd had time to mull everything over. He'd dropped the Marjorie relationship on Vivian like a bomb and then

vehemently denied killing the woman —
before the thought had even entered Vivian's
mind. And then there was the blackmail.

She suspected Graham hadn't told her the
half of what had gone on between him and
Marjorie. In fact, his whole explanation
seemed like a carefully orchestrated story to
establish his innocence — to get Vivian on
his side before something slipped out in the
course of the investigation. Maybe this
whole evening had been a setup — and not
just for the publicity. Maybe this confession
was the only reason he'd asked her out at
all. Graham Yarborough had more secrets.
She was sure of it.

"We'll have to do this again," Graham
said. "When all of this has blown over."

Vivian forced a smile. "Of course."

She shivered in the frosty fall air, and Graham reached over to pull her mother's borrowed fur more tightly around her shoulders. His hands lingered, fingers brushing
the side of her neck. She resisted the urge
to flinch at his touch. His dark eyes met
hers and held them.

"I guess this is good night," she said.

Vivian watched icy tendrils of breath form
at his lips, then disappear into the darkness.

"I guess it is."

Graham looked at her, the smile slipping

355

from his face. Then his hands moved from her shoulders up to her cheeks. He cupped her face in his hands for a moment before leaning in slowly, impossibly slowly, to touch his lips to hers. It was a brief kiss, over almost before it began. Vivian hadn't even time to properly close her eyes before he pulled away and they were illuminated by the headlights of the car pulling up to the house.

Graham stepped away from her. She glanced quickly at the car and wondered if Charlie had seen the kiss.

"I'll see you on Monday?" Graham asked, clasping her hands in his.

She nodded.

He squeezed them once and turned away. She held her smile for a minute as she watched him climb back into the waiting cab in case Graham turned again to look at her. He didn't, but she could hear him whistling very faintly before he closed the taxi door.

CHAPTER TWENTY-EIGHT

Vivian removed the ermine from her shoulders and held it up to the light of the foyer, admiring its perfect whiteness as she considered Graham's kiss. It had been nothing like the passionate, wild fumbling with Charlie in the closet. In fact, what Graham had done had barely registered as a kiss in the grand scheme of things. Now that Graham *had* finally kissed her, an event Vivian had been fantasizing about for weeks, she found herself trying to work up some enthusiasm for it. Frankly, it had left her flat, and not entirely because of all the horrible truths — or half-truths — Graham had let slip this evening.

Now that she knew more about the real Graham, his handsome face and charming manner no longer held much appeal. There was some relief in that. It would make it easier to work with him, for one thing. No more sweaty palms and missed lines. She shrugged before draping the fur carefully over one forearm, brushing it absently with her fingers. She'd have to sneak it back into her mother's closet before she noticed it was missing.

"Have a nice time tonight?" Charlie asked, banging into the foyer.

"Yes," she said.

"It certainly looked like it."

"Oh. Well, I . . ." she began, fumbling for a defense and not finding one.

He shook his head. "No need to make excuses. Yarborough's a charming guy." His tone was flat, and he stared into her eyes for one long moment before breaking her gaze to toss his hat onto one of the arms of the coat-tree. "Care for a nightcap?"

Without waiting for her answer, Charlie swaggered into the den and opened the liquor cabinet. He pulled out the almost-empty decanter of scotch and filled two glasses to the brim. He took a swig from his own glass before holding the other out to Vivian. She took it after a slight hesitation. The last time they'd shared a drink like this, Charlie had been about to tell her that someone wanted to kill her. She shivered at the memory.

Charlie slumped into one of the chairs in front of the fireplace and sighed. After a long moment he said, "Look, Viv, there's something you don't know about Yarborough. Something I think you're entitled to know."

Vivian held her hand up to stop him. "I know about Graham and Marjorie," she announced firmly. "He told me tonight."

Charlie's brow wrinkled. He opened his mouth to speak, but Vivian cut him off.

"He said it was a long time ago — before they came to WCHI and before she really started drinking." Vivian spoke rapidly. She was embarrassed at having to repeat Graham's flimsy excuse — embarrassed that it had been at all plausible to her when he'd told her. Graham had used Marjorie to improve his career, and it was very likely that's how he was using Vivian now. And what was worse, she was positive that Charlie already knew. He'd known it all along.

"He didn't mention any of that to the police."

"No," Vivian said. "He said he had never mentioned it to anybody . . . except me."

Charlie squinted at her. "Why not?"

"I asked him that," she said. She realized she was talking too fast. "I think it's embarrassing to him. It was long time ago. He didn't kill her, he said, so he didn't know why he should make a suspect of himself."

Charlie shook his head slowly, considering. "Good point, because I'd say that's exactly what that makes him."

Vivian swallowed hard. "And I think Marjorie was blackmailing Graham," she said.

Her stomach contracted tightly at the idea. She recalled Graham's reaction at Chez Paree at the hint of blackmail. There had to be something behind that. Why would he jump to that conclusion if it hadn't been true? "But that's ridiculous," she whispered almost to herself, part of her still not wanting to believe it.

Charlie shrugged. "Is it? Who better to blackmail than a former lover who's an up-and-coming star? It sounds like there's something in Yarborough's past he'd prefer to *keep in the past*." He looked meaningfully at her.

Just yesterday, Vivian would have responded that Graham was an open book, but now she understood she knew very little about the man beyond his current career ambitions and that the direct gaze of his dark eyes had once turned her to jelly. Charlie opened his mouth to say something else, seemed to reconsider, and took another long gulp of scotch instead.

They sat in silence for a few minutes, each

lost in their own thoughts. Vivian watched the liquor swirl in her glass and tried not to think about all of the holes in Graham's story, about the suspicions his behavior tonight had raised in her. The thought of Graham hiding something so huge made her uneasy. Even just sitting in the den again made her uneasy. She'd avoided it since the other night when Charlie'd let her know in no uncertain terms that she was mixed up in Marjorie's murder, whether she wanted to be or not. And now the person who wanted her dead might be Graham? She closed her eyes.

When she opened them, Charlie was studying her from across the room, his brow furrowed, his blue-green gaze level. He sat staring at her, unspeaking, long enough to make her uncomfortable.

"You know, I'm not sorry about what happened earlier today," he finally said.

An involuntary thrill traveled up Vivian's spine like a mild electric shock. "Which part?"

The corner of his mouth curled into a smirk. "You know which part," he said. "And I didn't like seeing you with Yarborough tonight," he added in a low voice. He stood and walked slowly toward her. "In fact, I hated it."

"Is that so?" Vivian's breath sped up.

"I didn't want you to go out with him at all," he said. He stopped in front of her and looked directly down at her. "And it didn't really have much to do with your life being in danger, truth be told. But I didn't think there was any way I could stop you. You're so goddamned determined."

Vivian narrowed her eyes at the detective. "I'll take that as a compliment."

"That's how I meant it," he said, brushing his fingertips along her jaw. "And if could stop you from ever wanting to see Yarborough again, I would."

Vivian felt herself go weak under the intensity of Charlie's gaze. "And just how would you do that, Detective?"

He leaned slowly down toward her, excruciatingly slowly, and kissed her. This was nothing like his chaste first kiss, or even the frantic scrabbling in Marjorie's closet. This time the kiss was slow, thorough, teasing . . . Vivian responded immediately but kept her hands at her sides, valiantly resisting the urge to wrap herself around him. He broke away after a few long, immensely satisfying minutes and straightened to his full height, raising his eyebrows.

"That's surely not *all* you would do . . ." she challenged, her voice husky.

He shook his head slightly in response and then bent and lifted Vivian off her feet, sweeping her up into his arms so quickly that she didn't have time to protest. One of her satin slippers fell to the floor with a clatter, and she managed a surprised squeak before struggling halfheartedly against his grip. She felt she ought to at least feign putting up a fight, for the sake of her dignity, though fighting was the last thing on her mind right now.

"Just what kind of a girl do you think I am?" she asked. She hit him in the chest with one ineffectual fist.

"The kind I like," he answered, grabbing her fist. Then he kissed her again, hard, before wordlessly starting off in the direction of the staircase.

Vivian relaxed into his embrace for a moment and let her head loll against his shoulder, relishing the feel of his strong arms around her. Then she stiffened as the reality of the situation struck her. "No!" she cried.

Charlie stopped walking and looked down at her, the disappointment on his handsome face almost comical. "No?"

Vivian smiled and ran a hand up his chest to his neck. She brushed her fingers teasingly along one of his earlobes and looked him directly in the eyes. "I mean, no . . ." she said, her voice nearly a growl. "Take me up the *back* stairs, Detective."

CHAPTER TWENTY-NINE

The next morning, Vivian found Charlie sitting in a chair in the den, intently reading the newspaper with a cup of steaming coffee near his elbow.

"Good morning," she said brightly. "You've eaten?"

"Hours ago," he said, his eyes just visible for an instant over the front page of the *Tribune.*

She glanced at the grandfather clock and did a double take to confirm the time, almost not believing her eyes. It was nearly eleven.

"You needed to regain your strength, Detective?" she teased, coming up behind him and running her open palms down his chest as she leaned down to give him a quick peck on the cheek. She rubbed her face across his freshly shaven cheek and resisted the strong urge to nip him in that delicious spot where neck met earlobe. She smirked at the tiny mark in that precise spot already turning a bright purple. She'd done enough nipping last night. She kissed the bruise lightly instead, and Charlie made a noise low in his throat, tilting his head slightly toward her. "Anything new?" she asked, standing again.

Charlie lowered his paper and gestured to the newspapers strewn over the coffee table. He raised one golden eyebrow and said, "See for yourself."

Vivian bit her lip and scanned the front page of the *Tribune* he was holding but saw nothing referencing her or Marjorie's murder.

She pulled the edge of the paper away from Charlie's face, a smile forming on her lips, sure that he was teasing her. "There's nothing —"

"Look again."

She followed his eyes to this morning's edition of the *Patriot* lying on top of the pile on the coffee table.

A photo dominated the top half of the paper — it was Vivian and Graham at their table at Chez Paree. She was half standing, scowling angrily (but not unbecomingly, she noted) at the camera. Graham's hand was raised as if to ward off the photographers, but she noticed that both of their faces were conveniently left uncovered. Graham's face sported a mild half smile, one eyebrow raised. This must have been the last photo taken of them before she begged Graham to run the photographers off — the one taken after they'd asked her about Marjorie.

Then she read the headline above the photo. "I'm Not Afraid," it trumpeted in bold, black type. She snatched the paper from the table with trembling fingers, feeling the heat rise to her face as she read the first paragraph.

Vivian Witchell danced the evening away at Chez Paree with her costar Graham Yarborough despite the peril of imminent death hanging over her head. She confirmed that she'd received a threatening letter just like the one received by the recently murdered Marjorie Fox, her costar at WCHI, but claimed with a defiant air that she was "not afraid of anything." Miss Witchell was seen dancing and canoodling with Mr. Yarborough throughout the evening as if she hadn't a care in the world.

Vivian threw the newspaper down onto the coffee table. It struck a bowl of sugar cubes and sent it crashing to the tile floor.

"Canoodling?" she said aloud, feigning

disbelief. Though she definitely had been canoodling at least in the beginning of the evening — and Charlie knew it as well as she did. "And I didn't say . . . I would never say . . ." She stopped suddenly, snapping her mouth shut, a fresh rush of heat rising to her cheeks. She *had* said those things, all of those things. She'd confirmed the second letter. She'd distinctly told the reporter that she wasn't afraid of anything. She hadn't realized the man was a reporter at that point, but she'd still done it. Her heart pounded with anxiety. If she'd seen this, then Mr. Hart had definitely seen it.

She squinted at the byline of the story — Mack Rippert — and snorted at the memory of the smarmy, bespectacled man who had begged a dance from her. Charlie had known, of course. He always knew. She owed Charlie an apology, but she had no idea how to begin. It wasn't like her to eat crow.

"Look," she said, worrying the hem of her dress. "You were —"

Charlie held up one large hand, halting her attempt at an apology, letting the scowl etched on his face do all the talking for him.

Vivian waited a long moment before beginning again. "I'm sorry," she said, not giving Charlie time to cut her off. She hitched in a deep breath. "I should have believed you about that reporter," she continued. "He was a snake in the grass." And she hadn't even gotten the two-page spread out of it, she thought with more than a little regret. Her eyes fell on the photo again. Graham looked handsome and something else . . . Satisfied? Pleased? She felt her anger rise again at the very idea. Graham had known about the photographers ahead of time, that much was certain.

"Any publicity is good publicity," she said mockingly, staring down at Graham's smirking face.

"Isn't that your philosophy too?" Charlie asked.

Vivian didn't answer. *It is,* she thought. *Or at least it was.*

She felt the urge to rake her fingernails over the photo and scratch Graham's handsome face into oblivion. She felt her knees buckle, and she collapsed into the chair opposite Charlie. She closed her eyes, putting her fingertips gently to her temples. She took a breath and forced the exhalation through her nose. After a moment, she opened her eyes to find the detective staring at her.

"Where's Mother?" she asked, her voice dull.

"Church," he said. "Then she mentioned something about surprising your brother at school. She took one of the policemen with her."

Vivian snorted. A surprise visit from their mother on a Sunday afternoon — Everett would love that. The clock on the mantel ticked loudly in the quiet of the room. She snatched the newspaper and scanned the remaining contents of the article, unable to help herself. When she was finished, she sighed and tossed it back onto the table, flipping it over so that the photo didn't show.

"It's not so bad," she said, forcing cheer into her voice. "I mean, it could be worse."

Charlie only grunted in reply, his face again buried in the Sunday edition of the *Tribune.*

Vivian glared over at the detective. She didn't expect much, but she thought a smidgen of sympathy for the precarious position she was in was justified, especially after what had happened between them last night. She'd expected, at the very least, that after last night he'd be in a better mood, but he'd barely even looked at her. "What gives?"

As soon as the words were out of her mouth, she had an abrupt realization about

Charlie's uncharacteristically dark mood. He clearly regretted last night. That's what. What else could it be? What had so drastically changed in the past few hours, despite the fact that she'd taken him to her bed? He hadn't said ten words to her since she'd come downstairs. He could barely look her in the eye. He was going to put that paper down any moment now, fix his steely gaze on her, and tell her in so many words: *Viv, it was a mistake. It was unprofessional.* Her stomach clenched at the thought.

"Charlie," she said before she could lose her nerve. She wanted to beat him to the punch, even though she didn't regret one thing about last night. But if she didn't say it, then he would. And she didn't think she could bear hearing it. "Last night was —"

The telephone rang and cut her off. They looked at each other while it trilled. *Last night was . . . wonderful, amazing, what you wanted too . . . Please don't say it wasn't.* She wanted to say all of those things, more, but nothing came out. Six rings in, she realized that no one else was there to answer the blasted thing. Charlie simply looked at her with those gorgeous blue-green eyes, his expression a strange mixture of curiosity and confusion. The ringing was insistent, rattling around inside her head so that she couldn't form a coherent thought. "Sorry," she said, jumping from the chair and rushing into the foyer.

"Hello," she said, clutching the receiver.

"Vivian, this is Mr. Hart."

Her stomach dropped, and she thought she might be sick just from the sound of his voice.

"Mr. Hart," she squeaked.

"Listen, Viv," he said. "About that story in the *Patriot* this morning . . ."

"Yes." She felt sweat break out along her hairline. "Let me explain about that."

"There's no need," he said.

Vivian felt a momentary rush of relief. Perhaps all of this would be swept under the rug. Perhaps it wasn't important after all.

Mr. Hart cleared his throat. "You can't be talking to reporters. We've discussed that." The anger in his tone was unmistakable.

Vivian closed her eyes. "Yes, Mr. Hart. We did. But what happened was —"

"I don't give a damn about what happened. The problem is that you talked to a reporter after I explicitly told you not to, Viv. And now the papers are going to be all over us like flies on goose shit."

Vivian tried to respond but her mouth felt sticky, glued shut.

"I'm afraid I have no recourse but to suspend you from all of your roles indefinitely," he said.

Vivian blinked, uncomprehending. "Suspend me?" she echoed. "But —"

"But nothing," he said. "You can and will be replaced."

The words echoed in her head. Around and around they went: *Replaced, Replaced.* She would be replaced.

"I . . . I . . ." she stammered. "I understand." The words seemed to be coming from someone else's mouth.

She heard the click as Mr. Hart hung up on her. Vivian rested her back against the wall and slid down the smooth oak paneling, coming to rest on the polished floorboards with a thump, the receiver still clutched in her hand.

Charlie poked his head into the hallway. His eyes widened with surprise and mild alarm at seeing her nearly supine on the floor of the entryway.

"Are you all right?" he asked.

Vivian didn't move. She blinked slowly, then met the detective's eyes. "I think I've just been fired," she said, her voice flat and disbelieving.

"Fired?"

"Mr. Hart is angry about the paper this

morning. About what I said . . ."

Charlie furrowed his brow. "Can't say I blame him," he said.

Vivian dropped her head into her hands.

"That's what he said? You're fired?" Charlie asked.

"Not exactly. He said I'm on an indefinite suspension from all of my roles at the station." Vivian blinked, tears springing to her eyes. She was barely able to force the next sentence from her trembling lips. "I just know Frances is going to be taking over Lorna Lafferty."

Charlie shook his head and offered a hand to help her up from the floor. She took it with reluctance, and he pulled her to her feet. He removed the receiver from her grasp and returned it gently to its cradle. Vivian stood unsteadily before him, wanting nothing more than to fall into his arms, to have him hold her and make everything better. She opened her mouth to speak, but Charlie beat her to it.

"You know, Viv, you give Frances too much credit. It seems like you are your own worst enemy. You brought this on yourself," he said.

Vivian wiped her eyes and met Charlie's gaze with her own fierce glare. "Where do you get off?" she asked, pushing his arms away.

"You talked to that reporter, Viv. You said those things."

"Yes, but . . ." she sputtered, her mind grappling for an excuse that made sense. "I was tricked."

Charlie shrugged. "Maybe," he said. "But it's your bed . . ." He lifted both eyebrows and left it to her to fill in the rest of the phrase. She blushed furiously at the mention of her bed.

"You're supposed to be on my side," she said, her voice dangerously low. She balled both hands into fists. She could feel the fingernails biting into the soft flesh below her thumbs, but she clenched them even harder. She glared at Charlie, who looked impassively back at her. He seemed almost amused by this horrible turn of events. As if he'd been wishing all along that she'd fail spectacularly. She was utterly humiliated — at being fired, yes, but mostly because of the callous way Charlie was treating her. They had been as close as two people could be, and now it was like last night had never happened.

"I *am* on your side," he said. "But you need to hear the truth."

She knew the truth. The truth was that

the goal she'd been so doggedly pursuing for the past two years, the stardom that was almost within her grasp, had been wrenched away after a few ill-chosen words to the wrong person. The truth was that everything had come crashing down on her, and Charlie didn't care.

"Leave," she said coldly.

"You know I can't," he said. "It's my job to keep an eye on you."

"I don't care." She unclenched one fist and raised an index finger to point toward the front door. "I don't want your eye . . . or anything else of yours . . . anywhere near me!"

Charlie leaned back against the door frame, both arms crossed over his chest. "This isn't the end of the world, you know."

He was right. Of course he was right. Damn him. She reached behind her, grabbed a vase of chrysanthemums off the end table, and hurled it at Charlie. He ducked smoothly, and the vase smashed into the wall just above his left ear, leaving a divot in the plaster. Charlie brushed a few glass shards off the shoulder of his gray serge suit. Then he lifted his head, his cold aqua eyes meeting her own.

"I think you need to practice your aim," he said.

Vivian glared at the detective, too furious to speak.

Someone knocked on the front door directly behind her. Vivian sucked in her breath but waited for Charlie to look away before she jerked her head toward the entrance. It could only be more bad news. The round face and cap of one of the policemen popped into the window that ran alongside the door.

Charlie rushed past her to answer it.

"Message for you," the policeman said gruffly, handing a folded piece of paper to Charlie. Charlie nodded and closed the door. He scanned the paper, a wrinkle appearing between his brows as he read.

"What is it?" Vivian asked, her hands ice cold.

"Looks like you're getting your wish after all," he said.

"My wish?" she croaked.

"I'm leaving."

"What do you mean *leaving*?" Vivian asked, panicked. "Where are you going?"

"Out." He stepped over to the coat-tree and grabbed his worn wool overcoat.

"When will you be back?" she asked as she scurried after him.

He shrugged his coat on and grabbed his hat. "Later," he said, glancing over his shoulder at her. He locked eyes briefly with her before saying, "The police guard is still outside. Stay here until I come back." Then he stepped over the threshold, pulling the heavy mahogany door shut behind him with a soft click.

CHAPTER THIRTY

Vivian awoke with a start and sat bolt upright in the darkened room. The telephone was ringing, an insistent trill that had pushed its way into her fitful dream.

She registered the utter silence of the house and realized that neither her mother nor Charlie had returned. The grandfather clock was just readable in the fading light: 6:10. Despite everything that had happened, she'd managed to fall asleep on the sofa. Now she felt lethargic, yet panicked. Her heart thudded wildly in her chest. Something was wrong. Very wrong. She stumbled to the front hall, each ring of the telephone filling her with fresh dread.

She went to pick up the receiver, but her fingers refused to grasp it, and she knocked it to the floor with a clumsy sweep of her hand. It clunked against the tiles, and a startled female voice was barely audible from the speaker.

"Hello? Viv? Viv?"

She clutched the receiver to her ear. "Imogene?"

"What's going on? Are you okay?"

Vivian sighed with relief at hearing her friend's voice, but that terrible feeling still churned her guts. "I . . ." She glanced at the window next to the front door. The policemen weren't visible. But they were there. Or had they gone too? "I don't know."

"What's wrong?"

Vivian swallowed. "Everything."

"Has something else happened? Are you okay? Viv, what's going on?"

"I'm sorry," Vivian said, noting for the first time the alarm in her best friend's voice. "I'm okay. Physically at least."

"Then what is it?"

Vivian felt the tears prick her eyes, and she bit her tongue to keep it together. "I think I've been fired."

"Fired? What are you talking about?"

"Mr. Hart called earlier. He saw that article in the *Patriot* this morning. Oh, Genie, I've been so stupid." She slumped against the wall and slid down, clutching the telephone cord to her chest.

"I'm sorry, Viv. But fired? I can't believe that. Maybe you misunderstood."

Vivian shook her head, unable to speak.

"Well, we'll fix this, okay? We're going to fix this."

Vivian felt a tear roll down her cheek. She wiped it away and hitched in a breath. Imogene understood. Imogene always understood. This was the reaction she'd wanted from Charlie, and he'd given her the opposite. And then he'd just left. She couldn't bring herself to tell Imogene about what had happened with Charlie last night . . . today . . . It was all too embarrassing.

"I can't talk about this right now, Genie."

"Sure. All right. I was just calling to tell you that I'm going down to the station. I'm going to look through those mailbags in the closet. Maybe I'll find something that will help — another letter maybe? It's a long shot, but I've been sitting here stewing about it all day, and I feel like I have to do something. I was going to see if you wanted to come along, but I suppose that's not the best idea right now."

Vivian sighed. "I suppose not."

"Would you rather I come to your place instead?"

"No, don't bother."

"I'll call you later, okay?"

Vivian didn't answer.

"Okay?"

381

"Okay," Vivian said. "Thanks, Genie."

She reached up and replaced the receiver on its cradle without moving from her seat on the floor. Her legs wouldn't work. All the energy seemed to have been leached from her body. She lowered her forehead to her knees and closed her eyes. Maybe she'd just go back to sleep, and when she woke up, all of this would have just been a bad dream.

Then the doorbell rang, and her head jerked back up.

A man's form was silhouetted in the window next to the front door. It looked like one of the policemen — Vivian could make out the sharp peak of his cap in shadow. She pulled herself to her feet and opened the door, keeping the chain latched.

"Yes?" she said.

The policeman touched his fingertips to the brim of his hat. "Letter for you, miss," he said. "Just delivered by messenger."

"A letter?" she repeated.

He pushed the slim envelope toward her through the crack in the door. "Unless you want me to read it first?" he asked. "In case it's, you know, another threat?"

Vivian shook her head and snatched the envelope from his hand. "No," she said. "That won't be necessary. Thank you."

382

She shut the door and tore the envelope open right there in the foyer. It was a clipping from today's paper — the photo of her and Graham, with the bold "I'm Not Scared" headline centered over it. She studied it, confused. Was it from a fan? Something for her scrapbook? And then she noticed the circle penciled around a face just visible in the background of the photo. She held the clipping up, squinting in the dim lamplight that filtered in from the street. Charlie's face was circled. He glowered at Vivian and Graham from over Vivian's shoulder, just one of the crowd at Chez Paree.

She reached into the envelope and pulled out another sheet of paper, her heart hammering in her chest. She read the message quickly, each typed word filling her with slowly growing terror.

```
You should be scared, you fool.
He lied to you. He knows what
Marjorie was. And I know what he
is. Get out while you still can.
```

It was unsigned. She flipped the paper over, but it was blank on the back. She brushed her fingers over the indentations left by the typewriter keys and flipped the paper back over. She glanced again at the message. The letters. They were off-kilter. Wonky. Just like the threatening letter that had been slipped into her script. The letters swam before her. She closed her eyes. Then she looked again at the circled face on that clipping. Not Graham's face, but Charlie's.

What he is. *What he is.* The phrase spun around and around in Vivian's head. What was this letter suggesting? What *is* Charlie?

In a daze, she found her way to the sitting room, turning on every lamp on her way, and snapped on the radio. The silence was suddenly too much. She was almost suffocating in her thoughts. The uproarious laughter of a live studio audience filled the air. It was the *Carlton Coffee Variety Hour,* live from WCHI. Vivian barely registered Sammy Evan's high-pitched voice. He was already hard at work in his new job. Things had turned out well for Sammy Evans, hadn't they? She snapped the radio off again, suddenly feeling sick.

Charlie had said he'd met Marjorie, but that he didn't know her. Had that been a lie? Had he been acquainted with Marjorie, as the note insinuated? Did he know what she was — whatever that meant? Had he *killed* her? Of course, that was ludicrous, Vivian thought. But Charlie had had the opportunity, hadn't he? He'd been a consultant on *The Darkness Knows* for months. He'd said he'd worked for Mr. Hart prior to that. He could walk into and out of that radio station whenever he pleased. And he could lie just like anyone else, couldn't he? Being a private detective didn't give him any sort of heightened moral compass. He could have been lying to her about all of it.

She didn't really know the man at all, did she? She'd met Charlie all of four days ago, and she'd already jumped into bed with him like a common hussy. That's what her mother would call her if she ever found out. And then he'd humiliated her and abandoned her without an explanation. *That's not something a man that cared for you would do,* she thought. *That's not something a man who cared about anybody but himself would do.*

On impulse, she went to the telephone in the hall, intending to call . . . to call who? Charlie's office? The police? As she reached down, the telephone rang, loud and insistent, under her fingertips.

Vivian jumped back, her hand clutched to her chest as if she'd been shocked. The telephone rang twice more before she could summon the courage to answer it.

"Charlie?" she whispered, hoping despite

385

everything that he was calling. She needed him to clear all of this up. She needed him to tell her that everything she'd just been thinking was wrong. She glanced into the dark entryway. She couldn't see the police guards from here, but she knew they were there.

"Viv?" a female voice asked tentatively.

"Yes."

"It's Peggy Hart."

Vivian's breath came out in a great whoosh of air.

"Viv, are you there?"

Viv felt the color flood back into her face, but she'd heard the note of panic in the girl's voice.

"Yes," she said, her voice stronger. "I'm here. What is it, Peggy?"

"Oh, thank goodness. I was hoping you'd be around," Peggy said. "Deena hasn't shown up yet. Joe was hoping you could come down to the station and fill in for her —"

"Which show?"

"*Murder & Mayhem.*"

Vivian glanced at the hall clock. *Murder & Mayhem* went live in little over an hour. Her immediate instinct was to respond that of course she would come down to the station, but she hesitated. Surely Peggy and Joe both knew that Mr. Hart had effectively fired her. Should she mention it or assume they already knew and were asking her anyway with his blessing?

"Peggy, I don't know . . ."

"You're our only hope, Viv," Peggy said, sounding as if she was on the verge of tears. "There's no one else."

Vivian bit her lip, thinking of Charlie's order that she stay home until he returned. She was suspended. She wasn't to come near the station. But if Vivian came in now and gave a professional, dependable performance on such short notice, maybe that would help change Mr. Hart's mind. She could prove to everyone that she was a professional and the actress they needed her to be. This was her chance to be a team player and to prove that she wasn't just a flighty chit who only looked out for herself.

"I'll be there," she said, her stomach twisting at the idea. Charlie would be angry with her for leaving the house, but he was already angry with her. And who knew if he was even coming back? She'd thrown a vase at him. She'd told him to leave — and he had, even though that's precisely what he was not supposed to do. He'd left her alone. He'd let her down, hadn't he? Maybe that had been his plan all along, she thought, glancing down at the newspaper clipping still in her hand.

"Thank God! Get here as soon as you can." Peggy hung up without saying good-bye.

Vivian thought of leaving a note for Charlie, but what on earth would she say? Instead, she wrote a few scant lines to her mother telling her where she'd gone. Her mother didn't know anything about the recent events, and she didn't need to know. Vivian took one last long look at the clipping and stuffed the envelope containing it and the warning message into her jacket pocket. She patted it, and another thought struck her. This could be another red herring, couldn't it? Someone who was just trying to keep her away from the station and Charlie?

But staying away was the last thing she'd do, Vivian decided. She would not be scared away. She may not know who was toying with her, but she refused to cower. She was going to go to that radio station and take matters into her own hands.

One of the policemen gave Vivian a ride to the station, and she walked through the empty lobby of the Grayson-Cole Building only twelve minutes after she'd hung up the phone with Peggy. She nodded to the night-time security guard, who eyed her warily.

Angelo sprang from his stool in the corner of the elevator, his eyes wide.

"Miss Witchell," he gasped. "What are you doing here?"

Vivian swallowed the lump in her throat. Was it possible that Angelo knew about her suspension too? "I'm filling in for Deena on *Murder & Mayhem,*" she said. "I need to hurry."

Angelo clucked his tongue and shook his head, but he closed the elevator doors behind her without comment. Vivian watched the dial move from floor to floor in silence, her stomach twisting itself into knots.

Just before the car reached the eleventh floor, Angelo pulled the brake and brought the car to a sudden stop. Vivian had to grasp his arm to keep from falling.

"What happened?" she asked, breathless.

Angelo didn't answer, and he didn't turn to face her. Vivian felt the hairs on her arm stand at attention as the goose bumps raced down her arms. She stared intently at the back of Angelo's gray head, willing him to turn around and smile. Willing him to act normally.

"Angelo," she said, fighting to quell the

panic rising within her.

After a moment, he did turn, but his eyes were locked on the floor of the elevator car.

"Angelo," she repeated, her voice rising. "What's going on?"

"I'm sorry," he said, eyes still trained on the floor at his feet.

Vivian swallowed. "Sorry about what?"

Angelo's caramel-colored eyes flicked up to her face. "It was me," he said, spreading his hands palms up before lacing his fingers together over his midriff as if in prayer.

Vivian tried to speak, but nothing came out. She swallowed and tried again. "*What* was you?" she whispered. She desperately wished that she'd accepted Imogene's offer to lend Vivian her gun. She had no way to defend herself. She glanced down to the brake and the lever beside it. She'd wished she'd paid more attention to how the elevator actually operated. Could she make a lunge for the brake? Set the car lurching upward and put him off balance if she had to?

"Mrs. Fox . . ." he began.

Vivian's heart stopped in her chest.

"Mrs. Fox," he repeated, shaking his head slowly, "was not a nice woman." He glanced up at Vivian again, as if needing confirmation that he was not the only one who felt

390

that way.

"No," Vivian whispered. "She wasn't."

She balled the fingers of her right hand into a fist but kept it hanging at her side. She'd never punched anyone before, but she was sure she could do it if she had to. And Angelo was small and slight, not much bigger than Vivian herself. She was sure that if she caught him off guard she could at least knock him off balance and make a break for it somehow. Make a break for it in an elevator, she thought with rising panic. How does one do that? She fought the giggle of hysteria that tried to force its way out of her mouth. This was no time to lose her mind.

"But that's no excuse," Angelo continued. "And it's no excuse at all for bringing you into it."

Vivian flexed her fingers. It was now or never, she thought. *Punch him. Knock him down. Release the brake. Save yourself.*

Angelo stared at the floor, shaking his head. Vivian clenched her fist tighter, but then Angelo looked up at her again. She decided she needed to hear it. She needed to hear his confession and know why.

"It was a lot of money he was offering," Angelo said.

"Who?" Vivian asked, her fist still tensed.

Angelo blinked several times. "That Mack

391

something or other," he answered.

"Mack? From the *Patriot*?"

"Yeah, that's it. The *Patriot*." Angelo grimaced. "He offered me fifty bucks just to feed him a little bit of information, that's all." Angelo looked at her, eyes pleading with her to understand. "Then I saw those stories, and I felt horrible. Mrs. Fox was a nasty woman, but you should never speak ill of the dead. And you, well, you didn't do nothing at all."

Vivian shook her head. She rubbed her sweaty palm on the side of her skirt.

"You were the *Patriot*'s inside source at the station?" she asked quietly.

Angelo nodded sorrowfully.

A sharp bark of a laugh escaped Vivian's throat, and the little man looked up at her, startled. "Sorry," she said, trying to get control of herself. "But that's all?"

"That's all?" he repeated, incredulous. "How can you ever forgive me, miss?"

"Jesus, Angelo," she said under her breath. Vivian took two long breaths. She pressed the palm of one hand to her chest. Her heart was indeed still beating. Then she looked him squarely in the eye and said, "You're forgiven. Now release that damn brake. I have a show to get to."

CHAPTER THIRTY-ONE

"Well, well, look what the cat dragged in," Frances drawled as she looked up from a huddled conversation she'd been having with Morty. "You look tired, Viv. Something wrong?" Frances's pretty face was a mask of false concern.

Vivian forced a smile to her lips. Frances was the last person she wanted to see right now. "Not a thing," she said in a breezy voice. "I was out late last night." She paused for effect, then said, "Dancing, oh, having a wonderful time . . ." She made a show of gazing off into the middle distance dreamily, as if recalling the reverie of the night before. She brushed the tips of her fingers against her lips and smiled.

Frances's blue eyes flared, and Vivian knew she'd seen the day's papers. *Let Frances think things are peachy between me and Graham,* Vivian thought vindictively. *Serves her right.*

"Morty," Vivian said, acknowledging the engineer with a smile.

Morty glared at Vivian, his hands jammed in his pockets. He'd apparently not forgotten what had happened the night before — or, more accurately, what had *not* happened. Anyway, Vivian seemed to have moved onto his no-longer-favored list. "I need to go check the microphone levels," he muttered before rushing off.

Frances smiled encouragingly after him. She looked down to her hands, fingering something that flashed golden in the light. Vivian recognized the object in Frances's hands as the same locket Morty had attempted to give to her a few days earlier. She blinked in surprise, slightly offended that she hadn't been Morty's one and only object of affection — but at least he'd offered her the locket first, Vivian thought with mild satisfaction.

"You know, I'm surprised to see you anywhere near the station," Frances said, a Cheshire cat smile creeping onto her face. "I'd be lying low if I were you."

Vivian narrowed her eyes at Frances, deciding whether or not to take the comment at face value. "I don't scare that easily, Frances," she said. Frances had looked annoyed by Vivian's appearance at WCHI

394

but not surprised. Maybe she *hadn't* sent the warning note to keep Vivian away. "And I'm most certainly not afraid of *you*," Vivian said, her voice a husky whisper.

Frances raised her perfectly penciled eyebrows in surprise. "I'm not talking about me, silly," she said. "I'm talking about Mrs. Gill-Davison." She paused dramatically as she spoke the woman's name, each syllable ringing like a hammer blow.

"Mrs. Gill-Davison?" Vivian repeated.

"I hear she's none too pleased with the unfavorable publicity you've drawn to yourself and the station," Frances said. She tut-tutted in mock sympathy before adding sotto voce, "She could ruin your career in a heartbeat, you know."

Vivian willed herself not to react. Frances could smell weakness like a hungry lioness, and Vivian was determined not to give her an ounce of leverage. Until this moment, she'd hoped that it had solely been Mr. Hart's decision to suspend her from the station. Now she wasn't so sure.

Before Vivian could respond, Frances continued. "You know, speaking of careers," she said. "I'd like to thank you for handing Lorna Lafferty to me on a silver platter."

Vivian felt the tingle of impending doom crawl up her spine. The false smile slipped from her face. Frances held the metaphorical knife above her head, ready to bury it to the hilt in Vivian's back.

Frances nodded as if she'd read Vivian's thoughts. "Mr. Hart called me into his office earlier and informed me of your little suspension. I told him I would be more than happy to take Lorna over for you. It seemed to ease his mind that he could rely on someone so capable."

Vivian's breath caught in her throat. So it was true. Her worst fears confirmed. Frances had indeed taken Lorna from her and was well on her way to stealing her entire career.

"Still," Frances continued, her voice light. "Graham and I have such wonderful chemistry *off* air. Imagine what we'll be like on the show." She smiled beatifically at Vivian.

"I won't be forced out," Vivian said, finally finding her voice. Frances's thin, black eyebrows arched effortlessly before coming together over the bridge of her nose in false concern.

"Oh, but, sweetie," she said in a low, soothing tone as if she were speaking to a small child, "I'm afraid you're already on your way."

Peggy hurried into the studio in a flurry of movement and audible sighs. She shoved a sheaf of papers at Vivian. "I can't believe Deena would be so irresponsible. She hasn't called or anything . . ." The words tumbled from her mouth in a rush.

For once, Vivian was thankful for one of Peggy's ill-timed entrances. She took a long, slow breath to calm herself. "Have you phoned her?" Vivian asked.

Peggy rolled her eyes. "A dozen times."

"She's probably had an accident," Frances chimed in, sounding rather pleased at the prospect.

Peggy shrugged. "I hope not, but the show must go on," she said. She pointed to the script in Vivian's hand. "Yours are under-lined, Viv."

Vivian scanned the script, flipping pages quickly forward, then quickly back. "*I'm* the murder victim?" she asked, incredulous. "You didn't mention this on the telephone, Peggy."

Frances hummed something jaunty and lighthearted under her breath. Vivian shot her a venomous look, but Frances's head was bent over her script.

"Sorry," Peggy said with a tight smile. "I guess it didn't occur to me. Now, shall we rehearse a bit? Time's running short." She nodded toward the control room. Joe McGreevey watched them intently, concern etched in every line of his face. "Let's start with page eight. There's been a last-minute rewrite near the end that I think we should concentrate on." She handed each of them two fresh pages copied onto pink paper to indicate a script revision.

"I won't stand for it," Frances began, her eyes skimming over the script.

"Stand for what?" Vivian asked. Her palms were sweating, the paper already damp in her hands.

"I won't stand for you taking what's rightfully mine," she said.

"Rodrigo was never yours," Vivian said. She glanced over at Peggy. The girl was standing just to the side, mouthing every word with them, a slight smile on her lips, clearly taking satisfaction in her own rewrite.

"He was, and you took him from me," Frances hissed, deep in character. "But it doesn't really matter anymore," she added with a shrug. "Rodrigo is dead."

"Dead?" Vivian asked, shocked.

"That's right," Frances answered. "He's floating in the duck pond out back. And you're going to join him."

"You can't do this, Evelyn. You'll never get away with it."

"Oh, I don't plan on getting away with it," Frances said. "After all, what's another murder? They can only hang me once." Then she leveled an imaginary revolver at Vivian and pulled the trigger. *Bang,* she mouthed, a smile of genuine satisfaction on her lips.

The two women stared at each other for one long moment before Joe's voice came over the speaker.

"Great, girls. Sounds great," he said.

"Joe," Frances called, glancing coyly over her shoulder, her voice dripping with sugar. "Would it be possible for Vivian and me to switch microphones? This one's giving me a tinge of feedback. And since I'm the star of this episode I thought I should sound the best."

"Surprise, surprise," Vivian muttered under her breath.

Frances's head jerked toward her. "What's that supposed to mean?"

"I mean," Vivian said, "you seem to want everything I have."

Frances's eyes narrowed. She waited a beat before saying in a low, even voice, "And I'll get it."

"Girls, we're live in fifteen," Joe interjected over the speaker with an audible sigh. "Why don't you both get some air, huh? Viv, you can use the time to review the rest of the script."

Vivian blushed and glanced at the microphone, which was obviously still live. Joe had heard everything they'd just said. She looked down at the floor and rushed from the room.

The twelfth floor was dark and deserted again, just as it had been the night Marjorie was killed. Vivian rubbed the gooseflesh down on her arms as she walked, trying to make as little noise as possible with her heels on the marble floor. She steered clear of the side with the lounge, the image of Marjorie's lifeless eyes creeping into her head for the thousandth time.

The lamp was lit at Imogene's desk, and the mailbags had been hauled out from the closet. One bag lay open atop the desk, the contents spilled haphazardly across the blotter, but Imogene herself was nowhere to be found. Vivian stood still for a moment listening, her eyes scanning over the letters and packages all addressed to Marjorie's alter ego, Evelyn Garrett. Her eyes fell on a mug of tea still steaming next to the lamp. Imogene couldn't have gone far. Vivian heard a noise from down the hall, and her head jerked in that direction. Maybe Imogene had gone to Mr. Hart's office for some reason. Maybe she was on to something after all.

Vivian rushed down the hall, but Mr. Hart's office door was closed, the room dark behind the smoked glass. Vivian stopped outside it and listened again, but all was silent. What now? She had to talk to someone. Instinctively, she reached into her bag and pulled out Charlie's card.

Charles Haverman Jr.
Private Inquiries
HAR–7998

Her heart thumped a little harder at the sight of it, and she turned back toward the telephone on the secretary's desk. She had no idea what she'd say to him, but maybe she could get him to explain himself — how he'd known Marjorie, and why he'd kept something so important from her. As she reached for the receiver, there was a click from inside Mr. Hart's office.

Vivian's attention snapped back to the door, and she peered in through the nearly opaque glass. She saw nothing, but now she heard it — the tinny sound of the radio. She snuck over to the door and listened for a moment but couldn't hear anything else. To her surprise, the door swung slightly open at her touch. It wasn't locked.

Mr. Hart sat at his desk, his back to the door. He didn't turn around when Vivian entered; he was listening intently to the radio, leaning toward it to concentrate. Vivian cleared her throat, and Mr. Hart turned slowly to face her. He was flushed and holding an empty glass in his hand.

"Viv," he said, surprised. "What are you doing here?" His words were slightly slurred, melting together at the edges.

"I was looking for Imogene," Vivian said, ignoring the larger question — what she was even doing in the station, given this morning's conversation. "Is she here?" she finished stupidly, seeing full well that she wasn't.

Mr. Hart blinked, then shook his head mournfully. "I haven't seen her." He tilted his head toward the radio. "Have you heard this?" he asked.

Vivian listened for a few seconds. The program was a man reading a news bulletin. She couldn't quite make out what he was saying. "What's happened?" she asked in a low voice, her stomach sinking with dread. She thought immediately of Europe. Had the war started?

Mr. Hart smiled and reached for the decanter of scotch on the corner of his desk. It was almost empty. "That Orson Welles is brilliant," he said, watching the amber liquid flow into his glass.

"Orson Welles?" Vivian asked.

Mr. Hart filled his glass to the brim and took a hefty swig before answering. Sirens suddenly blared from the radio speakers behind him. "My wife called in a panic ten minutes ago," he said. "She told me that the Martians had landed . . . in New Jersey of all places."

"Martians? Mr. Hart, I don't understand . . ." Vivian took a glance at her wristwatch. It was 7:19. She needed to get back to the studio. *Murder & Mayhem* would go live in a little over ten minutes.

"Oh, it's just a play," he said, waving his hand in front of his face. "*War of the Worlds.* H. G. Wells. Brilliant." He looked at her, eyes narrowed and piercing. He looked as if he wanted to say something else, but held back.

Vivian sighed with relief. "Well, I need to get back to the studio," she said, turning to leave. Mr. Hart was obviously very drunk and not making much sense. She also didn't want him to realize that he had effectively fired her just this morning and that she should be nowhere near WCHI.

"I'm sorry for what happened to Marjorie," he said.

Vivian looked back over her shoulder. "Me too," she replied automatically.

"No," Mr. Hart said impatiently. "It was my fault. All of it."

Vivian's hand froze on the doorknob. She stood still for a moment, hoping he wouldn't continue. But he did.

"She was so young then, Effie was," he said.

Vivian turned to face Mr. Hart, but he wasn't looking at her. He looked at his hands clasped tightly around his glass — empty again.

"I hadn't meant for it to happen. But I thought I loved her. I thought she loved me, and maybe I did, maybe she did . . ." He looked up to meet her gaze, his own watery blue eyes pleading with her to understand.

Vivian shook her head at him. "Mr. Hart, I . . ." she said helplessly. She glanced at her watch again. She had five minutes to make it to Studio B. She reached for the doorknob behind her. "I'm going to be late —"

"And I lied," he continued, seeming not to hear her. "I told Effie I'd taken care of it. I lied to everyone . . . even my wife . . . especially her. But I had to, don't you see? She's sick. She can't take this. I lied. I lied. I lied!"

Without warning, Mr. Hart raised the empty glass above his head and sent it crashing down to his desk. Vivian stood frozen for a moment in shock, her heart hammering in her chest. Mr. Hart eyed her wildly, just as shocked by what he had done as Vivian was.

Vivian's mouth opened and closed soundlessly. What exactly had Mr. Hart done? What was he trying to confess to her? And why *her* of all people? What did any of this have to do with Marjorie's death? Mr. Hart rose from his seat and started toward her, arms outstretched. Vivian yanked the door open.

"No! Don't go!" he begged as she ran down the hallway.

The door slammed behind her, and Vivian jerked at the sound. Her ankle twisted painfully sideways, and she lurched to a stop, muffling a cry with the back of one hand. Mr. Hart wasn't following her. She slumped back against the wall, her heart thudding in her chest. She put a hand to her sternum and forced two deep breaths through her lungs, feeling her diaphragm move up and down under her palm. She also felt something else, something flat and hard in the pocket of her jacket. Her hand slipped inside, and with her fingertips, she felt the worn leather cover of the Bible she'd taken from Marjorie's apartment.

She held it gingerly in the palm of one hand as if it were a living thing. *Holy Bible* was stamped in faded gilt lettering across the cover. She half expected the book to open of its own accord, its pages riffling by magic, but they didn't. The spine was still stiff, the book having rarely, if ever, been used. Vivian took another deep breath and opened to the flyleaf. A short inscription was written in a strong, ornate hand, stark black against the thick cream paper: *Presented to Euphemia Juergens upon the celebration of her first Holy Communion, April 25, 1900.* Vivian read the inscription three times before it hit her. Euphemia Juergens . . . Effie Juergens . . . Could that be the Effie that Mr. Hart had been so upset about? Before the connection could fully form in her mind, the elevator motor whirred to life. Vivian watched the needle over the elevator door slide from ten to eleven to twelve. Someone was coming up — it could be Imogene or even Charlie.

As the elevator lurched to a stop, Vivian looked down at her watch and gasped when she found it was only two minutes until showtime. She lurched toward the staircase, stumbling down the stairs on her twisted ankle, and made it into the studio just as the opening music began to play. Joe shook his head at her from the control booth. Vivian hadn't even looked at the script beyond the page she'd rehearsed with Frances. She would have to do the show cold.

Halfway through the script, Vivian thought that it was going as well as could be expected, especially as she could barely read her lines with her hands trembling so badly. She had to get ahold of herself. But she was holding her own against Frances, and Joe even seemed to have relaxed slightly in the control room.

"Talent opens a lot of doors," Frances growled.

"I don't play any games," Vivian replied in an icy tone.

"That's not what I've heard."

Vivian furrowed her eyebrows. There was something familiar about these lines of dialogue. Frances seemed not to notice. She was deeply set in her character, relishing the starring role of murderess, her eyes focused intently on the script in her hand.

Dave Chapman, as Rodrigo, stepped up to the microphone, and Vivian fell back a pace. She was out of this scene and had a moment to breathe.

Vivian's hand found the Bible in her

pocket. Effie Juergens was Marjorie Fox, she knew with sudden certainty. And Mr. Hart had done something horrible to Effie when she was younger . . . something that had gotten her killed years later? Had Mr. Hart killed her? He said he'd loved her, and Charlie had said it had been a crime of passion, a whiskey bottle to the head in a moment of exquisite anger.

Mr. Hart and Marjorie? Vivian could scarcely believe it. *Who didn't Marjorie Fox share a past with?* she thought. Then another, more upsetting thought struck her. Had Mr. Hart, the man who'd hired Charlie to protect her, been the one who'd wanted her dead all along? But why? What role could she have possibly played in any of this?

"I won't stand for it," Frances said, breaking Vivian out of her reverie.

"Stand for what?" Vivian asked, hurrying to find the correct place in the script.

"I won't stand for you taking what's rightfully mine." Frances's eyes glittered.

"Rodrigo was never yours," Vivian said vehemently.

"He was, and you took him from me," Frances replied, the anger in her voice unmistakable. Vivian looked up to find Frances glaring at her, both of them knowing they weren't talking about Rodrigo, but Graham. Frances finally broke eye contact and shrugged, still in character. "Doesn't matter anymore anyway," she said. "Rodrigo is dead."

"Dead?" Vivian asked, shocked.

"That's right," Frances answered. "He's floating in the duck pond out back. And you're going to join him." Frances pulled a gun from her pocket and leveled it at Vivian, the barrel aimed right between her eyes.

That's a real gun, Vivian thought. A real gun pointed directly at her. Oh God, Frances wasn't really going to shoot her during a live performance, was she? Vivian watched Frances's thumb move back, heard the hammer cock. Vivian's eyes darted around the room, but she found only disinterested stares. The soundman was lounging at his table as if this turn of events were the most natural thing in the world. Wasn't anyone going to doing anything? Did they all really think this was just playacting? Vivian's mind worked frantically.

Frances could shoot her in front of all of these witnesses and plead ignorance. She could claim someone had accidentally left a live round in the chamber and that Vivian's murder was an unfortunate accident. Vivian caught the director's arm moving in frantic

409

circles out of the corner of her eye. Dead air. She was blowing it. Again. Vivian swallowed and forced the next line out of her constricted throat, her voice a squeak of panic.

"You can't do this, Evelyn. You'll never get away with it."

"Oh, I don't plan on getting away with it. After all, what's another murder? They can only hang me once." Vivian didn't even have time to blink before the gun went off, shockingly loud at such close range. Vivian gasped in surprise and clapped her hand over her mouth. She glanced up to see Frances smirking at her. *Blanks.* The gun had held only blanks. Vivian let out a shaky breath, and the announcer stepped up to the microphone for the sponsor break.

"Are you feeling weak, irregular, not at the top of your game?"

Vivian looked down at her script in embarrassment. She really was on edge. It was almost all there, the solution tantalizingly close, but she couldn't make anything fit yet. Tears of frustration sprang to her eyes, making the text of her script swim before her. She blinked to clear them and surreptitiously wiped away a tear that was making a break for it down her cheek. She hoped Frances wasn't watching.

She tried to control her racing heart. Her vision was blurred again by persistent tears, and before she could wipe them away, a pattern formed in the fuzzy text. She stared at it for a long moment and then blinked the text back into focus. The Os, she thought. The Os in every word on this page were off. She flipped quickly between the pages. Yes, they were different on the pink revised pages Peggy had given her. The Os on the new pages appeared lower than all of the other letters on the line, just a fraction, just enough to mar the symmetry.

Just like the Os in the letters Vivian had received — the second threat and the one that had just been delivered to her house. Then it hit her like a thunderbolt. She knew exactly why this pattern was so familiar. Why hadn't she put it together before? She sucked in her breath and held it. These Os were made by the typewriter outside Mr. Hart's office. She'd used that typewriter for two years, and she knew its quirks like the back of her hand. The person who'd sent her the letters had used that typewriter. Her roiling stomach told her so. But she had to be sure. She had to go back up to that typewriter and test it.

CHAPTER THIRTY-TWO

"What are you doing up here?"

Vivian jumped, her fingers dancing above the typewriter keys.

"Oh, Peggy, hello." She sighed with relief and placed one hand over her thumping heart. She glanced at the girl and back down to the typewritten letters on the curled paper in front of her. She'd been terrified of running into Mr. Hart again. Terrified that he'd confess to Marjorie's murder or try to harm Vivian too. But his office had been dark when she'd returned to the twelfth floor. "Did you use this typewriter for the script revisions tonight?"

"I . . ." Peggy began. She swallowed visibly and continued. "I did."

Vivian nodded. She rolled the paper out of the machine and studied it. The O was definitely lower than the other letters — just like in that last message warning her about Charlie. "Have you seen anyone else using this typewriter?" Vivian asked.

"Just Daddy's secretary."

"Does Mr. — your father ever use it?" Vivian asked, trying to keep her tone neutral. She couldn't betray to Peggy that she suspected her father of anything.

A smile flitted briefly over Peggy's face, and she said, "I don't think Daddy knows how to type."

Vivian returned the smile. Peggy was absolutely right. It was impossible to imagine the debonair Mr. Hart hunched over a typewriter.

"Vivian, can I get you to listen to something?"

"Listen?" Vivian looked up.

"Yes." Peggy looked down at her feet. "I've written a lot for different shows, but I'd like to try my hand at acting . . . nothing big . . . just a bit part on a serial or something. Anyway, do you mind listening to me read and giving me some tips?"

"Oh, sure," Vivian said, looking nervously down the hallway. What if Mr. Hart was lurking in the dark somewhere?

Peggy motioned toward the smoked-glass door of Studio G, the little one no one used because it wasn't completely soundproof and the noise irritated Mr. Hart in his office next door.

"Now?" Vivian said. "I haven't got much time." She wondered for the hundredth time where Charlie might be. She supposed she'd just have to go home and wait for him. It was the only safe thing to do. She glanced down at the paper in front of her. There was something she was missing, a connection she wasn't making . . . Peggy had used the typewriter, as had Mr. Hart's secretary, but who else?

"Well, you're always so in demand," Peggy said with a smile. "I finally have you all to myself, and I want to take advantage of the opportunity. I promise it won't take long." Her gray eyes were bright, as if she was excited or about to cry.

Vivian smiled. She knew the girl was throwing shameless flattery at her, but Vivian never minded a little flattery, even at a time like this. "Okay," she agreed. "Just for a few minutes though. Then I really have to get going."

Peggy followed her into the studio and closed the door. The click of the latch echoed in the empty room.

The girl cleared her throat and straightened her shoulders, standing a bit taller. "You shouldn't have gotten involved." Peggy paused.

Vivian waited for her to continue her

414

monologue, but the girl simply stared at her, a slight smile on her thin lips. Vivian's smile faltered.

"Go on, Peggy," she said. "I'm listening."

Peggy's brow furrowed. "You shouldn't have gotten involved," she repeated. It was obviously a line she'd been practicing.

"Yes, all right, Peggy. That line sounds fine. What's next?"

Peggy shook her head, sighing. "No, Viv. This isn't part of a script. I'm saying, *You shouldn't have gotten involved.*"

"What do you mean?" Vivian asked, ice crawling up her spine as she realized they were completely alone on the twelfth floor — in an almost soundproof studio. "Involved with what?"

"Fiddling with the typewriter just now . . ."

"Oh." Vivian laughed nervously and took a step toward the door. "I know it's not my job anymore, but I can't seem to tear myself away."

"I know very well what you were doing," Peggy said in a low voice. She leaned back against the door and crossed her arms over her chest.

"Peggy, what's going on here? I need to get back to —"

"I suppose it really is my fault you're

415

mixed up in this, isn't it? After all, I mentioned you in the letter."

"The letter?" Vivian swallowed, her throat as dry as sandpaper.

"I picked Lorna Lafferty out of thin air, you know. Must be the alliteration in the name that makes it so memorable. I had nothing against you. I still don't . . ."

Details tumbled, clicking into place in Vivian's mind, little things she'd overlooked — expressions, choices of words, the Os, the typewriter, the threatening letters. It all suddenly came together in one thundering, inescapable conclusion. Peggy hadn't just typed the threatening letters. Oh no. She'd done far worse. "You killed Marjorie," Vivian whispered. "Why?"

Peggy shrugged, her eyes flicking to the floor. "Your dashing Mr. Haverman knows why."

"Charlie?" Vivian breathed.

Peggy smiled. "I *knew* there was something going on between you two," she said as if she'd caught Vivian confessing a sin. Then she frowned and said, "I suppose you *could* ask him, but I don't think he'll answer. Not now."

Vivian felt the hair on the back of her neck bristle. "Where is he?"

Peggy shrugged again.

"Where is he?" Vivian repeated, keeping her voice as steady as possible.

"Slowly suffocating in that shabby rented room he calls an office, I suppose," Peggy said. "It seems he's opened the gas line to end his guilt and misery over Marjorie's death — or, that's what it'll say in the papers tomorrow, anyway."

Vivian made a move for the door, but Peggy pulled a revolver from the pocket of her cardigan, aiming it dead center at Vivian's chest. "Don't even try it," she said.

Vivian stopped midstep and raised her hands reflexively. The weapon looked exactly like the prop gun Frances had leveled at her a few minutes earlier, but she couldn't take the chance that this gun held only blanks. Vivian's eyes darted around the room, looking for something, anything, to aid in an escape. There was nothing. The studio was empty except for the piano in the far corner. The small control room was dark behind the square pane of glass. Panic seized her. Peggy had killed Marjorie, and now she'd . . .

Charlie. Oh God, Charlie.

"His guilt and misery," Vivian repeated in a dull voice, feeling like her legs might give way under her. She looked at Peggy, at the gun, helplessly.

417

"Oh, I left a letter with Charlie too," Peggy said. "His suicide note explains how he'd killed Marjorie and how the guilt was making his life a living hell."

Vivian stared at the girl. Suicide letter? But why would Charlie have killed Marjorie? He didn't even know her, or she thought he hadn't. What had that letter said? What Marjorie was . . . What Charlie is . . . ? Vivian shook her head. None of this made any sense.

"*You* sent me that warning earlier tonight with the clipping from the *Patriot*." She watched the gun, watched Peggy's finger hover over the trigger.

"I did that for your own good."

"My own good?"

Peggy shifted the gun slightly, moving her finger away from the trigger. "It was an apology. I got you mixed up in this, mixed up with him, and I wanted to lessen the blow a little for you when he was found dead. You see, this way, you'd already have suspected him of being a murderer. And when it was confirmed with his suicide note confession, then maybe you wouldn't take it so much to heart."

Vivian clenched her hands into fists at her sides. *An apology? Lessen the blow?* Vivian regarded the girl through narrowed eyes.

Vivian felt sick, but she couldn't fall apart now. Charlie was out there — likely hurt, possibly dying. Vivian was the only one who could save him, and to save him she had to get out of this room. At the very least she had to get to the telephone on the desk outside and call for help. She glanced at the door behind Peggy. She had to get out there somehow. Vivian stared into the unblinking eye of the gun and stiffened her spine. She took a deep breath.

"You were wrong, Peggy," she said, trying to keep the trembling out of her voice. "I hadn't suspected. I had no idea."

Peggy's gray eyes flicked to hers, and she studied Vivian for a moment. "You didn't?"

Vivian shook her head.

Peggy sighed, pushing out her lower lip so that the wisps of fine brown hair around her temples fluttered. "But you were getting close. I could see it all over your face."

Vivian eased one foot tentatively off the floor, hands still raised, and Peggy cocked the gun, the metallic *click-click* loud in the empty room. "Don't."

Vivian's heart thudded painfully in her chest. Her eyes shifted to the clock above the window of the empty control room. It was already after eight o'clock, the second hand moving forward in merciless little

419

jerks. Charlie had gotten that note and left just shy of noon. That was eight full hours ago. She felt the warmth drain from her face, her entire body.

She wasn't going to be in time to save Charlie no matter what she did now. If Peggy had done what she'd said she'd done, he was already gone. Vivian's heart thumped once, painfully hard, and then seemed to stop entirely. *Gone.* And now she understood that Peggy likely had no intention of letting Vivian out of this room alive — not now that she knew the truth.

"I don't understand any of this, Peggy," Vivian said, her voice and her mind somehow still working.

"Haverman took you to the foundling home, didn't he?" The gun was still pointed squarely at Vivian, but Peggy's arm had visibly relaxed, the elbow bending slightly under the pistol's weight.

Vivian blinked. Nodded. *The foundling home.* She had to keep Peggy talking, keep her distracted. Find a way out. There had to be a way out of this. Peggy looked at her expectantly for a long moment. "You really don't know?" When Vivian shook her head, Peggy said, "Maybe you two weren't as close as I thought." She emitted another long sigh, and then the words tumbled out in a rush.

"Marjorie Fox had a baby. Of course, she was little Effie Juergens then, Father's dutiful secretary *and more.* Father likes his secretaries . . . but you know all about that, don't you?" Peggy's bland face crumpled with disgust. "Father didn't care a whit for her. I know he didn't. How could he? He already had Mother. So he took care of it, or at least he told Effie that he had. A member of the board of directors can easily get access to the confidential files."

Vivian's head was spinning. That explained it. She touched the Bible in her pocket. Marjorie was really Effie, and Effie had had Mr. Hart's baby when she was his secretary so many years ago. Mr. Hart had joined the Chicago Foundlings Home board of directors to cover up his own secret — an illegitimate child.

"He told Marjorie that the baby had died. But the baby hadn't died," Peggy said.

Vivian remembered Charlie's closed expression outside the foundling home, his hardened jaw, how he'd refused to look at her. He'd been protecting himself. How could Vivian have been so blind?

"You destroyed the letter Marjorie was carrying from the foundling home and replaced it with the fan letter, didn't you?"

Peggy raised her eyebrows. "I didn't replace the letter. She didn't have it when I confronted her in the lounge, and it wasn't really from the foundling home. I wrote it using some of Daddy's blank stationery. He keeps it in his desk, you know."

"*You* wrote it?" Vivian shook her head. "Why? What did it say?"

"That the child she'd given up had found out who she was and would go to the press if she didn't meet with him." Peggy was proud, Vivian thought. Proud of her complicated scheming. Proud to have someone to share it with.

"But Charlie didn't know then that Marjorie was his mother. Why on earth would you do something like that?"

"Why would I make it up, you mean? I knew that was her worst nightmare. Marjorie was never the maternal type. And she still had ambitions to go beyond radio, deluded as they may have been, especially at her age. A scandal like a bastard child would have sunk her. So I wrote that letter to shake her up, to show her what it felt like to be harassed — just like she harassed my father, my mother, me. Then I found myself alone with her in the lounge, and I decided to needle her about it. I just wanted to get a rise out of her. But she didn't play along." Peggy shrugged. "I got angry, and I hit her with whatever I could find."

"The whiskey bottle."

"Ironic, really. We all knew the bottle would get her someday." She smiled. "Anyway, that was an accident. I hadn't meant to do it." Peggy was so engrossed in her story that the barrel of the gun had wandered slightly to the right, no longer centered on Vivian's chest. Should she make a break for it?

"And when you realized she was dead, you rushed to the typewriter and cranked out some nonsense to throw the police off."

"Good, wasn't it? A red herring, and apparently it worked like a charm. You really believed there was a Walter that couldn't live without you."

Vivian ignored the dig. "And then you snuck out down the back stairs."

Peggy nodded, and something else clicked into place for Vivian.

"You took Graham's cuff links, didn't you?"

The shock on Peggy's face was almost comical. "He left them in the studio. I just picked them up so I could return them to him," she said defensively.

"Of course," Vivian said. "And you

dropped one in the stairway, or hadn't you noticed?"

It all made sense, all of the little things along the way that had tripped her up and kept her from guessing the truth. Kept her suspicion aimed mistakenly at Graham, Frances, Morty, Mr. Hart, Charlie — nearly everyone in at the station except the real culprit.

"You know, Marjorie showed that fake letter from the foundling home to your father. I heard them arguing outside the ladies' room." Vivian thought of the smell in Mr. Hart's office when she'd woken from her fainting spell after finding Marjorie. He must have taken the letter and burned it in the ashtray on his desk.

"I should've known she'd run to Daddy," Peggy said, her face twisting with annoyance. "I didn't want to get him involved."

"Is that who Marjorie was blackmailing? Your father?"

Peggy laughed suddenly, a sharp bark in the silence. Vivian jumped. "Marjorie Fox was blackmailing herself," Peggy said.

"Herself?"

"She was always trying to manipulate Daddy. That's how a drunk like her kept a plum role like Evelyn Garrett," she said. "She'd come to the house begging for favors, money . . . It was disgusting. And Daddy went along with it because he felt he owed her something. And he didn't want Mother to find out . . . to upset her . . . She's so terribly sick." Peggy's voice cracked.

"One evening a few weeks ago, Marjorie showed up with a silly note cut from some letters in a magazine and convinced Daddy she was being blackmailed over their *secret*. That's when I got the idea for the letter from the foundling home. That horrible woman deserved to get a real scare. And that's all I really meant to do," she said, her voice shaking. "I just meant to scare her."

Peggy shook her head, her face reddening. "But she underestimated me," she said, sticking out her lower lip like a petulant child. "Everyone underestimates me."

"You shot at me outside the masquerade."

"I didn't shoot at *you*."

"Charlie," Vivian whispered.

"I knew Daddy knew about Charlie, but I didn't know until the night of the masquerade that Charlie knew about Daddy. I overheard Charlie confronting Daddy. Charlie was trying to weasel in on our family too. He wanted my father's attention, his recognition. He wanted too much. I'd already killed Marjorie and gotten away

425

with it. What was another murder? But then you got in the way and I missed my shot — literally. But that led to an even better idea. Soon they'll find Charlie's lifeless body next to the suicide note confessing his murder of Marjorie. Two birds with one stone."

Peggy shook her head, giving Vivian a small smile. "You know, it wasn't planned, but it really was fun watching you think this was all about you. You do have quite an ego. You stole all of the attention for yourself." Peggy tipped her head to one side. "You're a lot like Marjorie, you know," she said.

Vivian narrowed her eyes at Peggy. "Is that an insult or a compliment?"

Peggy smiled briefly. "Oh, it's a compliment. Marjorie was a talentless drunk, but she knew what she wanted. And she knew how to get it . . . just like you."

Vivian glanced toward the door, catching a flicker of movement behind the smoked-glass panel, the distinct shadow of someone passing in the hallway beyond. Passing and moving on. *No, stop,* Vivian pleaded in her mind. *Come back, whoever you are.*

"I'm sorry to have gotten you all mixed up in this," Peggy said, raising the gun at Vivian again. "But you have to understand I can't let you go now."

"What if I promise to never say a word

about any of this?" Vivian said, making every effort to keep her voice steady.

"Then I'd say you're a liar."

Vivian's stare shifted from the barrel of the gun to the girl's cold, gray eyes. Peggy watched Vivian expectantly. It was now or never, Vivian's only chance. She hitched in her breath, opened her mouth, and screamed. It was truly bloodcurdling, one of her best.

Peggy winced, letting the gun drop. "That was right on cue," she said. "You know, it's as if this were all a scene written for *The Darkness Knows.* I couldn't have imagined it playing out better. But Harvey Diamond isn't coming to save you. No one can hear you, and no one will hear this." Peggy raised the gun again, biting her lower lip in concentration as she took aim.

The heavy oak door flew open behind Peggy, making contact with her backside with a satisfying thump and knocking her off balance. The gun flew from her hand and skittered across the parquet floor. Vivian watched it land near the piano bench, spinning twice before finally coming to rest. The spell broken, Vivian lunged forward. She felt the heel of her right shoe snap off and the pain shoot up her leg as her already tender ankle twisted again. She crawled toward the gun, her hand reaching it a split second before Peggy's did. Vivian kicked out savagely with her left leg and made contact with Peggy's stomach. Vivian struggled to her feet, the loaded gun in her own hands. She pointed it down at Peggy, trying to look as if she knew how to use it.

Imogene stood in the doorway, open-mouthed with shock.

"What —"

"Oh, Genie, thank God," Vivian said. "Call the police. Ask for Sergeant Trask and tell him to get to Charlie's office right away. He's in terrible trouble."

Imogene glanced from Vivian to Peggy and back again. Then she nodded, eyes wide, and scurried from the room.

Vivian swallowed and tightened her grip on the gun. She narrowed her eyes at Peggy, who curled into the fetal position on the floor, her arms over her head.

"That was close, wasn't it, Peggy?" Vivian said, her voice shaking. "You almost got away with it."

Peggy lowered her arms and glared at Vivian, teeth bared in a snarl. "Your beloved detective is still dead," she said. "That's all I really wanted."

Vivian knew it was a taunt, just empty bravado, but her stomach dropped just the

428

same. Charlie could very well be dead, and what would she do then?

CHAPTER THIRTY-THREE

Vivian nudged the hospital room door open, heart thudding in her chest. There were two beds in the room, Charlie's nearest to the door. He was lying on his back, eyes closed. She watched automatically for the rise and fall of his chest. Her fear was irrational, of course. The police had already told her they'd gotten to his office in time. But she watched anyway, only satisfied when she saw his chest rise and heard a tiny rumble of a snore drift toward her. She stepped into the room and eased the door closed behind her.

What she wanted to do was climb into the bed with him, rest her head on his chest, and feel the reassuring aliveness of him. Instead, she glanced at the shriveled man in the bed next to his and then quietly pulled the curtain closed for some modicum of privacy. As she turned back to Charlie, he opened his eyes, gazing directly at her like he'd known she was there the whole time. He smiled at her, his lips slightly lopsided. There was a bright purple bruise on his left temple that would turn nasty in the next few days, but beyond that, he looked unhurt.

"I'm so glad you're all right!" she blurted out, her voice sounding strange and high-pitched. For just a moment she thought she might cry out of sheer relief. She rushed to the bed and kissed Charlie as passionately yet delicately as possible, wary of his injury and everything he'd been through in the past twenty-four hours.

He groaned in pain anyway.

"Sorry," she said, her fingertips hovering over his temple before lowering to touch his unblemished cheek.

He smiled and winced slightly, closing his eyes briefly before saying, "No, it's okay. I appreciate the enthusiasm."

Vivian blushed and straightened up. She never lacked for enthusiasm. "Are you really all right?" she asked. She didn't like seeing him this way, so helpless.

"Well, I have a splitting headache, but the doctor tells me I'll live," he said, his deep voice husky from the gas inhalation.

"Thank God." Vivian sighed, closing her eyes. When she opened them again, he was frowning at her in that familiar way.

"You didn't listen to me, Viv," he said.

Vivian blinked.

"I told you to stay home yesterday," he said, his voice stern. "And you went to the station anyway."

"Yes, well, I . . . They needed me," Vivian sputtered, feeling guilty at how inane that sounded. She'd put herself in such danger for the sake of her silly career. Flustered, she sat in the chair by Charlie's bed and tugged at one of her gloves. She winced as she heard the fabric tear along one of the fragile seams.

"Thank you," he said in a voice almost too low for her to hear.

Vivian looked up, confused. "I'm sorry?"

"Thank you for being stubborn and contrary and self-absorbed . . . and for saving my life," he answered. He closed his bloodshot eyes briefly, and then they opened and fixed on hers.

Vivian opened her mouth to reply, but her throat felt tight.

"I . . . Well, you're welcome," she said finally, the words completely inadequate. She waved one hand dismissively. "I don't even want to think about what might have happened if I . . ."

"What *did* happen exactly?" he asked, his

brow furrowed over his dark blond eyebrows. "I'm a little cloudy on the details of my near-demise."

"The police haven't told you?"

"Just bits and pieces," he said. "And frankly, what they did tell me doesn't make much sense."

"Well," Vivian started and then realized she didn't really know how to begin. It was still a muddle in her own mind. "It was that note you got at the house yesterday that started everything, wasn't it?"

"The one that arrived after you nearly clocked me with the vase of flowers, you mean," Charlie said, one corner of his mouth curling. "Yes, it said that Mr. Hart wanted to see me in my office and that I should tell no one."

"But that message wasn't really from Mr. Hart. It was from Peggy."

Charlie touched his forehead lightly with the tips of his fingers and winced. "I went to my office and waited, but Mr. Hart didn't show." Disappointment showed on his handsome face for an instant and then was gone. "There was a folder on my desk. My folder from the orphanage . . . the one Sister Bernadine had told me was burned in that fire. I started to leaf through it, and the next thing I knew, I was waking up in the hospital."

"Peggy was waiting for you in your office. She knocked you out and opened the gas line," Vivian said. "And if she hadn't been so proud to tell me about it afterward, you would have . . . well, you would have . . ." She swallowed the sudden lump in her throat. "She left a fake suicide note with you, Charlie. It said you had killed Marjorie. She wanted to pin the whole thing on you."

"How do you know all this?"

Vivian bowed her head. "Peggy told me."

"She told you?"

Vivian nodded. "After you left yesterday afternoon, Peggy called me to fill in last minute on *Murder & Mayhem.* I know you told me to stay at home, but she told me Joe McGreevey was frantic and that he asked for me specifically. You don't refuse Joe McGreevey," Vivian said with an apologetic shrug.

"And you never turn down an opportunity to make your mark," Charlie said, crossing his arms.

Vivian smiled wanly. "Yes, and Peggy knew that too," she said. "I'm fairly certain now, of course, that Peggy lured me to the station to keep me from interfering in her real plan."

"Of offing me," he said.

Vivian swallowed and nodded. She thought of Peggy's secondary goal of getting Vivian to spar with Frances. She felt her color begin to rise at the very idea and decided that was a detail Charlie didn't need to know — not now anyway.

"I went to Mr. Hart's office before the show and found him there alone. He was drunk and rambling on about Orson Welles and his own sick wife and how awful he felt about what he'd done to Marjorie so long ago . . ."

Charlie blanched and turned his face to the window.

"He called her Effie," Vivian continued. "What he'd done to Effie . . . How he'd loved her and thought he'd taken care of everything. I didn't make the connection immediately, but that was the name in the Bible in Marjorie's apartment: Euphemia Juergens. Marjorie had been Effie Juergens."

Charlie fixed his gaze on the window. "How did you see that?"

Vivian glanced down at her hands. "I took it after you left her bedroom. The look on your face told me there was something important about it."

Charlie stared at her for a long moment and then smiled wryly. "You really *aren't* the flibbertigibbet I thought you were." But then the smile faded, and his attention shifted back to the grime-smeared window. "And Effie, as we both know now, was the woman who gave birth to me. I had seen the name in the files in Mr. Hart's home study a few weeks ago. It was the same file I found on my desk yesterday. Evidently, Peggy had seen that file too and had connected the dots long before I had. I didn't connect the name with Marjorie until I found that Bible in her apartment."

"You've been to Mr. Hart's home? Seen his files?" Vivian asked.

Charlie shrugged. "I snooped around."

Vivian placed her hand lightly on top of Charlie's. "So you've known since we were in her apartment that Marjorie was your mother?" she asked quietly.

Charlie nodded.

"You could've told me."

"It wasn't related to your threatening letters. Well, I didn't *think* it was related."

Vivian felt a stab of shame. None of this had ever been about her.

"You could've told me anyway." She paused. "So then you knew this whole time that Mr. Hart was your father?"

"I started digging into my adoption after my mother died a few years ago. I'd known

I was adopted, of course, but I knew it would have hurt her for me to be so interested in finding a birth mother that hadn't wanted me — you know, when she so obviously had. I've been to the foundling home maybe a dozen times since then. The first ten times or so, Sister Bernadine told me the standard line — all files prior to 1930 had conveniently been destroyed in a fire. Then something happened on the eleventh visit."

"What was that?"

"Well, she started to aggressively discourage me from digging any further. Tried to make me feel guilty for even wanting to know about my birth parents. It was then that I knew I was on to something and that that something had to be pretty big. I looked into the workings of the home, the board of directors. I found out that Mr. Hart was on that board. As luck would have it, I'd already been doing some detective work for him, so it was easy enough to snoop around his home office, and that's where I found my file."

"There wasn't any luck involved. Mr. Hart knew who you were the whole time. He'd hired you for those jobs and suggested you as the special consultant to *The Darkness Knows* so he could meet you, see what you were like," she said.

Charlie looked down at the sheet covering him. Then he jerked his head sharply back up at her. His eyes blazed. "Then why did he deny everything when I confronted him at the masquerade?"

Vivian searched for an answer but couldn't come up with anything that made any sense.

So Charlie *had* confronted Mr. Hart at the masquerade. And Peggy had been listening. No wonder the dialogue in last night's script had sounded so familiar, Vivian thought. Now she realized it matched a conversation she and Frances had had days earlier almost word for word. Peggy had been listening, all right. She always had been.

He pursed his lips. "How did you get Peggy to spill all of this anyway? How did you even know to ask?"

"Well, it was sort of an accident . . . I did the show, and after my character was bumped off, I had some time to think. It was then that I noticed that the Os on the new pages of my script matched the Os I'd seen on the threatening letter I'd received. And I thought those Os matched what I remembered about the typewriter I'd used as Mr. Hart's secretary for two years. So I went up to test it to make sure. That's when

Peggy showed up and assumed I knew more than I did." Vivian looked down at her hands, remembering the feeling of fear and panic when Peggy drew the gun. "She trapped me in a rehearsal room to confront me, and the only way out was for me to keep her talking."

"And she spilled the whole story just like that?"

Vivian shrugged. "I think she really enjoyed telling someone. She said I was the only one who knew everything. I suspected that Mr. Hart had helped her, but now I think she did this all on her own. She thinks she's exceptionally clever."

"Not clever enough," he said, grimacing. "How did you get out of it?"

"I screamed," Vivian said, deciding to give Charlie the abridged version of events. "I saw a shadow go past the door behind Peggy. When I screamed, that person came back, flung open the door, and knocked the gun right out of Peggy's hand. That person turned out to be Imogene, of course. She always comes through in a pinch."

Charlie smiled and shook his head in disbelief.

"I know. Just like a script for *The Darkness Knows,* isn't it?"

They smiled at each other.

"Have you spoken with Mr. Hart?" Vivian asked.

"No, and I don't expect to. He made it perfectly clear the night of the masquerade that he wants nothing to do with me."

"Maybe he's changed his mind."

"I wouldn't bet on it. Frankly, I'm not sure I want anything to do with *him*. He doesn't have the most upstanding character. Not to mention that his daughter tried to kill me."

"Several times," Vivian added unnecessarily.

Charlie gave her a withering look, and then his expression softened. "Listen, Viv, thank you again for what you did for me."

"Well," Vivian said, suddenly growing shy, "I'd like to keep you around." She placed her hand lightly on top of Charlie's. She squeezed it, and he flipped his hand over and squeezed hers back.

"By the way, I believe you still owe me for services rendered," he said.

Vivian glanced sharply at him. "Services rendered?" she said indignantly. "*I* saved *your* life, mister. Besides, I don't recall ever coming to terms on your fee."

"Still, a debt is a debt." Charlie gazed seriously at her for a moment, then broke into a smile — or as much of one as he could muster. "But I'm sure we can work out some sort of a payment system."

Vivian felt her palms go sweaty at the suggestive tone in his husky voice. Before she could respond, there was a knock on the door.

Graham burst into the room. Vivian pulled her hand away from Charlie's. She hadn't told Graham about what had happened between her and Charlie yet, and she didn't want him to find out like this.

"Chick!" Graham exclaimed, unable to hide the shock of seeing the detective laid up in bed. "Hell of a thing that happened to you," he said, frowning. "How are you doing?"

"Oh, I've been better," Charlie said.

Graham shook his head. "Peggy," he said in a low voice. "Who would've guessed she'd do something like that?" He looked at Vivian and Charlie expectantly.

Charlie touched the garish purple bruise at his temple gingerly.

"Well, I'm glad to see you're on the mend," Graham boomed. "And I hear that's all due to our little Viv here." Graham placed both of his hands on Vivian's shoulders and squeezed a bit too hard.

Charlie closed his eyes for a moment. "Indeed," he said, smirking. "She'd make quite a private detective."

Graham laughed at this a little too readily, and Vivian shot him an irritated look over her shoulder, which he failed to notice. Instead, he glanced down at his wristwatch, and his brown eyes widened.

"Viv," he said. "We'd better hurry."

"Hurry?" Charlie said.

"To the station," Graham said.

Charlie's eyes shifted back to Vivian. "You got your job back?"

Vivian glanced toward the window, but the blind was drawn and left her nothing to focus on. So her eyes flicked to the floor, and she shrugged one shoulder. "Well, no," she said, her voice strained. She hadn't. But now that his daughter had been arrested for murder and was stewing behind bars in the Cook County Jail, Mr. Hart would likely take a leave of absence from the station to withdraw from the scandal. Vivian knew she had a better chance of pleading her case with Mr. Langley, who would certainly take over leadership of the station. And if that didn't work, well, then she didn't know what she would do. She didn't have a Plan B yet, but she'd think of something. WCHI wasn't the only station in town.

"Just a formality," Graham said with confidence. "We're heading in there now to talk some sense into Langley. Anyone in their right mind would see that letting Viv go would be a huge mistake."

Vivian's eyes moved to Charlie and held his gaze briefly before she glanced away again.

"I mean it," Graham continued, giving her shoulder another squeeze. "I'll walk if he doesn't bring Viv back on board."

Vivian looked sharply up at Graham. He'd walk? She didn't know if that was the truth or just bluster for Charlie's benefit. Very likely bluster, she thought, but she appreciated the sentiment. She smiled at Graham, but the truth was that she wasn't as thrilled about this turn of events as she should be. Yesterday, Lorna Lafferty had meant the world to her; today, Charlie Haverman did.

She opened her mouth to explain everything to Graham — everything that had happened between her and Charlie in such a short time. Then she snapped it shut. Because she couldn't do that, could she? She needed Graham on her side to get back onto *The Darkness Knows.* Everything had happened so fast. She'd been on a date with Graham just a few days ago, a date that had ended in a kiss. She had no idea how Graham thought their relationship stood. He might truly care for her, and she couldn't afford to alienate him with the truth. Not now.

"Right. We should go," Vivian said, standing. "You need your rest."

"Ready, doll?" Graham asked, taking Vivian's arm in his.

"I, uh . . . I suppose I am," she said.

Charlie's eyes were closed, his head sunk back onto the pillow. Maybe he'd already drifted off. Still, Vivian took a step forward and leaned down toward him, hoping she sounded as sincere as she felt. "I hope you feel better very soon," she said quietly. It seemed inadequate, but she couldn't think of anything else to say. Actually, she could think of plenty of things to say. The problem was finding the courage to say them.

Charlie's eyes opened a crack, red-rimmed but still a lovely shade of blue green.

"I guess I'll see you around," he said. "You have my card. Call me when you need me."

When she needed him, she thought. Not *if.*

Vivian smiled and nodded. Charlie understood the bind she was in, she thought. She'd make this up to him when she wasn't in such a hurry. She brushed her fingers quickly over his hand as she backed away from the bed. Then she turned, took a deep breath, and put on a brave — but properly reserved — face for the reporters lingering outside. Chicago hadn't seen this kind of front-page material in years, and Vivian was determined to make the most of it. If she didn't get her job back with *The Darkness Knows,* then at least she'd get her picture above the fold of the papers today. All the papers. And then, by God, she'd catch on somewhere. Because she was too damn determined to let things end here — not when everything was just beginning.

READING GROUP GUIDE

1. Vivian tells Charlie that she'll do anything to succeed as an actress. Do you think that's true? Why or why not?

2. A career woman, of any kind, was a fairly unusual thing in the late 1930s. Why do you think Vivian is so focused on being a radio star? Where do you think that drive comes from?

3. Vivian claims to be an independent woman, and she is to a point, but she also lives with her wealthy mother and doesn't fully support herself. How do you think she justifies these dualities? Does she think about it at all?

4. Vivian certainly isn't a shrinking violet, yet she's mortified of her mother finding out what she's been up to with Charlie. How do you think societal pressures were

different in Vivian's day? How were they the same as today?

5. Vivian and Charlie clearly come from different classes and backgrounds. How do you think this affects their relationship?

6. Compare and contrast Vivian's relationship with Imogene to her relationship with Frances. Why do you think she relates to the two women so differently?

7. Radio has famously been called the "theater of the mind." How do you think the medium of radio drama compares to that of novels or movies? How would a story be told differently depending on the medium? How would this story be told differently as a radio play? As a movie?

8. Vivian's father died at a very impressionable time in her life (her late teens). How do you think his death affected her? How do you think it affected her relationship with men? With her mother? If you have experienced the death of either of your parents, how has it affected your life?

9. What do you think draws Vivian to Char-

lie? Charlie to Vivian?

10. What do you think draws Vivian to Graham? Graham to Vivian?

11. The murderer in this story turns out to be someone fairly unlikely. How do you feel about this character? Can you sympathize with the murderer in any way?

12. What traits do both Vivian and Frances share? Do you think Vivian is proud or ashamed of these? How do these two women differ?

13. Vivian has feelings for both Charlie and Graham. How do the two differ? Have you ever been in such a situation?

14. What does the author use to create realism in the story? How does she make the time period authentic? How would this story differ if it were to take place in present time?

15. What do you think is in the future for Vivian and Charlie?

A CONVERSATION
WITH THE AUTHOR

How old were you when you wrote your first story? What was it about?

I started writing stories as soon I could read. I used to have my dad haul out our ancient manual Underwood typewriter to the dining room table so I could hunt and peck out my stories about cats. My dad called me the Mad Typist. The first real story I can remember writing and finishing was called *The Mouse That Didn't Believe in Santa Claus* in the third grade. I illustrated it as well. I still have it.

What do you love most about writing?

I love world building and doing historical research. I got really involved in figuring out the particulars of what Chicago looked like in October 1938 — how it would have felt to walk down the street; how it would have sounded, smelled; what was playing at the movie theaters. It's a way of time travel-

451

ing. Writing is also a way of living vicariously through my characters. I can make them do anything . . . to a point.

What inspires you the most as a writer?
I'm a curious person by nature. I'm always on the lookout for interesting stories (especially historical), and I love learning. I never really know what little tidbit of information will strike my fancy or spark a story idea.

Who are some of your favorite authors? Why are they your favorites?
My Antonia by Willa Cather was the first real grown-up book I read. It had a major impression on me since it's not a romance and it doesn't have a (completely) happy ending. I read Tim O'Brien's *The Things They Carried* during a short story writing class in college. It has such perfectly specific detail you'd think it was a memoir and not fiction. In the historical romance genre, I love Anya Seton. Then, on the complete other end of the spectrum, I really love a good Stephen King book. I read *It* as a twelve-year-old (likely *way* too early in the grand scheme of things), and it thrilled and terrified me. The setting/world he created is so intricately detailed. Basically, I just like to be entertained, no matter the genre.

When do you know the story is finished?

I think the mystery genre is a little easier than others — the bad guy/girl gets caught or the mystery is solved. But in my head, the story is never really over. The characters keep going, keep interacting, keep having adventures. But I suppose, in a story's structure, you just feel that the time is right to wrap this particular chapter up.

What advice would you give to aspiring writers?

Write what you want to read. And let yourself get bored. My best ideas are born from boredom, when I just let my mind wander and I'm forced to entertain myself.

What is one thing you know now that you wish you knew when you started your writing career?

Patience is required. Getting published is not a quick or easy process. If someone had told me when I started to write this book that it would take seven years for it to be published, I may have quit then and there. There were so many times in this long process that I could have given up, but I didn't. It's not the published book that I'm most proud of — it's not quitting.

Did you always want to be a writer, or did you start off in a different career?

I've always wanted to be a writer, but by virtue of having to pay the bills, I've found myself in a career completely unrelated to writing. The reality of it is that very few people are lucky enough to make their living as a writer. I've never wanted to be a starving artist. I like to eat too much, and health care is a nice thing to have.

If you could spend one day with an author, dead or alive, who would it be, and why?

Probably Dorothy Parker or Mark Twain — someone who doesn't take themselves too seriously.

What are your favorite genres to read?

I love historical suspense/mystery with a touch of romance (obviously). But I also love horror, YA, historical fantasy. Really, I'm just a sucker for good storytelling.

How would you describe your writing style in one word?

Light.

What is the most challenging part of being a writer?

Keeping at it and not getting discouraged by failure or rejection. Writing is a very solitary thing, and it's easy to convince yourself that no one will like what you're putting down on paper. Letting people read what you write and getting feedback is terrifying, but necessary.

What research or preparation did you engage in before writing this book?

I'm a huge fan of old-time radio shows. I have been since I saw Woody Allen's *Radio Days* in the eighth grade, but it was hard to get access to them back then. Then a little thing called the Internet came around, and I realized I could listen to old radio shows whenever I wanted, which meant at my desk at work. The time period and the speech, I think I learned through osmosis from all that listening to old radio shows and watching old movies. I also really delved into how radio shows were produced and the radio scene in Chicago, trying to find firsthand accounts if I could. I found old *Radio Guides* on eBay and poured over the gossipy articles — "The Tattler" in the *Radio Guide* was a real thing! I learned so much from those about what things were like for actors and actresses, as well as listeners. I also researched what Chicago was like in 1938.

The Loop was a much more vibrant and lively place then. People came downtown to go shopping. There were movie palaces everywhere. There were streetcars clanging down State Street. Chicago 1938 is very much alive in my head.

Which character do you feel most closely connected to?

Vivian. She's everything I'd like to be myself — sassy and confident . . . and petite. I've always wanted to be petite.

Are any of your characters inspired by the people around you?

Not overtly, but I suppose I subconsciously use the personality traits of people around me for my fictional friends.

ACKNOWLEDGMENTS

Thanks to my agent, Elizabeth Trupin-Pulli, for believing in this little book in the first place. Thanks to my editor, Anna Michels, for molding my story into something better than I ever thought it could be. Thanks to my entire extended family — but especially to Barak and Kate for understanding and giving me the space to write . . . and just stare off into space sometimes. Thanks to Kerri Ricker and Julie Shaner Jones for always encouraging me in this writing dream.

Thanks to all of those who put together the fantastic *Nostalgia Digest,* whose back issues were instrumental in my research of radio and the prewar period. Thanks to the National Novel Writing Month (NaNo-WriMo) organization, which lit the fire under me to start this book so many years ago. (This book was the only time in three tries that I "won.") Thanks to the RWA Kiss

457

of Death chapter for sponsoring the Daphne du Maurier Award for Excellence in Mystery/Suspense, which, at long last, helped me find my people.

And finally, a huge thanks to all those marvelous radio stars (and production crews) of yesteryear that made me fall in love with the medium and the theater of the air. Your performances have kept me such wonderful company, and I hope I've done you proud.

ABOUT THE AUTHOR

Cheryl Honigford was born and raised in the Midwest and currently lives in the suburbs of Chicago with her family. *The Darkness Knows* is her first novel.

The employees of Thorndike Press hope you have enjoyed this Large Print book. All our Thorndike, Wheeler, and Kennebec Large Print titles are designed for easy reading, and all our books are made to last. Other Thorndike Press Large Print books are available at your library, through selected bookstores, or directly from us.

For information about titles, please call:
  (800) 223-1244

or visit our Web site at:
  http://gale.cengage.com/thorndike

To share your comments, please write:
Publisher
Thorndike Press
10 Water St., Suite 310
Waterville, ME 04901